Deep State is vying for global control...

Political
Deception

Geoffrey **Bott**

An Award-Nominated Author

Solihull Publishing

Acknowledgement

To my long-time friend, Dr. Rich Kondrat, who had been diagnosed with prostate cancer, that was fortuitously detected in time. As Rich seeks medical assistance for life's next journey, he once again guided me through a grueling, complex manuscript. The comments, thoughts and suggestions – most were kind, lol - were hugely beneficial as chapters progressed, and their numbers escalated. His encouragement enabled me to keep writing. Not once did he ask, "When does it end?" Well, he may have done but I wasn't listening. Thank you, Rich, as I spread hope for your successful treatment.

Also, I must thank the growing number of readers who are entertained by the stories. Without you, there simply would be no personal satisfaction since I use writing to help me recover from my own traumas in life.

Again, to my children who help me steer through this sometimes-crazy world.

Acknowledgment

1

Explosive Beginning

Perched on a mountain side overlooking a military airfield, Cross has his infra-red binoculars pinned to his eyes as he scans the tarmac below. Partially hidden under suspended camouflage netting are two private jets. Surrounding those are military planes dotting the scene that is illuminated using sparce lighting.

He drops the binoculars tethered to a lanyard hanging around his neck and removes the phone. Cross now extracts the text he had received two days earlier to confirm what he is looking at. In front of him sits the corporate jet in question, and the same one found in Panama Taylor had taken pictures of before incapacitating the Asian clones.

The registration number is bogus but once Granfield had transferred the data to him, he had quietly pursued ownership. It took some delicate and time-consuming effort because it was wrapped in multiple shell companies. The registration started with VQ-B, which is Bermuda, but the trail of corporate shells left Cross stunned in the end, but not technically surprised.

He returns the phone back into his black thermal jacket pocket and confirms via the binoculars what he is examining. Now verified, he scans the lighted buildings adjacent to the aircraft. There are guard shacks also, manned by armed soldiers. Parading the fenced perimeter are more personnel displaying AK47s. Some are walking with attack dogs.

"Jesus Christ," Cross mumbles. "Time to move."

He returns to his electric all-terrain vehicle, puts the night-vision goggles back on and navigates closer to the facility through trees, bushes and a steep descent. He is thankful for the terrain map his friend had provided.

"Where the hell do you get this material," he had enquired, but never got an answer. Perhaps best he didn't know, he concluded.

Escaping the tree cover, he approaches the compound perimeter and parks. It's very dark this side which facilitates his next moves. He retrieves a sniper rifle from the rear of the 4x4, attached with a night scope. He removes the goggles and now uses this to scan the immediate vicinity.

Pop, pop, pop, pop. Four shots, four dead. He moves the vehicle closer to the fence and steps out. Next, he retrieves wire cutters and proceeds to create an opening in the fence. Once big enough, Cross climbs back on and drives through. He faces more armed security soldiers and shoots them. So far, so good, but his anxiety builds and heart rate quickens as he gets deeper into the airfield. Mountain darkness has kept him well hidden, but this will change very soon as he reaches life.

He heads toward the parked aircraft and finds a location where he can hide the 4x4 behind a mound of some sort. He climbs out and scans the area. The private jets are close, and the stairs are down with two guards posted at the bottom of the Gulfstream G800 his operation is pursuing.

Cross hesitates and thinks about his next move. Surprise has brought him this far but anything he does now will remove that precious commodity. The structure housing a secret meeting the said text message two days earlier had brought to light can be seen across the other side of the aircraft parking area. He needs to act fast but not without thought.

"Think, dammit."

Done.

He grabs his trusted CIA-sanctioned firearm from his ankle and screws on the silencer. He silently manoeuvres behind a military F-16 where he can see the two guards. He takes aim and fires two shots. He runs over and drags the first casualty away from the area and into the shadowy darkness provided by the paltry lighting, and behind a fueling vehicle. He heads back and drags the second one away.

After re-examining the area, he walks back and quietly climbs the stairs to the cabin with his gun pointing forward. As he gets to the top, he peaks his head inside. The cockpit door is partially closed but he can hear two pilots talking. They are preparing for their imminent departure, it sounds like to Cross, as they run through a checklist. He twists his head to view the cabin and a hostess is also preparing the aircraft.

"Shit."

This changes everything. He quickly but softly retraces his steps down and runs to his offroad vehicle. He searches in the back for something and finds it. He grabs it and adjusts some altitude setting on the device before returning to the Gulfstream. He jogs over to the rear right wheel well, climbs the wheels and secures the device inside, lodging it behind some electrical wires and hydraulic pipes. Scurrying back, he climbs onto the 4x4 and heads for darkness and the hole in the fence. More armed soldiers are approaching, but they cannot see or hear him. He shoots them too, along with their dogs.

As soon as Cross exits the perimeter fence, he stops and dismounts the vehicle. From this vantage point he views people leaving the building. The individuals are shaking hands and filling the air with tainted laughter. A small group walks over to the corporate jet and ascends the stairs. No one seems to observe, notice or care about the missing guards, as the cabin door is secured behind them. In the background he hears the whine of the G800's engines spinning up. As they increase in revolution, a man in fatigues wearing headphones removes the wheel stops. The same person then guides the Gulfstream out of the holding pad and in the direction of the taxiway.

Cross is fixated as the aircraft taxis to the end of the perimeter and the pilot guides the nose to line it up with the runway's arbitrary centre line. Low-wattage ground-lighting had been activated to illuminate the strip and, without stopping, power increased to full thrust as it starts to barrel down the tarmac. Once it reaches sufficient velocity and aerodynamics activate, the nose wheel lifts, and the Gulfstream departs into the night sky. Its initial climb is steep to clear the surrounding mountains and Cross tears off his balaclava as he stares at it and waits.

Off in the distance and at two thousand feet above the terrain – the setting he had dialed the detonator to - the wheel well explodes which in turn ignites the fuel tanks. A large fireball escapes the wheel hatch, ripping off the right wing. Loss of lift forces the plane to bank hard right and it plummets to the ground, blowing up on impact into thousands of pieces and eerily lighting up the darkened vicinity. A swath of heated air washes over the valley and bathes his stony, naked face in a satisfactory warmth.

Now with a big smile, Cross climbs onto the electric ATV and exits back the way he came, and into the alpine forest.

2

Political Posturing

Cross is sitting on a rug on the floor. He is in a hotel in Westminster, London, meditating. After the escape from near-death experiences in Shanghai and the Korean Strait, he had sought professional help on deeper meditation exercises. There is some mysticism surrounding practices in hidden schools in the Tibetan and Nepalese mountains. However, it had taken some months to adapt the methods they apply, and he is rapidly seeing results. He will need to focus and gain clearer perspectives on his next, and hopefully final, missions.

The hotel is situated on a long, straight street lined with terraced properties, and packed either side with parked vehicles. Some dwellings are shops, but most have been converted into small, boutique-style hotels and B&Bs. His room is small, large enough for a single bed, side table, closet and a bathroom with shower just big enough for one person. A small window, partially opened, overlooks a narrow strip of garden that backs to more terraced properties. A flat screen TV is mounted on the wall above a dresser. He had tuned onto a local news channel but with the volume muted.

As he squats with legs crossed underneath him, his mind is empty. The mission last night was successfully executed, and he was pleased. The private flight back into London was uneventful and he had remained incognito.

Cross takes a break and relaxes. As he does so, he turns his head to face the television. The news of one of the richest men in the world being killed in a plane crash yesterday evening is portrayed so he reaches for the remote and disengages the mute option.

"…as the plane exploded shortly after take-off. No word yet on the cause but grief is being felt globally at the loss of one of the world's charismatic personalities." The news presenter looked shocked.

"Fuck him," mumbles Cross, with no remorse. "He deserved it, the aristocratic arsehole."

The female presenter switches topics and this piques Cross' interest even further.

"The runoff in the French presidential election is gaining momentum. The incumbent, President Dubois, has lost considerable gains to a relatively unknown opposition party and its leader, Philippe Marchant. Mr. Marchant is a local billionaire from Paris and has known ties to powerful business entities. His fortune derived from the suspicious death of his father eighteen months ago who had built a fragrance empire. His party, the Democratic Union, is pushing for liberation of the people from Dubois' autocratic control and socialistic ideals. The French people seem to be rising to this narrative and their growing frustration over immigrants from North Africa." Turning to her male counterpart sitting next to her, she adds, "This is a developing story which may have implications throughout Europe and beyond."

Cross has done listening and turns it off. He sits for a while and ponders this revelation, before heading to the shower.

Wu is enjoying a bottle of thirty-year Hibiki Suntory Japanese whiskey at his home when a call comes in.

"Mr. Wu, have you seen the news?" asks the person on the other end.

"Yes."

"We have located security personnel at the mountain base killed with precision shots. They were found inside the perimeter. The perpetrator excised a hole in the fence and there are tyre marks indicative of a small offroad vehicle. Two guards were added to the count, and they were hidden behind a fuel truck. It looks like whoever did this had intelligence on this facility, sir, and knows how to kill."

"I see. What else?"

"Nothing, sir. I was informed by you to keep you updated. We are actively searching for whoever did this." Feeling the requirement to rapidly change subjects, "Oh, and Mr. Marchant is gaining popularity in France, it seems."

"Yes, he is. Keep me posted," and hangs up the phone.

Wu doesn't care much for the plane crash or death of one of his sponsors. He saw him as an arrogant wanker and detested his very existence. His vast wealth was beneficial to the cause and regarded as a necessity but that doesn't matter anymore. He is, however, concerned about the circumstances in which the plane went down.

There is a buzz on his home's intercom.

"Your dinner date has arrived, sir."

3

Assassination in Westminster

Cross exits the shower and dries himself off. He had already arranged his flights back to California so now just needs to get ready. He picks up his phone to organise airport transportation but there are messages pending.

'Where are you?' came one from a new trusted source.

'Westminster, leaving for home this afternoon.'

'I've identified another target. Luckily, it is close to you.'

The trusted source leaves minimal directives and it is now up to Cross to decipher what to do with them.

"Shit." Is about all he can conjure up.

He punches his reply into the phone. 'Let me get back to you shortly.'

The virus and vaccine were a ruse. However, had they worked, it would have been purely academic moving the clones into place and taking over. That part would have been simple enough. Destroying their ability to orchestrate the first phase meant the second phase was deployed, but not as they would have liked.

The island in the South China Sea was obliterated and ceased functioning – as did the clones - but Wu was not found anywhere. He just got up and disappeared for the second time. Cross had deliberated over this circumstance for some time and felt it isn't over yet. There is too much power and money involved. It can't be over.

Their plan had to change, and he is beginning to pick up vibes here and there that are hoisting big red flags. The political stage is altering too but no one outside of what he knows will see it and connect the dots. Someone or some entity is forcing this shift. Now he is faced with another dilemma and one he must act on if he is to definitively end it.

He messages back. 'Forward more specific details and I will follow up,' is all he types.

His phone starts vibrating as the information is received. Cross reads it and gulps.

"What the hell."

Cross leaves the hotel in black clothing just as the sun is setting and heads as directed. The London air is unseasonably warm and a tad humid. As he approaches the Thames River, he locates the bridge and sees a trash can as instructed. He leans over and pulls out a plastic bag. Inside is a balaclava, scarf and a marksman's precision pistol with a telescopic night-vision sight. Cross inspects it to ensure no signatures or identification numbers are present. The handle is fingerprint-proof. He tosses the bag and walks over the bridge. As he does so, he looks north up the river and sees the Palace of Westminster and Big Ben lit up.

He checks his Rolex since timing is essential. He needs to hurry so ups his cadence.

He navigates onto the Thames Path which runs alongside the river and walks toward Westminster Bridge. Once he reaches it, he climbs the stairs to Westminster Bridge Road. Across the other side of the river and adjacent to Palace of Westminster, a large crowd has gathered. This was part of the details, so he is expecting it. It will allow him to do what he needs to do with fortuitous advantage of cover. Now he waits.

Ten minutes pass when a small convoy of cars slowly approaches Parliament from over the bridge. Two police motorcycles followed by a police car headed the procession. Behind that is the vehicle Cross is interested in; a black long wheelbase Jaguar XJ-L. Behind it is another police car. The people are immediately energized upon seeing the motorcade and start moving in unison. Those congregated on the bridge start running to engage with the large crowd. The noise level has also advanced in decibels as people are screaming and shouting. This leaves Cross unimpeded as he quickly puts on the balaclava and prepares the pistol.

The procession is right next to him, and two people occupy the back seat of the Jaguar. Once they pass, he points the gun and fires two high-caliber shots; one directed at each head. The rear window shatters in the process as blood and brain tissue splatter the interior before they slump over. The police car behind them doesn't have time to react as Cross pumps two more shots at the driver and passenger through the side windows.

He quickly removes the balaclava and retrieves the scarf to wrap around his neck. The gun he tosses into the Thames as he runs toward the crowd so that he can blend in and hide.

Several hours later Cross is back in the hotel room lying low. He has turned on the TV and is watching the chaotic scenes being displayed outside of Parliament. The crowd has accumulated vast numbers and it is madness. People are being interviewed in tears as the nation descends into shock.

He picks up his phone and a message is displayed.

'Excellent work.'

'Heading home.' Cross replies.

After only a few hours of sleep, he is now on a private charter to Reykjavik, Iceland where he will resume normal commercial flights back to California.

Wu just happens to have his laptop open when the news flashes over the internet. He grabs his phone.

"What can you tell me?"

"Henry Mitchell was assassinated outside Parliament last night along with his chief of staff. It took some hours before their deaths were confirmed. They were being driven to a protest where Mr. Mitchell was the keynote speaker. They even had police escort and two of their men were killed. There were thousands of people at the event. Someone pierced their skulls with two single bullets. I mean precision stuff. The police canvassed the area, but the assassin likely fled through the mallee. As soon as the public began to hear, they swarmed the area making it even harder to find anything. Whatever evidence they had is likely gone now."

Wu is angry.

"This can't be a coincidence. Two deaths in as many days."

"Yes, sir. I concur."

"We have our newly elected official under control in Romania. We have illicit information on the Latvian prime minister to keep the Baltic region in check. We will have problems if this continues so find out what you can, and quickly."

"Yes, sir."

"Prepare my plane. I will leave soon."

The phone goes dead.

4

Unofficial Proposition

Cross is home in the kitchen with Sadeghi and they have just finished making love numerous times.

"Why are you so beautiful," Cross enquires.

"I've missed you."

"Me too." He moves closer and wraps his arms around her. "How are the wedding plans coming along?"

Before she can answer, his phone buzzes. After kissing her he lets go, walks over and picks it up.

'Where are you?' the CIA Director messages.

"Sorry, my love. It's David and I need to take this."

She doesn't flinch or negatively react. "Tell him I say hello, please. Wedding plans look rather good." She smiles at him.

He departs the kitchen and heads for the office. Now seated, he dials Granfield.

"Sorry, Daniel. We need to talk. I'm down the street at a café in Meyers."

Cross doesn't bother asking how he knew he was home. He dons a jacket and leaves.

The café is empty and quiet when he enters and immediately locates Granfield in the corner. He walks over and seats himself before they shake hands.

"This is a surprise, David. I signed documents relinquishing my contract with CIA and releasing me of further liability and potential health threats."

"Nice to see you too, Daniel." He laughs, as only he knows how.

"Welcome to Tahoe, my friend." This time he stands up and they bear-hug each other. "I've missed you, but the last assignment beat me up."

"You look good and healing well, it seems." He's being genuine. Cross looks magnificent, considering. "How are the leg and shoulder?"

"Functioning reasonably well and I'm recovering as expected."

"Excellent."

"I'm involved in meditation and have modified a room in my home to accommodate that. It is really helping me."

Granfield raises his eyebrows a tad. "Modify a room for meditation? You must have added a punching bag with a picture of my face on it."

Startled at his frighteningly accurate insight, "How did you know?" and they both heartily laugh.

"Damn, I've missed you."

"Whilst I appreciate the genuine warmth, you didn't fly all the way out here for lunch in this dodgy café because you missed me, David."

"Very astute," and chuckles. He shuffles his backside a little as he adjusts for the next part. "I came here to solicit your opinions and extract some knowledge." Getting right to it, "What do you know about Evander Cartwright?"

"One of the richest men in the world, you mean?"

"Yes."

"Well, he is one of the richest men in the world." He grins.

"Very funny. Seriously, what can you tell me?"

"Is this on or off the record?"

"Off. This meeting today doesn't exist. I am not here. It never happened. Understood?"

"Yes, of course," and he relaxes a little. "Cartwright has a lot of money which affords him many luxuries. I'm not referring to material luxuries either. His contacts in the elite world are extensive and he has considerable clout, even on social media. He commands millions of followers."

"Keep going." Granfield is entranced and can listen to Cross all day.

"He has many political allies. However, those allies seem suspicious to me. He aligns himself with people often referred to as Deep State, or Globalists. Take the guy in Romania for example. He financed his recent campaign. There are rumours on the street he is financing the potential threat in the coming UK elections, and doesn't he control Marchant in France? Who is another political pariah. All these affiliations are dangerous."

Granfield listens. He knew or guessed – he would claim a knowledgeable guess – that Cross hadn't stopped after he blew up Wu's island. This is now too personal for him. He had been nearly killed a number of times and that can beat a man up. It changed him. Granfield also knows he must tread very cautiously here. Cross has to be a man living on the edge and his temperament could illuminate rapidly if a fuse is set.

"Do you watch any news?"

"No." Obviously Cross is being disingenuous but he doesn't know Granfield's angle of attack or where he is coming from. Why is he here? Cross knows already or suspects he does. In any event, he isn't admitting anything yet.

"Evander Cartwright is dead."

A vision of Cartwright's plane nose-diving into the ground and exploding comes to Cross' head. "Really?" Trying to act shocked.

"His plane crashed in the Swiss Alps three days ago. Tracking suggests it had departed from an unused military base there."

Granfield is attempting to gauge Cross' reaction but there isn't one.

"I wonder what happened. Planes crash often. Remember the Germanwings flight that slammed into the Alps?"

"This wasn't suicide, Daniel," as he raises his tone. "His aircraft blew up. Investigators found the right wing separated from the rest of the debris." His eyes dart around the café realising he needs to remain calm.

"Oh." He gives away nothing.

"It was examined, and explosive residue was detected." He takes a microsecond break. "This is causing quite some controversy and fingers are being pointed."

"Being pointed where?"

"Everywhere. This has serious ramifications." Granfield takes a breather and then continues. "You mentioned the popular UK opposition leader. What is your take?"

"One of the newest members of Parliament, who is destined to win the forthcoming UK election by a major landslide. I question his funding sources. However, his major contributor is now dead apparently."

"He has other sources too."

"The new political characters all seem to be towing the same autocratic line. I believe it to be all bullshit. They all spout off about democracy and how it has been curtailed and controlled under previous or current administrations and leaders. This is nonsense. Didn't we get help too from those same leaders who they claim are destroying human rights and abusing freedoms? They helped us stop the One World Order rhetoric. So, the narratives are arse-backwards."

Granfield isn't stopping him. Cross is animated and when he gets this way, let him spill the beans.

"The French guy is the same. Who did I say he is?"

"Marchant."

"Yes. Him. He wants to control immigration. What he means by that is stop it. The EU doesn't like that idea at all, and Marchant is anti-EU because of it. But read between the lines of what he is saying. He doesn't want to give the French their freedom and remove them from socialism. He wants to control them by installing a more draconian system. It is obvious but they don't understand the difference.

"These people have massive sponsors and their campaign funds are huge. No one knows who they are but it's pretty evident if one looks."

This is what Granfield was waiting for and why he flew here: Cross has been researching.

"Henry Mitchell was assassinated two days ago, along with his chief of staff. Two police officers were also shot and killed."

Cross goes silent now.

"He was scheduled to be a key speaker at a protest rally outside of Parliament. I'm obligated to ask you, do you know anything about these two deaths, Daniel?"

Cross is still silent and impossible to read. Granfield takes a hand and reaches across the table, placing it on one of Cross' arms.

"I know you, my friend. I don't want you to answer that question. You flew back from Iceland yesterday morning using an alias. It doesn't take a surgeon to figure it out. Please don't answer the question I posed."

Granfield removes his hand and requests fresh coffee. Their server comes over and tops both mugs.

"It isn't Kopi Luwak." His humourous injection works.

Cross looks at him and grins. "Can't beat that taste for sure."

"I will take your word on that since I'm not into drinking cat droppings." He smiles and continues. "Those two deaths have compounded an already difficult political mine field. They may in fact start a war.

"You are very accurate with your acquired knowledge." He leans back in the chair. "You are very learned, but I knew that. One of the corporate jets Leslie took photos of in Panama belonged to Cartwright." Granfield looks directly into Cross' eyes. "That is the one that blew up."

Cross doesn't flinch, nor blink. He just stoically sits there, silently meditating but inhaling every syllable as Granfield talks.

He removes his gaze. "We compiled our own research too and did some further digging. He was there in Panama, we believe, to observe if his funding was being used effectively. He likely wanted to see the Tainan explode. This guy is good at hiding things, and I'll give him that. He partly funded the viral development which meant he sponsored the robots too. He formed an integral part of Deep State."

Cross identifies a break and picks up his coffee mug. He wraps his hands around to warm them up since his body has gone cold all of a sudden.

"I don't care if you killed them both. I will be the first to congratulate you. Hell, I will even give you a medal. However, you signed off on our contract and, therefore, you have no legal or diplomatic protection, and these killings were on foreign soil." The crescendo changes as he reaches the final words, to directly reflect his annoyance level. This isn't a game anymore.

Cross starts to open his mouth, but Granfield prevents him from uttering any objection.

"I've got your back, Daniel. I will always have your back. I came here on my own recognisance to remind you of that fact."

He simmers down and injects diplomacy. "Please don't go rogue. We also know what is going on, but we can't officially be going around killing heads of state and international political opposition leaders at will. People get upset and there would be dire global ramifications." He smiles and gathers his thoughts. "But unofficially, we can do what the hell we want." He stops and takes another breather as he takes a sip of fresh coffee.

Looking directly at him, he adds, "I have a proposition for you, Daniel."

Cross looks Granfield directly in his eyes. "I'm listening."

"Officially, we aren't contracting with you. We will sign no legal tender. This is off the record but people in the agency will know. Some do already."

"Wait." Cross stops him this time. "I haven't agreed to anything."

"I know you. I admire you more than anyone else on the planet, my friend. I don't know who helped you facilitate the assassinations, but this tells me you have people in special places."

"I can't reveal sources. And helped me do what, exactly?" His expression is hard.

Granfield smiles. "Unofficially, let's coordinate and get these bastards, before Deep State takes control. They tried unconventional methods and those were unsuccessful. Now they intend to develop the more conventional route, a way that has worked for centuries: the political method incorporating corruption, money laundering, fraud, bribery, sex, coercion and death."

"My objective is Wu. He can't keep escaping."

"Then we have a mutual and amicable objective, Daniel."

They both stand and shake hands.

"Great work, by the way, in private." He laughs.

Cross walks into his home and heads for his meditation class, but not before first conversing with Sadeghi. He enters the meditation room, closes the door behind him and turns up the heat. He then removes his clothes, except for the briefs and walks toward the padded wall. Time to implement his own version and lifts the arms, steps one foot back and starts pounding the pads. He pummels them with first the left hand, then the right, then the left. The installed soundproofing allows him to vent and scream as much as he wants. The mirrors display the damage and scars these blowhards are causing to his physique.

When he is finally spent, he squats on a mat on the floor and sits quietly as the forced sweat is pouring from his body. His mind is now clearer.

He murmurs to himself, "Wu, I am coming and I will eviscerate you, so fuck you too."

5

Wu's Mountain Retreat

Wu steps off his plane that has landed at a private, secure airfield in the mountains. He is greeted at the bottom of the stairs by his chief of staff, Bao. It is dark and extremely cold.

He looks around to verify other prominent members of the group are present. He visually confirms their aircraft, but some have even driven there or arrived via helicopter. The various modes of transportation are hidden under camouflaged netting and bunkers built into the rock formations.

"Hello, Mr. Wu."

"Good evening, Bao."

"Most are present, sir, and are awaiting your arrival."

Wu brusquely walks toward a sheltered compound, purpose built for this engineered take-over. The explosive-proof window coverings are shut but as he enters the steel structure built into the side of a mountain, he's greeted by faces he recognises. They are seated at a large conference table immersed in muted conversations, but Wu's entrance stirs them into life as they stand to greet him.

Plastered with pins to poster boards mounted on one wall are pictures of recent events. As Wu ignores the pleasantries and walks passed, he surveys the collage. On a similar board on another wall is a dramatic overview of Europe with portraits of their representatives pinned to countries they already control or soon will. Henry Mitchell has a red X drawn across his picture pinned to the UK. Next to that are maps of the US, Russia and China. At the top of this wall are portraits of their sponsors. Cartwright has a red X on his face.

Wu takes his position at the head of the table and they all then re-seat themselves. Wu starts up and gets right to it.

"What happened to Cartwright's Gulfstream?"

Handcock, who is English and oversees Wu's European aspirations, takes the floor next to the photographic wall.

"This is the main crash site." He points using a red laser pen. Shifting to the photograph next to it, "And here is the right wing. They are separated by several hundred metres which means the wing came off and the plane had enough forward momentum to carry it beyond its aerodynamic stall. The wing separated after an in-flight explosion. Six perimeter security men and two dogs were killed with single bullet holes. Two aircraft guards were also killed this way. The assassin entered the perimeter through this self-spawned hole in the fence." He points with the laser pen to other photographs as he narrates. "There are tyre tracks which trace the vehicle through the forest. However, those get lost when they enter a normal alpine patrol area."

"What about Mitchell?"

Handcock moves to the next album of photographs.

"Mitchell, accompanied by his chief of staff, was scheduled to speak at an unauthorised rally outside UK Parliament. A large crowd had gathered also. As the motorcade passed the assassin on Westminster Bridge, they opened up, again with single-shot penetrations to each head."

"What further information do you have on this?"

"Nothing, sir. Our police found nothing. The assassin disappeared."

"Only one?"

"We presume only one, based on the physical evidence."

"What about security cameras?"

"The police we aren't bankrolling took the tapes. This is something on which we are working. However, we have evidence they were tampered with even before the event started. The security cameras in the area were disabled by an external source, we believe."

"So, this was a professional operation?"

"That is a justifiable conclusion to draw, sir."

Wu is calm, despite mitigating circumstances.

"Thank you." He looks over at the second in command, Kowalski, a Polish national, who also controls the finances for this renegade. "Where do we stand?"

"The loss of Cartwright, although unfortunate, poses no requirement for a financial risk assessment. His funds are in-house and assigned. As you know, the other sponsors on the wall will address any unforeseen shortfall. In any event, I have already spoken to them."

"Yes. My concern isn't financial. My concerns are who did it and what are they going to do next."

"We are pursuing leads and evidence, sir. However, as with Mitchell, this seems to have been a professional hit implemented with dexterity and precision."

"Well, this diminishes the number of possibilities to what, every country in the western hemisphere?"

"Point taken."

"I am not here to make points, Jan. This is serious." He is raising his voice and stands up, walking over to the wall with the maps. "I want to know what the impact of these losses is, and will they continue?" Gesturing and hovering over eastern Europe. "We have Romania. We lost Mitchell, which is a big loss. The Baltic states are still a concern."

"Yes." Kowalski agreeing. "This is a problem area we will need to defuse. There is growing unrest here and war looks pre-emptive and imminent."

"Who is orchestrating this push?"

"Lithuania. Latvia's prime minister is pro-Russia but him sleeping with Moscow's current governor's wife really hasn't helped." He grins but knows he shouldn't. "It didn't exactly endear him to the Kremlin, and they frown upon such behaviour. However, Lithuania already has a pro-Russian border with Belarus. If we add Latvia, then this makes them extremely nervous."

"I thought we blackmailed Ozolins?"

"We did but word got out in Latvia. Someone can't keep their mouth shut, I guess."

"Then deal with that aspect. Find out who leaked this delicate information."

"Yes, sir."

Wu stops and thinks for a moment, holding up his hand to prevent others from distracting his thoughts. "Perhaps a Baltic war will help us by immiserating the populace."

"Who will fund that?" Sanchez asks from the other side of the table.

"Oh, that answer is easy. If we do this right, then NATO will have to protect their own member states. It will not cost us anything financially, but we will gain politically." Wu answers.

"Brilliant strategy," replies the Spanish gentleman who offered the question.

"What about Russia's response?" asks their German representative, Schmidt, sitting next to Kowalski.

"Let me manage that, Paul. So, what do we do about Mitchell's replacement?"

Handcock pipes in. "I have someone lined up already, sir."

"Fill me in later, when this is confirmed."

"Yes, sir."

"Marchant looks a shoe-in. The French people are tired of immigration policies enforced by the EU. This could be our catalyst, so we need to focus on this inevitability."

"The Germans are also watching this election. They too have had enough of the de-facto-capital Brussel's interference in their national borders," Schmidt adds.

Wu is happier now than when he walked in. His chosen group has their shit together. "Loss of Germany would ruinously impact the EU. What else?"

"The US?" asks Anderson, Wu's gorgeous female chief assigned to North America.

"Cross rescued Prime Minister Walkman in the South China Sea. His popularity as a result markedly increased to our detriment. Keep doing what you are to manage this, however, and we will continue the discussion privately, Florence. I will reach out before you fly back to the States tomorrow and fill you in."

"Of course, Mr. Wu."

"Thank you all for attending. I sense we covered everything. Any questions?"

None were forthcoming.

"Let's head over to our dining room."

Drinks, hors d'oeuvres and dinner plates have been prepared in their kitchen. The dining room is a separate area but accessed through a concealed tunnel.

Wu is impressed and quietly relieved. His meticulously selected group seems to have been coordinating and are administering minor setbacks. He had chosen the political route at the beginning but was overridden by the sponsors, who preferred tens of millions of strategic deaths. Even his political allies, some representing governments in their respective countries, had agreed with them and he was vetoed. Political conspiracies always win. He chuckles.

Anderson walks up next to him as they enter the dining area.

"I will seat myself next to you."

Wu is happy with that announcement. She is stunning and will be beneficial for what he has planned in the US.

"Good. We can discuss tonight what I want you to do and then you can leave at your leisure after dinner."

When they are both seated, she places a hand on his crotch.

6

Deep State's Emerging Influence

Cross wasn't expecting another assignment, even if this one is unofficial. After meditating, he has dinner with Sadeghi whom he loves. She fills him in on their wedding plans which are coming up in a month. She isn't happy with his change in circumstance, but she understands the reasons. She adores him and her heart aches for his touch.

"This will not end until you find Wu. I understand, honey. Please return less damaged than the previous two assignments."

This is all she asks for as Cross picks her up and ravages her as only he can, right there on the dining table. Sadeghi also loves his power, poise, energy and control. She melts whenever he moves inside of her. She's aware there is nothing that can be done or said until this is over. Then, perhaps, they can share a life of their own, if he is still alive or not in a wheelchair.

She has also noticed Secret Service agents from time to time. The airport fire truck opened her eyes, and she is even beginning to fear for her own life.

After leaving the dining table, he walks to his office and flops in the chair. He sighs, "When will this end?"

He opens the laptop and retrieves the data file he has been compiling. In it are lists of people he has assigned to Deep State and their countries he believes they represent. The complexity is mind-boggling as he stares at the flowchart he extrapolated on a wide screen monitor mounted to his desk. He presses a few keys and adds one red mark each next to Cartwright and Mitchell since they are now unequivocally deceased. Unfortunately, their influences aren't.

He passionately believes Wu is involved and doesn't second-guess this theory. It is pretty evident when the dots connect. If it looks, walks and quacks like a duck... The pictorial presentation on his display must form part of Wu's team, which is why his name is inserted at the top.

The irony is that a significantly high percentage of people on the planet don't believe in Deep State. However, here he is, staring at its very foundation.

He flips to the next page in the file and on the screen appears President Walkman. Cross found him curled up in a cell and saved his life. That life must surely remain in danger.

Underneath his picture is a list of Free Socialists, the opposition party, to potentially replace him in an election. The problem is a US election isn't imminent. Unlike other nations, including those in Europe, their election timetable is rigid. So, Cross added a name from the Federal Republic Party who he believes stands out.

He types in that name in his search engine, out of curiosity, to find out if anything has changed in the past few weeks. A link of interest pops up, so he clicks on it:

'Jason Briar (FR-CO), a member of the House, filed a motion to vacate the chair which would challenge the leadership of Speaker...'

Cross stops reading, types in another search and finds a link from the Washington Standard:

'Control of the House changed after three Free Socialist representatives died within days of each other. Nothing was found to link their deaths but two were deemed suspicious even though age was a credible factor in each. The third died in a horrific car accident. A Federal Republic wave that swept the US after President Walkman's rescue in the South China Sea facilitated the House' majority switch in party representation.'

Cross messages Granfield, who quickly responds.

'Two died from cardiac arrest. The third got t-boned by a drunk driver.'

'Did anyone perform toxicology reports?'

'Not that I'm aware of.'

'I would like to request their bodies be exhumed and samples taken.'

'What's your thinking?'

'They were murdered so Federal Republics could have a Speaker of the House installed. Free Socialists should have replaced those seats but didn't. Coercion took place I believe.'

'For what end?'

'Jason Briar, a Federal Republic congressman from Colorado, has filed a motion to replace the current Speaker.'

'And?'

'Briar is on my list.'

'Shit. I will get those reports but it's common opinion in Washington that Deep State members are Free Socialists.'

'Usually, but not anymore, I guess. Power, money and control are not restricted to partisan lines.'

Cross puts the phone down and continues with his evaluation. There are overtures evolving from the Baltic states. Something is brewing over there that clearly needs to be addressed. The French election is also a genuine problem and the person he has listed under Mitchell's name is surely the one who will take his place in the UK election.

It is quite a quandary. Who does he go after first? The risks and complexities will be existential with increased security at any political event from now on. This will get worse if they eliminate the elected patrons one by one.

He switches off his computer, walks over to the bar in the living room and finds Balvenie 21. He half-fills two tumblers and moves over to the sofa, handing one to Sadeghi who had been waiting for him.

She had been watching some Iranian show but turned it off when Cross entered the room. A phone message had sent him immediately packing and scampering overseas. Four days later he returns, and two important figures are dead. Sadeghi is a smart lady and can read between the lines. Neither of them can say anything, so they don't. She harbours deep concern because she sees this heading into serious international politics involving heads of state, where anything goes. Before it was a dangerous, collaborative and well-funded private entity but now this is different. With governments' sovereign wealth and personal power at stake, there are no rules of law or restrictive boundaries whatsoever that control them, and the gloves come off.

She leans over and kisses him on the lips. "I love you, Daniel Cross."

7

Orchestrated Chaos, Vilnius Lithuania

Cross is in Vilnius, Lithuania observing a peaceful rally organised by an anti-Latvian coalition. It is a cool September Saturday. Banners are being held in a well-orchestrated march against Latvia's Prime Minister Ozolins and his country's close affiliation with Russia. The Baltic states used to form part of the fifteen soviet republics and now Lithuania, independent since 1990, has most of its borders lined with pro-Russian countries. This makes the people exceptionally nervous. Its accession into the NATO alliance came in 2004 and, consequently, the EU is monitoring the situation very carefully.

Cross volunteered himself to be a participant in the process too, with Granfield's approval, partly in anticipation of possible retaliatory action for the deaths of Cartwright and Mitchell. The other more important reason is the increased volatility in the area's political environment. The situation had degraded into a cesspit of accusations and innuendos emanating from Lithuania's leader in his desire to solidify power and control. Cross wants to oversee the scheduled protest rally, to ensure it remains within the confines of controlled stability. Anything less would light a military fuse.

He is in the Old Town district which is one of the oldest surviving medieval towns in Northern Europe. The streets are narrow with historic two-three storey terraced buildings and footpaths lining each side. Old churches with ornate domed spires regally populate the area. Cross is standing on the balcony of his room at Alexa Old Town observing the procession as it approaches.

Suddenly, off in the distance, what he perceives to be firecrackers are heard. He doesn't quite understand until faint screams echo.

Alerted to this, he hears more shots. Swiftly, he exits his room and runs downstairs, then departs the hotel and heads in the direction of the shrieking.

Approaching cobbled streets, he passes people running in random directions. In front of him are dead and dying citizens laying in their own pool of blood. Stepping to one side, he quickly scans the area. Most of the buildings have their windows open with occupants just staring. Some are crying and in shock, not even sure what they are witnessing.

The streets are chaos. Unexpectedly, two more pops and two more people close to him drop. He swivels his head to find where they came from and sees a sniper's rifle being withdrawn from a nearby window opening. He notices two other snipers escaping over the roofs. Armed already, Cross aims and fires. The one in front flees but the second is hit and rolls off the roof onto the street below.

He must react quickly so darts off into the building the snipers came from. He runs up the stairs and enters a back room which has the door ajar. Inside is a window that is open, with the drapes wafting due to a disturbance. A trailing leg disappears out the window frame and Cross runs over to find a third assassin on the tiled roof. He has his gun drawn so points and fires. One shot ricochets off a chimney whilst the second penetrates the leg. The assailant cries out, loses his balance and falls some distance to the ground.

Cross climbs out of the window and scales the red ceramic tiles.

He leans over the edge and looks down. The murderer is attempting to get up but is struggling. He expectantly sees Cross peering over and shoots, just missing him. Cross is pissed and leaps off the roof, landing on the back of the shooter causing his spine to break.

Cross climbs off, rolls him over and starts hunting the body for any material item of consequence. There is nothing but surveys him as he keeps searching. He does not look Lithuanian, Cross thinks. Finally, in the jeans rear pocket is a folded sheet of paper. Pulling it out, he stuffs it in his own trouser pocket.

In the background are sirens and car horns as emergency vehicles make their way. Abstract mayhem and confusion have descended on the scene which is a signal for Cross to vacate the area. He disappears into the frenzied crowd and in the general direction of his hotel, but not before he injects one more bullet into the killer.

8

A Beautiful News Anchor

"Two of our people were killed, sir." Handcock says.

Wu is on his corporate jet and had been observing the rally in Vilnius.

"I saw it was peaceful until we applied external influence. What do we know?"

"So far, the predictive reaction is as expected, if our media influence is credible. The journalists are the voice, and a local news anchor has been coerced into spewing what we tell her to."

"Are our men prepared?"

"Yes, sir. There are huge local and international condemnations. The communities believe the assassins emerged across Latvia's border in order to disrupt a peaceful protest against their prime minister."

"Good." That part of Wu's plan is working. "Any further developments on the deaths in the Alps and London?"

"We are delving into satellite imagery. However, it is difficult, and this person is a professional hitman. We have located a possible suspect in London from photographs, but he wore black clothing and a balaclava before leaping into the crowd."

"Keep looking."

Cross is back in his hotel room and has been watching local news with captions. He calls Granfield.

"David, the rally was purposely sabotaged. The local news anchor is reporting it as propagated by mercenaries from Latvia but no idea where she got that information from. Surely too early to tell who organised this."

"Do you have ideas?"

"I killed two of the active shooters and one of them certainly wasn't Latvian." Cross is keeping quiet about what he found since he has yet to research anything. "It is something I hope to find more information on before I leave here."

"We need to find out if this is retaliatory and if Wu is connected."

"That's my plan?"

"Good, you have a plan," Granfield injects.

"So far." They both laugh. "My gut tells me they are trying to influence politics in the Baltics with a war. A war will be yet another distraction and more of democracy's deceptional bull. They aren't looking for democracy: Deep State is looking to secure control of people and assets through their imperialistic tendencies. We need to investigate Lithuania and Latvia leaders. The latter prime minister may already be in trouble and a war erroneously provoked by his country will push it over the edge. Deep State will replace him with one of their cronies."

"We have looked into the Lithuanian leader, and he is allegedly pro-EU. They might not want that either, but he could perhaps be swayed if he hasn't been already."

"Yes. This is obviously a concern."

"Let me know when you leave the country and what you find. Congressman Briar is moving with his push to be House speaker. The vote is coming up."

"I saw that. Mitchell's underling is also making waves in London."

"Get back to me."

The phone goes dead.

Cross pulls out the paper he extracted from the assassin and opens it. It's a Vilnius hotel check-in receipt, so he types the address into his phone's GPS.

The taxi pulls up outside Artagonist Hotel, which is close to the university and just north of Old Town. He steps out and walks into the lobby. He leaps up the stairs, avoiding the need to answer hotel workers' questions, and locates room 24. He puts his head to the door and hears nothing.

"Good."

A door key scanner is inserted into the lock and lights start flashing. In a few seconds, a green light illuminates and Cross rotates the handle. He quietly pushes the door open and sees the room is dark. Gun in hand, he enters, and then closes the door behind him before turning on the light.

A single bed occupies the room. Clothes are scattered and a small bag sits on a chair. He scours the room, closet and bathroom to confirm he is void of unwanted company. The travel bag has a few shirts in it and an airline ticket, which he stuffs in his back trouser pocket. Next, he walks over to the desk and on it sits a small yellow notepad. Scribbled are the name Janina Gabrys and her telephone number. He is familiar with this name since he watched her on the local news this afternoon. Underneath are shorthand notes about times, street names, buildings and, presumably, last name of associates with reference to the protest rally and the area where Cross killed the hotel guest. He rips off the first few pages of the pad and stuffs those in his jacket pocket. Next to that is the pen that was used so he solicits that too; hopefully, it has fingerprints on it.

Exiting the room, he shuts the door behind him. He was cautious not to disturb anything, so no one was going to suspect it was trespassed.

Standing across the street from the hotel he dials Gabrys' number. She picks up and answers in Latvian.

"Do you speak Russian or English?" Cross enquires.

"Both," she replies.

"I am sorry to bother you, but my name is Gerald Callum, and I am an English reporter from the Associated Press. I was at the protest rally this lunchtime and was there when the shooting started. I have some questions I would like to pose and would be honoured to discuss them with you."

"How did you get my number?"

Cross is winging this one but the airline ticket he found is a roundtrip from Barcelona. "Your friend from Barcelona passed it on."

"Mr. Sanchez?"

"Yes." He also noted the name and hopes she doesn't know he is dead. He might not even be her friend.

"There is a bar I frequent, and people know me there." She proceeds to pass on instructions.

Cross has an hour to find it and then prepare.

He is sitting at the end of an imposing dark wooden bar facing the door when Gabrys walks in. He recognises the face from the news and waves before standing up to greet her.

"Hello, Ms. Gabrys. It is an honour to make your acquaintance."

"Hello, Mr. Callum. It is an honour for me too. I researched your name for my protection, and you have a reputation to savour." She takes his hand as she speaks. "Please, call me Janina." Her English is very strong although accented with a Baltic twist.

"Thank you. Call me Gerald."

She removes her fur-lined, white linen jacket and hangs it on the back of the chair, then sits herself.

Her curly blonde hair and makeup are immaculate. The black Italian wool dress sits above the stocking-covered knees and rides further up as she crosses her legs. The dress' V-neck is modest and she looks impeccable. Expensive watch and jewelry grace her slender body, and a large diamond ring pronounces her marital status. Cross would have guessed a TV personality had he not already known.

"Welcome to Latvia, Gerald."

They order cocktails before Cross starts the conversation.

"Thank you for agreeing to meet with me, Janina. I saw you present the news this afternoon and you look more beautiful in person." He places a business card in front of her.

"Thank you, Gerald." Her smile radiates genuine warmth. "It was a sad day for Lithuanians." She visually scans the card before putting it in her Gucci handbag.

"How many casualties have been confirmed?"

"The newsroom has confirmed fourteen dead and thirty-seven injured so far. A majority of injuries were induced by the panic and those numbers are expected to climb. Some were crushed."

"This is obviously political. I understand there is rising tension between the two countries."

"Yes. I have word that the assassins were Latvian which would add complexity to a volatile situation."

Now Cross is happy she brings up this very topic.

"How do you know the killers were Latvian?"

This question rattles Gabrys but she controls herself; though not enough. Cross observes her shift in manner as she takes a sip of her cocktail.

"I am a reporter so cannot reveal sources. You understand this, Gerald. However, it was information called into the newsroom just after the shootings."

This answer conflicts with data Cross had already obtained and doesn't explain her name written on the killers' notepad. It is his turn to take a sip of the Stumbras-derived cocktail as he analyses this.

"I called contacts in the journalist world, and they don't have that information yet. They can only guess based on the politics."

"I report the news five days a week and I know what is going on in my own country." Troubled by his comments, she takes another sip. She turns her head to look at him. "You likely know Lithuania's affiliation is with Brussels. To the north and east of us we have pro-Russian countries on our borders. This isn't healthy for our citizens, nor does it encourage political stability."

She seems irritated by Cross' questioning, and he needs to reassure her in order to stimulate and maintain a constructive but serene dialogue.

"I understand the dilemmas facing the Baltics and must apologise for my naïve and pretentious positioning." He smiles at her. "It is a sensitive topic, and I should have crafted my words with more discretion." Wishing to change subject, "Who is your friend, Mr. Sanchez?"

Gabrys places her hand on his arm. "I'm sorry for my tone," then removes it. "I only met him two days ago. He called me out of the blue, just like you did. We met for drinks at this same bar actually. He is an unofficial member of the Catalan separatist movement in Barcelona, but he is officially a representative of the Spanish prime minister's party in the Upper House, or Senate. I researched this also. The ruling monarch is a ceremonial head of state in Spain, and some want to change that."

Why the hell would a Spanish political figure be assassinating people in Lithuania? Cross asks himself. "Yes, I'm well versed on the political layout." Now he is even more confused.

He changes subjects. "I'm hungry, are you?"

"Yes, we can order food. Do you have any preference?"

"No," replies Cross.

It is obvious the bartender knows her as she passes on their order by requesting 'the usual'.

They continue discussing politics even after the array of organic food arrives. Cross feels comfortable but there is something wrong here. Gabrys knew about the events before they happened. She had to since she knows one of the killers, who isn't Latvian. He doesn't know if she was paid off, is part of the revolution or was pressured because of who she is and what she knows. He suspects the latter. However, she was told to report the involvement of Latvia before anyone else knew anything.

After they finish eating and order another cocktail, Gabrys excuses herself and heads to the bathroom, but not before she adds an anecdote in a whispered tone.

"There is something going on in this country and I'm scared. Let's go somewhere else when I return."

When she doesn't return Cross becomes deeply concerned. He waits a few more minutes before mobilising himself, and strides to the ladies' bathroom.

He walks in and one of the stalls is locked.

"Janina, are you in there." No answer. This time he shouts. "Janina?"

He doesn't ask a third time and forces the door open. It is empty but her Gucci bag sits on the floor. He hurries out of the bathroom area carrying her bag and scans the bar and restaurant. She isn't anywhere and has vanished.

He runs out of the building and just as he does, he notices a vehicle leaving. It is dark outside but in the back seat is Gabrys with the silhouette of a gun pointing to her head.

9

Attempted Kidnapping

A taxi is waiting across the street so Cross runs over and leaps into the back.

"Следуйте за автомобилем со светловолосой дамой сзади." Follow the car with the blonde lady in the back, he says in Russian. The driver looks it, thinks Cross, so hopes he is.

"Ok, but I speak a little English."

The driver sets off behind the black BMW, careful not to get too close. He looks bemused as if cab drivers lay in wait for such an occurrence.

Cross needs to think. Wherever they are going, he must stop this endgame before they kill Gabrys. He types the license plate into his phone and sends a message. Thirty seconds later, a response is received.

'It is a Lithuanian government vehicle.'

He reads the rest of the abbreviated text. "Shit."

"We need to stop this car before it gets to the Presidential Palace." He says to the driver.

"I know a shortcut."

The driver removes his vehicle from the tail and speeds off toward Old Town. Streets are still blocked off from the afternoon turmoil, but he seems well versed on where he is heading. Cross hopes his own intuition is accurate.

The driver pulls over and points. "Over there is vehicle entrance to Palace, sir. Here is only access point and there is security. BMW will enter from this street." He says, in a strong accent.

"Great. Please wait for me."

Cross climbs out and views the Palace. He locates a recessed entranceway to a university building across from security, and out of sight. A few minutes later he sees the BMW approaching and wastes no time. He lifts his gun, points and fires.

The windshield shatters as the velocity of the special bullet penetrates the driver's skull. The instantaneous death as a result of the head exploding causes the BMW to veer off the road and in Cross' direction. He jumps out of the way as the vehicle slams into the building that is providing him cover.

He runs around the back and pulls open the rear door. Inside are two passengers who have been momentarily shocked from the sudden and violent impact. The interior is covered in human brain, skull fragments and blood. Gabrys is still alive but moaning and in tears. Her dress had been pulled up and Cross is livid. He removes his jacket and places it over her head.

"Sorry. This isn't going to be pleasant."

He looks at the guy slouched next to her, points his gun and shoots.

"Fuck you too."

The taxi pulls up alongside as Cross drags Gabrys free. He shoves her into the rear of the cab and climbs in as the car takes off. He looks behind and notices security stirring. They are too slow as the cab driver disappears into the night.

Gabrys comes around and tries to focus.

"Where are we?"

"In the back of a cab." Cross replies.

"Take us here," and supplies an address. "I know the owners."

Cross transfers the information to the cab driver and off he goes, seemingly engrossed in all of this with a desire to help them.

Gabrys exits the shower, dries off and pulls on clothing her friend has supplied. She walks into the living room and sits next to Cross on the sofa. Her demeanor equates to someone still in shock and the wet hair only enforces it. Two mugs filled with hot tea sit on the coffee table, so she takes one.

"Who are you?" she enquires.

"Where are we, first, and is this place secure?"

"My friend and I went to school and college together. This is their family's summer home in Trakai, thirty kilometres west of Vilnius. This is an extremely close community, and we are safe here. Everybody watches everything. They even have a boat on the lake for our escape." Attempting to inject some levity.

"Thanks for this consideration." They both laugh. "You look much better after removing brain fragments."

"I didn't think being a news anchor would afford such extremities." She has an infectious smile but is mildly shaking. "Thank you for saving my life and I don't wish to sound ungrateful, but who are you?"

If she has credible testimony, he's going to have to trust her, at least to a certain degree.

"I'm a mercenary from the US and unofficially working with the CIA. However, I make my own rules because they will deny everything." He hesitates and gauges her reaction before continuing. "I am Daniel Cross."

She goes silent, deep in thought and doesn't say anything for a few minutes.

"Thee Daniel Cross?" with emphasis on 'thee'. "The scientist?"

"That sounds auspicious, and I was forgetting I used to be."

"You don't look and dress like any international journalist I know, but you have seen things in your life. I could tell that the first time I saw you. Well, well; the infamous Daniel Cross just saved my life. My employer is certainly not going to believe this story," and chuckles.

She sits in confused, benevolent silence whilst studying him.

"I can't tell you what I have seen and been through. But I can tell you I never want to see another damn robot again, ever."

"Yes, Daniel. I can't even begin to imagine your experiences. So, who is Gerald Callum? That was an impressive profile."

"I have friends in low places," and laughs, more as a release.

"Yes, I can see."

"You wanted to tell me something in the restaurant. You do realise I rescued you from entering the Presidential Palace?"

"I was partially incapacitated and pulled away as I made my way into the bathroom stall. They stuck a needle in me and then a gun in my back so had little choice. I have been doing my own journalistic research lately. As an anchor on the most popular TV news channel in Lithuania, I also see and hear things." She sighs and continues. "Obviously you know who Lutkus is?"

"The Lithuania prime minister? Yes."

"His name keeps coming up in my research. He is pro-EU, but in reality, he isn't. I read between the lines of news I am paid to promote but most of it is nonsense. It is fabricated bullshit."

Cross hasn't heard her use profanity before, and it doesn't seem to match her feminine, angelic personality.

"Lutkus is dangerous and aligned with Deep State. He tells us what stories to promote and how to angle them. Our network is controlled and censored, yet we are supposed to be a democracy."

Cross has a question mark on Lutkus in his flowchart and happy she validates that.

"Democracy is just an illusion in this case. You confirm my research too although I admit I wasn't one hundred percent on him. So, who is Sanchez?"

"Lutkus' switch in political persuasion is recent. Like I told you, Sanchez called me, and we met in the same bar. He threatened to throw me in a lake tied to a concrete block if I didn't do what he asked. I had to convince the news network my information came from a reliable source."

"Do you have children?"

"Yes, but I'm divorced."

"Your ring is impressive."

"This is simply for cosmetics. The network wouldn't allow me to be single, so this is their image, their illusion. It also helps to keep some lunatics at bay, but not all," as she looks at him wearing a sly grin.

He smiles. "Yes, well, some aren't deterred." Returning to the subject matter, "The prime minister was kidnapping you. What was the Palace's aim? It wasn't because you were talking to me."

"Correct, it wasn't. They asked who you were, so I told them. I wasn't expecting to live so I faked a name." She looks into his eyes. "You are welcome." She waits for his reaction but there isn't one. "Unfortunately, I convinced my employer that Latvia is involved so this will be the narrative they pursue." She sips her tea and then continues.

"Sanchez wants to start a war and this misinformation will likely do that. A war will achieve two goals: 1) allow Lutkus to control the people and make them dependent on him, and 2) overthrow Ozolins. My research suggests they have someone to replace Ozolins." She takes a breather and hasn't expressed any of her findings to anyone else before.

"I did what the Palace wanted me to do which is promote the beginnings of an uprising. Lutkus, I suspect, wanted to rape me before terminating my life. However, Deep State is into the insidious sexual exploitation of children so don't quite understand that part."

She starts to sob and Cross tries to comfort her with words.

"Come on, Janina, you are simply gorgeous, intelligent and a strong woman. These people are sick freaks."

She retains some of her composure. "Thank you, Daniel."

Working exceptionally hard to maintain his own emotions, he gets up, pulls a facial tissue from a box sitting on a mantle and hands it to her, before returning to the sofa. He understands after seeing his own life flash before him, so he has empathy for this poor lady.

"You also confirm this part of my research but why is a Spanish senator involved?"

"I couldn't figure that one out either," as she gathers herself.

"Wait. I need to do something quick." He picks up his phone and types a message. "Sorry. My contact in low places needs to update Callum's profile picture, just in case." He grins. "The Lithuanian government will be looking at security footage from the bar and scrutinising the credit card I used. They will know the name you provided is fake. Before you arrived, I convinced your friend behind the bar to move all the camera angles. They will be a tad perturbed when they see we are out of view." He plants a big grin on his face. "They think they are dealing with amateurs, and the bartender wanted to protect you too."

"I need a real drink." Gabrys stands up and walks over to the alcohol cart.

"Me too. Lithuanian vodka if your friend has some."

She brings back two glasses and hands one to Cross, before sitting back down.

"Thank you. What happens to you now?"

"Obviously, my life is in danger. I must work to correct the narrative and attempt to salvage my tarnished reputation. It may be too late to stop the war now the incendiary fuses have been lit. But I can at least try to limit the potential fallout."

She is, of course, frightened, Cross can tell.

"We can help you. I can help you if you need anything. They are going to be looking for you for sure. Get your children out of the country too. Deep State has already infiltrated some select countries and they are preparing others."

He stops for a moment to let her digest what he is telling her. Then he continues. "You must know about Cartwright and Mitchell?"

"Yes. I read about them and reported their news. Cartwright is, sorry, was a big sponsor of all this and Mitchell was set to win the upcoming UK election. It appears they were both murdered."

"Poor choice of wording but yes, it appears so."

"I found out Mitchell was killed with an explosive projectile, just like the driver tonight."

She abruptly stops talking and Cross sees her brain churning and connecting dots. This lady is smart and her eyes light up.

"You assassinated him?" Gabrys shifts to the edge of the sofa and rotates her whole body to face him. Her bottom jaw is on the floor. "You did it?" Sounding rather startled at her own revelation.

"I'm not going to sit here and admit to anything, but I don't play around either, Janina." His blood pressure is a little elevated. "They have tried to kill me several times and came after my fiancée too. She has special protection because of it but I am livid. They are playing games with the wrong people. Sorry, but there is a special place in hell when we are finished with them."

"I am sorry. I wasn't accusing you."

She lifts her glass and Cross reciprocates.

"I know, but I have one final question though: does your research bring up Wu's name?"

"Yes," is all she says.

10

Hotel Rendezvous, Washington, DC

Anderson is on top of Briar in a luxury suite in Washington, DC. She had arranged to rendezvous in a lavish hotel restaurant that evening before adjourning to his room to spend the night. He isn't aware she has been trained and this is the result of it. It is morning now and their third sexual go-around since last night. He calls it passion, but she doesn't.

Anderson climaxes just as Briar releases his final push and she waits a few seconds, then rolls off him onto the bed sheets. Wu had instructed her how to properly satisfy these narcissistic, power-induced, despicable arseholes and her technique works to perfection. It has turned into a source of amusement even though she gets off on it, sometimes. She faked the last three orgasms.

"It isn't too difficult," Wu had told her. "It might even be the simplest artform to discover." He was correct. "These men and women clamour for attention and are easy to seduce." She has satisfied both.

Briar rolls over and tries to hug her. "I love you, Florence."

"I love you too." She doesn't and is repulsed by his grotesquely large physique. She detests his very existence.

He is much older but obviously a man of power and wealth. She climbs out of bed and walks over to the bathroom. Briar follows in all his flabby nakedness. He had removed his condom and is about ready to ingest another blue pill.

"You won't need that."

Anderson was a model and met Wu two years ago whilst escorting. He convinced her to quit, which she did. She never knew her father, who walked away when her mother was pregnant. Two years into her life, she was abandoned so never knew her mother either. She was left in a basket outside an orphanage in Cincinnati where she was taken in. The adopted parents looked after her and provided a real life until they became abusive in her early developmental teen years. She eventually ran away.

Anderson became aware of her own beauty and the strength it holds, so taught herself how to extort the virtues of it. Soon after moving to New York City, a modeling agency had noticed her when waitressing and she signed a contract. As it turned out, it was an afront for an exclusive escort agency serving affluent men and women around the world. She was only nineteen but later learned some were underage teenagers. Wu had paid for her to fly to Taiwan, and he ended up treating her like no man ever had before.

Wu has provided an important role and one Anderson must flourish in. She is being asked to sequester the purposely chosen politicians and elevate their dynamic strengths as they manoeuvre into strategic political sanctuaries. In essence, she must use her beauty to control and keep them in check, to ensure they don't falter or be distracted. On one hand, seducing these self-possessed morons was the easy part. She is an expert at seductive mind games and knows how to dress the part. On the other hand, overseeing and regulating their conceited activities will turn out to be much more problematic.

For now, she is their dream and fulfills their perverted fantasies.

"Your campaign to become the next Speaker of the House has

gained significant momentum. It will be purely academic."

"I'm going to divorce my wife once I become Speaker."

She is brushing her teeth to remove his nauseating taste after kissing him. "I want you focused on the House voting."

"I'm being serious."

"Me too."

She gets dressed and rummages through her night bag. She pulls out bundles of hundred-dollar bills strapped together and tosses them on the bed.

"You are being paid well to become Speaker. I suggest you earn it."

He is what Wu termed 'besotted and confused' which he said will happen. "I love you."

"I will be in contact soon," and departs the suite.

A twin-turboprop Cessna Conquest I has been arranged for Cross at Paluknio Aerodrome, south of Trakai, where it will take him directly to London. Gabrys and he had covertly traveled to Vilnius in the middle of the night to find her children. Fortuitously, they had been with Gabrys' friend whilst she was having drinks with Cross, a friend that was not known amongst her acquaintances or family. They had to be careful because of curfews authorities had imposed after the unrest. Gabrys had called a very close friend who is a local police chief, and he is helping them. Cross was uncomfortable with this idea, but their options were limited. She had assured him of his integrity and trust.

The chief is using his own patrol car to advance this mission. After picking up the two children, they navigate back out of the city and toward the aerodrome. Cops and military are everywhere.

Cross' vigilance is high, but he is justifiably concerned. Surely the Palace must be looking for Gabrys and he is combing the vicinity for government vehicles, or any vehicle for that matter. The government has vast resources at its disposal. They made it back out into the countryside and away from the big city. It is still dark, so it is easier to spot someone following although he has been known to be wrong.

The chief had decided on a longer but less-traveled alternative to the main thoroughfares and headed southwest out of Vilnius. Now on the A4, they are heading north toward the airfield. Cross had been earlier notified the plane was ready.

As they edge closer, Cross sees a row of vehicular lights coming from north of the aerodrome heading south. Before he says anything, the chief has also spotted them and puts his foot down.

They turn into the aerodrome and Cross sees the Cessna with its engines idling, ready. Now the traffic coming towards them has closed in, fast.

"Over there, Chief," as Cross points to an aircraft at the end of the grassy field.

"Oh, God." Murmurs Gabrys. "Hurry, Filip."

He pulls up to the aircraft's door and Gabrys and her children, along with Cross, immediately pile out of the patrol car.

Cross shakes his hand and follows the others onto the plane via a step. The chief speeds off as the parade Cross has been monitoring enters the airfield. He latches the cabin door as the Cessna powers up its twin engines and embarks on its rapid escape. It is too fast and lifts off just as the convoy arrives. Cross sees military people exiting the army vehicles with guns in hand but those are now futile.

"Hold on," shouts someone up front.

With enough distance between it and the ground, the plane's pilot banks hard right.

Soon after departure, a message on Cross' phone appears.

'Safe?'

'Yes, thank you.' He responds. 'Just…'

'See you in London.'

An hour into the flight his passengers are all asleep, so he messages Sadeghi. She is safe, thank God, but Cross worries. She knowns now what is going on and he fears for her life more than his own.

He messages Granfield. 'Escaped Lithuania.'

'Good.' Comes the reply. 'See you when you return from UK.'

11
Meeting Old Friends

"Sanchez' death has been confirmed and Gabrys left Lithuania from a private airfield west of Vilnius in the early morning hours, sir. She had help."

"Help from whom?" Wu is incensed. Too many events suggest they are controlled and not random.

"The credit card indicated a Gerald Callum, who is apparently an award-winning freelance reporter for the Associated Press. We verified his existence and accessed security footage from the bar. However, the camera angles were not correct."

"Explain."

"They did not show people coming in and out nor focus on the bar area they were sitting at. It was as if someone knew. She was removed by two of Lutkus' security details, but they were shot dead during an automobile incident. Lutkus was going to terminate her since she had served our purpose."

"Automobile incident?"

"Someone stopped the car entering the Palace compound and took Gabrys."

Wu's body temperature is escalating. "The person who helped her is from the Baltics? They know she is accusing Latvia of involvement. Could it be someone trying to shut her up?"

"That's a possibility because this looks like another professional operation."

"So, where is she now?" Wu senses who it is but is desperate for proof.

"We haven't been able to track the Cessna Conquest I."

Wu slams the phone down and clears his desk with one swift move of his right arm. God, he is pissed. A lieutenant comes running in to see what the commotion is.

"Get the hell out."

The twin-engine plane lands at a private airfield northeast of London. The sun is just trying to lift off from the east under heavy cloud cover. It is a cold, damp morning. Cross steps off first and is greeted by Jennings.

"Hello, Nick."

"We meet again, my friend." They embrace.

Cross helps Gabrys step down with her two children and introduces them.

"Nice to meet you, Janina."

"Likewise, Mr. Jennings." They shake hands.

"Nick is fine, ma'am." He smiles at her.

Behind Jennings are two Range Rovers and they walk over to them.

"Janina, my associate Agent Richards will take you and your children to a secure facility. We will provide your style of clothing, showers and access to the internet. I'm sure you need to reach people back home and your employer is interested in hearing from you. We need to calm people down.

"My boss at MI6 has a recording studio to facilitate you broadcasting nightly news 'from a remote location'. Lithuanian citizens will react if you disappear, so it is imperative you continue. Your employer already knows. As an added benefit, we like to mess with Wu and his cohorts."

"Thank you," as she attempts to laugh.

"I told you he is insane," pipes in Cross as he smiles at Gabrys.

Jennings grins and continues. "This is temporary. However, we need to advise you on what you can and cannot say from this point forward. This is vitally important. The altercation in Vilnius may spark a war and this is what Deep State wants. We are unsure if we can diffuse that even with proper caution, but we may be in a position to mitigate it somewhat. There are many things in play here with unknowns out of our control, unfortunately."

"Yes, I know." She smiles, kind of, but she is very tired.

"Daniel filled me in and I'm sorry this happened to you. Our response needs to be coordinated."

Agent Richards steps forward. "Come with me, Ms. Gabrys. I'll take care of you and your family."

"You look tired so get some rest. You will be looked after, and Daniel and I will be in contact shortly." Jennings adds, "You have Daniel's number so message him later."

Cross and Jennings walk over to their vehicle and climb in.

"I have an interesting idea for Janina and will explain later. But first, I have some friends who want to see you."

An hour north they arrive in a small country village. It is discrete and away from prying eyes and ears. Cross loves these places as they drive on narrow country lanes, pass decades-old hand-built stone walls and white-washed homes constructed centuries ago, complete with thatched roofs.

After reaching their destination, Jennings parks in the back of a quaint English pub nestled off a beaten track. It is a place only locals are likely to find. They step out of the Range Rover and walk inside.

The owner acknowledges Jennings as they walk on heavily varnished uneven floors and past the worn hand-carved wooden bar before entering a quiet corner. Sitting at a square, antiquated mahogany table are Moore and Moore Jr. Cross is taken aback and he thought he couldn't be shocked anymore.

They stand up and vehemently shake hands and hug tightly.

"You saved my life, Daniel. I have waited so long to thank you."

Moore, still wearing his black thick-rimmed glasses, looks healthier than when Cross rescued him off the island. Much healthier in fact, but the ordeal and constant torture evidently took a toll. He has aged and his speech is slow and hesitant.

Cross stares at him, smiles and then looks for his birthmark on the neck.

"Sorry, just checking." Everybody laughs. "I knew you had one. Those robots nearly drove me over the friggin edge. You are dressed significantly better and have a nicer watch. I never understood that part and it left me perplexed." He looks at him with admiration because he can't imagine the tortuous pain and what it took to recuperate, if he ever will. "My friend, you look fantastic."

"How are you, Daniel?" asks Moore Jr.

The owner brings over four beers which encourages them to take a seat.

"I am good, thanks. The information you are providing me is causing major problems. I think we're onto something here. The set-up in London was masterclass."

Moore Jr. laughs, but barely. "Your executions, pun intended, were brilliant and yes, we are. They must be panicking by now."

Cross hesitates as he venerates the Moore's.

"Wow, thank you, Nick. I'm shocked. It is so nice both of you came to see me. I'm honoured." Cross is rocked. "You look good, Graeme. I'm so happy to see you are improving from when I saw you last."

"It's been a slow, arduous process but every day I see improvement."

"How is Helen?"

"She's recovering also. Harder for her psychologically because of the type of abuse. Thanks for asking. She sends her love and says thank you. You saved her from untold persecution, pain and horror."

With a pained expression, he turns to face Jennings. "I'm shocked. Thank you, Nick, for arranging this." His linguistic ability briefly deserted him as he repeats himself.

"Thank you for saving my parents. We owe you a debt of gratitude."

"No. No you don't." Cross answers shaking his head. He puts his hand up to stop him, but Moore Jr. shakes it instead. "It is the price we pay, and this isn't over yet."

"You look like you have recovered also from being shot at twice. You look good." Moore adds.

"Yes, it also took time, but thank you. I can't go through metal detectors now though." He shrugs, and grins.

Cross is parched so takes a few gulps of his beer. Jennings turns and takes control.

"They have delectable pub food here so let's order before we discuss anything further."

Soon after they finish eating, the plates are cleared, and Jennings brings out his laptop and turns it on. His back is against a wall for maximum privacy. He clicks on a file and accesses the flowchart Cross had sent him. The three move closer to view the screen.

"We all agree this is the structure."

"Yes," answers Moore. He doesn't need to study it. "Graeme and I have been compiling the same data."

"Janina, whom I met in Vilnius," looking at Moore and Moore Jr., "has also been working on this. She shared similar information."

Jennings is calm and is being serious. "We must figure out what the next phase of their plan is. As far as I can see, they have political nominees in UK, France and US all vying for position."

Cross studies the flowchart and looks to see where he can insert Sanchez.

"I killed an assassin in Vilnius named Sanchez. His profile came up as a member of the Senate from Spain. Why would a politician be involved in the killings on foreign soil? That is a huge risk to facilitate and implement, surely?"

Moore removes his eyes from the monitor and faces Cross. "Understand something, Daniel. They didn't swap all people with clones. He could be just assuming the identity of Sanchez."

"Jesus. Now we are looking at clones who are real people."

"Clever, isn't it?"

Cross sighs, leans forward and bangs his head on the table. Then he repeats the exercise. "I think I need more beer to cope with this crap," and orders another round. "I left my prescribed medication at home too."

"That isn't all," Moore adds. "They replaced body parts such as facial features, limbs and organs. I was deeply medicated through-out my ordeal, but I still could partially hear. I also saw things."

Jennings quips. "They…"

Cross abruptly sits up and puts his left hand on Jennings' right bicep to stop him.

"Wait. Sorry Nick." He twists to face Moore. "Hold on a second. What did you just say, Graeme?"

"They had the ability to replace body parts."

"So, not only do we have people to replace people, but some are enhanced with artificial body parts?"

"That is precisely what I'm saying."

Cross picks up his second pint and downs the whole lot. Then he lets this new information marinate for a few minutes as the others look at him. "I've had enough of this shit already. I need to reserve my straight jacket in a mental asylum."

Jennings looks at him. "Daniel, I am way ahead of you on this. I reserved it for you months ago."

Everyone starts laughing as the owner brings another round.

"This round is on the house, gentlemen." Jennings nods his appreciation.

"One question remains," Cross interrupts. "Do you know where his hideout is after the loss in the South China Sea?"

"We are working on this with the information we have. However, we feel it must be somewhere in Europe," Moore answers.

They each grab another pint as Jennings goes through in precision format what Intelligence wants to do next. When he finishes, he leans back in the chair and folds his arms.

"That should just about do it," he adds. "I've had enough of this shit too."

"No unforeseen event is going to interfere with that plan," adds Cross as he laughs his head off.

12

The Next UK Prime Minister

Cross retrieves a message from his phone as Jennings drives them back to London.

'Thank you for rescuing my family. We are safe now.'

'My pleasure. Good, so I can sleep better later.'

'Thank you, yes. I have been briefed and will go on air in Lithuania tomorrow.'

'How is the newsroom? Did they believe your story?'

'Which one? Lol.'

'You are very funny, considering what just happened.'

'Ladies at the newsroom all want to meet this infamous Daniel Cross. The men don't believe me.'

'Men are smarter, lol.'

'Lol.'

'This is witness-protection protocols for now. We can't have dinner yet.'

'☹.'

'They will not even tell us your location. For your safety too.'

'Yes, I understand.'

'You can message any time and I will watch your broadcast tomorrow.'

'I will tell you when.'

'Ok, I must go. Good luck. Glad you are ok.'

'Thanks.'

Cross puts his phone down.

"I didn't want to disturb your text conversation," injects Jennings as he drives.

"It was Janina. She is very funny considering she escaped death. She is in protection mode."

"I don't even know where they put them, and it's safer this way. She is beautiful and different compared to most TV anchor women I have met. Men also, for that matter. They typically have this air of arrogance and narcissism, believing they are so important."

"I agree. I only met her a little over twenty-four hours ago, but she seems normal."

"Yeah, anyone is normal next to you. Even someone from a mental asylum." Jennings laughs.

"That seems a fair assessment." He looks over at Jennings and grins. "I meant down to earth. She broadcasts tomorrow and it will be interesting how the government in Lithuania will take it."

"Unfortunately, I think a war is on the narrowing horizon. They must replace the PM in Latvia because Russia isn't part of Deep State. Wu has no choice, and we can't react fast enough to stop it. All we can do is attempt to limit the casualties and destruction of infrastructure.

"The militaries are already mobilising and that commenced the early hours of this morning when you were in the air.

"We can't go around eliminating heads of state or soon-to-be elected officials. This must be methodical, as I laid out earlier."

"But I can, as a renegade."

"Indeed," Jennings replies and they both laugh.

"Let's go and see this dick MP who claims to be replacing Mitchell in the election. He gives his speech tonight. We have so many names, I have forgotten his; Daven something-or-other."

"Port."

"Huh?" asks Jennings.

"Davenport. The dick's name is Charles Davenport."

"Another bloody rich wanker."

"They all are, and all sponsored by the same richer wankers." Cross sighs. "His talk tonight will be interesting."

Outside the hotel hosting the event are riot police on horseback along with armed guards and parliamentary security. Police and military hardware are everywhere. Taped off in one area are media outlets and news crews with reporters and cameras. Roads are coned off. It is a shit-show on steroids. Behind them is a mass crowd hoping to catch a glimpse of the new candidate.

"Holy crap," Cross says as he is eyeing all the activity. "This is like a military exercise."

"They must have heard you are on the guest list."

"They are going to need all this then," and chuckles. "We need to avoid any cameras though. Wu must have people here."

"Agreed."

Jennings flashes his credentials, and he sees Cross present the ID he had just given him. They avoid the metal detector and frisking, with access through a private door. They enter the building together, then walk straight downstairs to the conference centre.

The hall at 45 Park Lane is packed and invitation-only. Security is everywhere with armed police randomly questioning people, even after passing the vetting procedure upstairs. It is conceptual insanity.

"MI6 personnel don't need invitations," Jennings quips. "I see a few shadow MPs, secretaries and ministers here. I am looking for just one of his sponsors but can't find any."

"They are all cowards and hide. Are these events always this crazy?"

"Yes, but your recent activities may have heightened their insecure anxieties."

On the wall before entering the vast room is a portrait of Mitchell with his family. Underneath are lists of his achievements, endorsements and letters of condolences.

"The quintessential family man. What bullshit. What he was trying to be part of has nothing to do with family. I wonder what happened to the list of women he cheated on his wife with?"

"You are hilarious, Daniel. Perhaps they didn't have room on the wall, and some of them might be here."

They are about to enter the hall when a stunning blonde accidentally bumps into Cross.

"I'm so sorry. I wasn't looking where I'm going."

"No, it is my fault. Please accept my apologies," says Cross. "We are all in a hurry to listen to more rhetorical political horseshit."

"Yes but coming out of a different mouth makes it sound less phony." They both laugh and then the lady disappears to find her seat.

Cross turns to Jennings. "That lady had an American Midwest accent."

"What lady?"

"Where are you? You are supposed to be an agent."

"That is precisely why I brought you." He chuckles. "Sorry, I'm scanning the room. Let's stand off to the left against the wall over there," as he points. "Less traffic it looks like."

They walk over, lean against the wall and wait for Davenport.

Ten or so minutes pass and then Cross sees the curtains ruffle behind the podium, which is sitting on a small stage. Someone pulls back a curtain and out stroll three males and two females. The audience stands up and starts cheering. It is obvious to Cross which one wants to be prime minister because his suit is in the five-thousand-dollar category. French cuffs and two-thousand-dollar shoes with layers of facial makeup compound the image. The greased hair gives it away, and something he has seen before. He is tall, much larger in girth than he should be and a foreboding figure on the small stage. He has the typical air of arrogance and confidence all politicians exude.

"These fucking arseholes are all the same."

"I know that. Keep scanning the crowd."

Cross looks around and sees the blonde lady who bumped into him. She is focused on the stage, as she finishes taking a few photos with her phone. He wonders how an American got to attend a British invitation-only political party in London. With her exquisite beauty and the elegant way she is dressed, he can perhaps guess.

In front of the podium microphones have been set up but off the stage are more news reporters and cameras. Microphones and small electronic recording devices are pushed forward to record Davenport's every word.

"Ladies and gentlemen, I wish to introduce you to our next UK Prime Minister, Member of Parliament Charles Davenport." There are loud cheers as one of the ladies who made the announcement steps back and makes way for Davenport. The other lady moves forward and stands next to him.

"Are they allowed to say that anymore?" asks Cross.

"Say what?"

"Ladies and gentlemen?"

"Who the hell knows. Fuck the woke morons too."

"That must be his wife standing next to him."

Davenport begins. "Thank you all for activating your invitations and showing up at my fundraiser. First, I wish to extend my condolences." He pauses, placing the right hand over his heart. "Sorry, *our* condolences, to the gentleman who couldn't be here tonight…"

Jennings looks at Cross. "See what you caused."

With the sympathies, pleasantries and introductions now over, Davenport is into his well-prepared monologue written by lawyered speechwriters. Cross doesn't believe any of it and is trying hard to focus, but he keeps drifting and looking over at the blonde lady. She ignores him which breeds confidence that she didn't recognise who he is, so Cross smiles.

"…Prime Minister Clark has a lot of questions to answer. She has failed in her fiduciary responsibilities as head of this country. Our liberties have been eradicated, people are poorer, good paying jobs are scarcer, inflation and energy prices are skyrocketing, house prices are astronomical and unaffordable for the average worker. She has abdicated her civic duties…."

The audience is lapping it up and cheering Davenport on.

"Are we done yet?" Cross asks Jennings.

"No. Stand, listen and learn something. You might run for prime minister one day, and you can plagiarise his speech." He faces Cross and grins.

"I can't spew this shit fast enough," and rolls his eyes.

"Hahaha. Don't you believe it, my friend."

"…it is time we put our own citizens first." A big cheer erupts. "Elect me as your Prime Minister and you will see changes from my first day in office…"

"Oh God help us all." Cross adds.

"…I will remove the Royal Family from hierarchy and return their assets to the people." Another big cheer and it is bedlam. No one is bothering to sit anymore as they are clapping and yelling. Davenport has to elevate his voice to be heard and raises his left arm above his head with a clenched fist as he punches the festering atmosphere. "Government departments will be minimised or removed. I will eradicate power from the few and Western oligarchs will disappear. Everyone will be equal." Another huge cheer erupts.

"This is a form of communism, only on a bigger scale." Cross says.

"This is precisely what Deep State is."

"He is trying to add a veneer of legitimacy. There isn't much variation on the surface but dig deeper and it becomes a dissonance of lust, greed, power, mind-game control, asset-stripping, and death. Adding to that is an astounding compliant populace who believes this garbage."

"That, my friend, is what the vast majority of people don't understand."

13

MI6 Headquarters, London

Cross had never been to Vauxhall Cross Houses before, located on the edge of the Thames in Vauxhall in the southwestern part of central London. It is the headquarters of the Secret Intelligence Services, UK's foreign intelligence agency. He had seen the building in films, but never in real life.

Jennings' office is high up in one of the towers and overlooks the river.

Cross is peering out viewing the river's activities. "Nice location."

"I have served my time and get perks for my loyalty and defense of liberty."

Gabrys had messaged him earlier that morning and was somewhere in one of the buildings setting up her news broadcast. They weren't allowed to know where, but he wished to view it on a TV somewhere. Jennings was facilitating this request.

Cross has strange feelings about the American lady he bumped into last night. "Call it a hunch," he had told Granfield, after Davenport's public showcase. Something wasn't sitting right.

He asked who has the invitation list but even Jennings wasn't sure, so he is researching it.

"Surely our Intelligence needed to know who was attending the event?" he protested.

He is waiting whilst admiring the view.

"Got it. An associate just emailed it to me," announces Jennings, sitting at his desk.

Cross grabs a chair and wheels it over to the computer before sitting on it.

In alphabetical order, sitting near the top is Anderson. "Florence Anderson. Never heard of her. She is listed as a 'Personal Guest' and known to Davenport. Interesting. What else can we find?"

Jennings scrolls down the list. Skipping through parliament members, security, media and the like, he reaches the bottom.

"That is it. Other females on the list were legitimate invitees, allegedly."

"So, who is Florence Nightingale?"

Jennings types in her name and Cross leans over to see which one she is.

"There," as Cross touches the computer screen. "She appears younger in that photo. New York City driver's license and a passport photo soon after were her last known government-required identifications."

Jennings reads her profile. "Poor girl was adopted after being left outside an orphanage in Cincinnati. She moved to New York City and became a waitress. Then she signs on as a model at nineteen and after that, nothing."

"I told you her accent was Midwest. How does she know Davenport? It also makes me wonder if she knew Mitchell."

"Let me ask," and sends an email.

While waiting, Cross messages Granfield.

'Find out what you can about a Florence Anderson, please,' and fills him in on some particulars.'

'Ok.'

14

Florence Anderson's Arrival

On the TV set up by Jennings is Gabrys sitting behind a news desk. She looks exactly like Cross remembers her when they first met in the bar. She is wearing her news-anchor dress code and makeup.

Behind her on a banner is the station's name, TV5, and its logo. Next to that is 'On Location'. Cross is impressed. She is talking in her native language, but it is being dubbed in English on this particular TV.

"Good afternoon and welcome to TV5 news. I am Janina Gabrys coming to you live from a remote location.

"Two days ago I reported on a peaceful protest through the streets of Old Town Vilnius. Unknown assassins purposely disrupted the rally. As it currently stands, sixteen people are now confirmed dead and forty-one injured. Those numbers have increased and are likely to change again. A number of those injuries and deaths resulted from the panic that ensued afterwards."

As she reads, the news feed turns to a video of the scene displaying chaos and people laying on the ground shot, with blood running into the gutters. The feed returns to Gabrys.

"I reported at the time the assassins were Latvian mercenaries. This information has proven to be inaccurate. Two of the killers were shot dead by security. One is a Spanish citizen, and another is local, from Vilnius…"

"Hey." Jumps in Cross. "I wasn't security." Talking to the monitor mounted on the wall in a conference room.

Jennings slaps his arm.

"…got away. No information is available yet on what the motives are. However, since Lithuanian and Latvian military forces have been mobilised, it is fair to conclude that their intent is to promote a conflict neither country relishes. We will update this as the data filters in.

"As an extension, a strict curfew is being enforced by the Lithuanian government and this will continue for the immediate future." A video is now showing quiet streets after-hours being patrolled by police and military vehicles. "No news has been forthcoming from the Palace, despite our repeated requests." A video feed now shows the Presidential Palace lit up at night.

"In more news…"

Jennings mutes the sound.

"The authorities over there will block the transmission." Cross finally says.

"The reality is, they can't. This is broadcast on airwaves we control. This is a feed from one of our satellites that we moved into place last night, and it will take some time for the government to realise we had help from their own people."

Wu picks up the phone.

"Turn on Lithuanian channel TV5."

He does and watches. "Where is she broadcasting from? Why can't we disable the feed?

"We don't know where the feed is coming from yet. Their escape aircraft has a range of around sixteen hundred miles, but they could have refueled also, or modified it."

"She referenced our Spanish contact. Haven't we found a camera with their saboteur on it yet? What is Lutkus doing?"

"No, not yet and Lutkus is preparing their military. Even with this news being broadcast, it would be impossible to stop the war."

"We need to suppress this version of news with our own propaganda. We need to consider cross-border incursions."

"Yes, sir. This is being arranged. The first feed will go out tonight and incursions are already on the agenda."

"Has Florence reported in yet?"

"Yes. She arrived in London and was at Davenport's event last night. Supposedly she will be with him later today."

"Did she provide any useful information on other attendees?"

"No. It was news, media and invited guests only."

Cross and Jennings are scouring the lists of attendees at some of Mitchell's last parliament events. They are even watching videos.

"There she is," as Cross points on a video from a speech Mitchell gave in Manchester two months before his death.

"This is crazy."

"Surely you didn't expect anything different. The hair is dark brown but that is definitely her."

"Good point and yes. And stop calling me Shirley."

Cross chuckles. "Do we have the list of attendees for that event?"

"Yes, I saw it so let me find that document." He brings it up on the screen. "F.P. Anderson."

Cross sighs. "I wonder what P stands for. How is she listed?"

"Special guest."

"Why not change the last name to Walker, Wilson, Yalden, Yaleman? I mean remove the name from the top of any list that would be alphabetical."

"Easy, Daniel: they don't expect to be caught."

Cross calls Granfield from Jennings' office.

"How was Davenports' event?"

"I will hang myself if I have to listen to another politician talk."

"Then let's avoid that scenario," and laughs.

"David, look for video feeds and guest lists from the last couple of speeches Congressman Briar has given. Perhaps even forward me those lists, please."

"I can do that."

"Anderson seems to be friends with men high-up who are on our list. No way this is coincidental."

"Ok. Your wedding is in a few weeks, right?"

"Yes."

Sometime later in the evening a text message arrives on Cross' phone.

'Daniel, long time no hear. I understand you are causing trouble again.'

'Leslie Taylor. To where did you disappear?'

'Spending my most recent US government contractor check.'

'Ha-ha.'

'Me too, at MI6.'

'David just messaged. He wants me to meet you at the next Rep. Briar speech in Washington, DC in two days.'

'News to me.'

'Apparently, whoever a Florence Anderson is, she is on the guest list to attend.'

'Is she now? Interesting. This lady gets around. I wonder what happens when all the politicians she is fraternising with show up to the same party?'

'I don't want to find out.'

'Ok. Will text when I leave London. See you in Washington.'

15

Baltic War Commencing

It is a cold, dreary morning in London and Cross has enjoyed a quiet evening in a local hotel. It helped him catch up on meditation.

Circumstances and events are escalating as the push for global control is taking unprecedented political steps.

Gabrys messages him.

'Lutkus started his propaganda media push last night after my broadcast in the afternoon.'

'Yes. I saw that. He is refuting your reporting and undermining your credibility as a news anchor.'

'Yes.'

'This we expected. The propaganda war machine is something to behold with the advent of social media and the internet. It is difficult these days to believe anything reported by mainstream media, particularly when one looks at who owns most of the companies.' His thumbs are working the keypad so fast, and people tell him they have never seen anything like it.

'Lithuanian media is controlled by the government.'

'Yes, you told me. But then who controls the government? That is the question.'

'Hold on, I am being messaged by my boss.'

Cross waits, but he needs to get home via Washington. He doesn't even want to listen to Briar tomorrow and needs to prepare for his wedding. He is also desperate to see Sadeghi again. His phone rings.

"Janina, you aren't supposed to call my cell."

"The government closed down TV5's newsroom and then arrested my manager and her staff. They have been released with gag-orders, but the studio is closed."

"Are they ok?"

"Yes. They now believe my story."

"That's good," and they laugh. "We can keep broadcasting."

"I told her that and she encouraged us to do so."

Another ping on Cross' phone. It is Jennings.

'Meet me at the café down the street from my office in thirty minutes.'

"Janina, I must go. Good luck with the news and will message you later. Kids ok?"

"Yes. They are finding this exciting. Bye."

Cross exits the hotel and drives over to the café in a Ford Focus concierge let him borrow. He parks and finds Jennings already seated. Two coffee mugs occupy the round table.

"Good morning, Nick."

"I wish it was, Daniel. Lithuania started some military incursions last night over the border with Latvia."

"It is starting. Janina called, against protocols. Her associates were arrested and then released with a gag order."

"We have already notified our prime minister. These are NATO countries so the Alliance must be involved. Deep State will never control the Kremlin, but they need their man in Riga's Castle, home of Latvia's president."

"Shit." Cross pauses as he thinks. "So, let me get this straight, Wu is starting a war that NATO will ultimately end up financing. Then, the fallout will be his appointee moving into Latvia and a stronger leader in Lithuania."

"A fascinating world in which we reside."

"In the meantime, he has more arseholes with small penises vying for positions in other prominent NATO countries. Did I get all that correct?"

"I can't vouch for their disproportionate phallic appendages, but the rest is fairly accurate."

Cross sighs and picks up his mug of coffee.

"By the way, our Florence Nightingale is in Washington, DC tomorrow to hook up with Briar. I didn't tell you that part. She isn't limiting herself to UK politicians evidently. Leslie text last night and meets me off the plane tomorrow afternoon."

"Indeed, a fascinating world," and rolls his eyes. "How is Leslie?"

"She took a leave of absence for a while."

"I don't blame her. I figure Anderson must work for Wu. That is why her profile ends abruptly and why she keeps meeting with prominent politicians."

"Sleeping with, you mean?" Cross looks directly at Jennings and smiles.

"I was trying to be diplomatic."

"She is a Wu mule which is my conclusion as well. She is seducing their weak, fragile minds or paying them off. Likely both."

"What's Marchant up to these days? Too many other things going on to keep track."

"We have time with him but who knows anymore. His election in France is a month away, at least."

16

A Lesbian Affair

Taylor steps out of the free-standing marble bathtub and dries off. Her expensive Cartier watch indicates she has two hours to get ready.

She had confirmed a reservation in the Townhouse Suite at the luxurious five-star hotel as soon as she researched the name on a guest list. She had done some poking around once Cross had filled her in on a Ms. Anderson. Taylor didn't believe she would use the same name for every occasion. Discretion is desirable for someone in her position.

She had looked at a video from another politician's recent event and saw Anderson. On that occasion she was frolicking with a state senator. The accompanying guest list had her name as Laura Inglewood. Taylor then went searching for a luxury hotel around the Washington, DC area who had a reservation for Inglewood. She found one: Rosewood in Georgetown.

She decided on white for this occasion and wears a short Versace silk dress with laced high-heel shoes. A multi-shade red silk scarf wraps around her neck and she settled for no stockings. Finally, the last item she delicately fixes to her head. The strawberry-blonde wig contrasts nicely as she monitors herself in a reflection in the full-length door mirror. She sprays Creed Aventus perfume as a finishing touch. She admires herself in white, offset against her pure black skin.

Taylor steps outside the room and walks over to the hotel bar. It is modern, contemporary and warm as she locates an empty chair at the end of the counter. She seats herself and orders a vodka martini.

The bartender seems very friendly upon seeing a stunning lady sitting at the bar on her own. This always amuses Taylor, but sometimes in a good way. Bartenders frequently have enlightening and funny stories for anyone interested in listening to them.

During check-in, Taylor had verified Inglewood's reservation and left a note at the front desk. The note was simple: meet me at the bar around eight. However, she had no idea if she would get the note never mind show.

Her watch's hands display eight-ten when Ms. Anderson walks into the room. She strolls around with an air of confidence, but Taylor ignores her as she surveys the surroundings. Not finding anyone interesting, in a bar mostly void of people, Anderson walks over and sits three down from Taylor. She orders an aged whiskey, neat.

Anderson is immediately on her phone punching messages to someone.

Taylor gives herself time before ordering two more drinks: one being an aged whiskey. The bartender prepares them and hands one to Anderson.

"This is from the lady at the end of the bar."

Anderson looks over and smiles. "Thank you."

Taylor looks her up and down. She is incredibly young and beautiful, but she knew that already. No wonder politicians fall all over her. Her body-clinging black Gucci dress is knee-length and has two slits. Her thick black hair has been curled with an iron and her makeup is meticulous and spotless, boasting bright red lipstick. She can't see an ounce of fat and her image portrays that of women in the 1940s and 1950s when they cared about their appearance and dressed in class and style. She is simply breathtaking.

"Are you on your own?" enquires Taylor.

"Yes. I'm in town for an important talk tomorrow."

"Oh, me too."

"That's interesting. Being in Georgetown, it must be politics, right?"

Taylor laughs. "Unfortunately, yes. How did you know?"

She shuffles over two chairs and sticks her hand out. "I'm Evelyn Brooks. Nice to meet you."

"I'm Laura Inglewood. Nice to meet you too," and they shake hands.

"I'm a Georgetown lawyer and do investigative research for elected officials. It is important they get their facts aligned, which has a touch of irony since most lie through their teeth."

Anderson laughs. "Wow, you got that straight. Most are lying cheats, and pathetically obese."

An interesting comment, thinks Taylor, coming from someone who helps them cheat.

"Health isn't on their agenda, I guess."

"I'm studying political science at Georgetown University and have been invited to Representative Briar's speech tomorrow. I'm excited having never been to one before. I did some research, and he is going to be the next Speaker of the House."

Taylor admires Anderson already. She read her background and being an orphan is not an encouraging start for most in that situation. However, she seems particularly well-mannered, articulates with perfection and her knowledge are all well suited for politics. She certainly doesn't look or sound twenty-one. Except she isn't Laura Inglewood, and she doesn't study political science at Georgetown, nor does she live around here. Taylor is fascinated with this girl.

"You are beautiful." Anderson is staring and it is her turn to look a fellow bar patron up and down.

"It is so important to look after oneself, don't you think?"

"Absolutely. In politics, beauty is power, Evelyn. Even for men, handsomeness opens doors, which some don't get."

This girl is intelligent too and understands her position in the role Wu has provided. As Taylor looks at her, Anderson fixes her gaze. Taylor sees how she is marginalised and abused by her perfect youth which further encapsulates her. Anderson moves her arm and places the left hand on Taylor's naked right leg. She doesn't move, nor does she feel a desire to exercise that option.

"You have beautiful dark skin. It is soft too."

"Thank you."

They carry on talking but hidden underneath the bar is Anderson's foreplay. They had moved a little closer and ordered another round. Taylor is loving the touch from experienced youth and her body is gyrating. On occasion, to keep the bartender guessing, Anderson will bring her hand to the table in order to take a sip of her drink. It is then Taylor's turn to drop a hand onto Anderson's leg now exposed by the convenient slit.

They continue to discuss politics and recite stories of their past whilst sexually stimulating the other lady. It is choreographed and neither of them is aware they have both been trained in this field of elicit erotic psychosis, the seduction game, to draw the other person in and manipulate as required. Or perhaps they don't care.

After a couple of hours of intense discussions, one of them takes the lead.

"I have more drinks in my room, Evelyn. Why don't you join me? I'm finding your company to be remarkably stimulating and we can order food."

"Yes, I would enjoy that."

Anderson is asleep as Taylor effortlessly slips from under the satin sheets and removes herself from the California king bed. She quickly picks her clothes up off the floor, puts on a silk robe and departs the room.

17

Formulating Plans

Cross is sitting on a government plane on the way to Washington and is deep in thought. What if? He picks up his phone.

'Graeme, we managed to remove Cartwright. We need to work on the other sponsors. Your thoughts?'

'Yes,' came Moore Jr.'s response. 'This is problematic because they are recluse.'

'Understood.'

'It isn't the person either. We must also bring down their ability to fund, which is more challenging.'

'Give it some thought, then get back to me. I have ideas.'

'Of course you do. Ok.' Moore Jr. understands Cross' request.

Cross stops texting and calls Sadeghi. She is so happy to hear his voice.

"I will be home in a few days, honey."

Their wedding plans are small and will take place on the edge of Lake Tahoe. For fear of provoking unwanted and unnecessary attention, Sadeghi had agreed. Cross promised a larger affair when the world stage is quieter and was surprised when she accepted that without hesitation. He isn't aware her fears are real and more pronounced than his since she hasn't told him.

Cross clicks off the phone.

The Gulfstream lands at Ronald Reagan National Airport and Cross disembarks. He walks through the private terminal and Taylor is there to greet him outside. They embrace and he kisses her on the cheek.

"Daniel, you look fantastic. No bullet holes either."

"You do too. Your vacation worked and you look more relaxed. Yeah, I vowed in the next phase of my life I will avoid being a target."

"How is that working out for you?"

"It isn't so far and needs time to develop." They both laugh.

"I have missed your suits. You do, you look handsome and very happy to see you well recovered from the excursions in Asia."

"I need to be presentable for Briar's event. I sought professional help and doing advanced forms of meditation. It has helped me a great deal." He looks at Taylor. "You look beautiful, and I've missed you."

"Thank you. Me too. I have heard about advanced classes. Let's go find a coffee house near the hotel where the event is being hosted."

They climb into Taylor's white Maserati GranTurismo, and she navigates away from the airport, toward downtown. He loves her interesting taste in automobiles.

She is sitting in Grace Street Roasters and sees Cross walking over carrying a tray with cappuccinos and sandwiches. She clears room so he can place it on the table.

"Thank you, Daniel."

"Sure," and smiles at her before sitting down.

"I have been doing some research into this Ms. Anderson character. She has a storied background."

"Yes, we investigated her too. Nick says hello, by the way. Poor girl has a history."

Hearing Jennings' name warms her heart. "Thank you. How is he?"

"Doing good."

Returning to the current topic of the day. "Florence had a poor start in life."

"Indeed, which created her vulnerability and why we believe she works for Wu."

"I concur. The results from my research suggest she approaches politicians in powerful and influential positions. Ones who will benefit Deep State's goals. She doesn't pick them based on their debonair looks for sure." She giggles. "It is likely, I feel, she blackmails them after they become sexually involved. She could also be paying or buying them off. This is a dangerous game for her since these are powerful men, and women." She looks at Cross for reaction to the latter reference.

"I'm confident she is bisexual. She is using her breathtaking beauty to control, and women love that too." Taylor hides her blushes. "She learnt that trade escorting. They must purposely select the candidate because this isn't some random game she is playing. Once selected, she is in for the kill and then Wu finds the sponsors to endorse their campaigns before putting them on payroll."

"Precisely." Taylor looks at her watch. "We have time yet but perhaps we should head over shortly to do some pre-emptive surveying." She smiles and winks. "David couriered the passes this morning."

"Yes."

"We go as separate people. We can't be seen together at this event."

Taylor shows her pass to the police officer who then lets them through.

"It is less militarised than Davenport's debacle in London."

"He is a congressman and not running for president. At least nobody knows that yet. Speaker of the House puts him in line which is what this is about."

"Yes, it is."

"I will let you out here and you can find the private entrance. See you inside," as she stops the car.

"Ok."

Cross walks through security, displaying his badge. Today he is a certified member of Capitol Hill and chief of staff to some congressman he has never heard of. This is going to be interesting; he thinks. There is time yet, so after meeting some people and chatting, he goes looking for the bar.

As he approaches, he abruptly stops and steps off to the side. Hiding his face behind a small group of people standing, he takes a peek. He recognises Anderson sitting at the bar, even with her hair now black. He would recognise her anywhere. As he looks, he can't believe who walks up and sits next to her. From Anderson's tender reaction, it is pretty obvious they know each other. The bartender brings her a drink.

Cross doesn't know what to do. He is momentarily shaken and decides to vacate the bar area. There is a reason for this, and he needs to calm down.

"Come on, Daniel. Get a hold of yourself." He would slap himself if it wouldn't look so silly. He tries to recall the conversation this afternoon and something that was said: 'men *and* women'. Suddenly a light goes on.

"Dammit, Leslie, you could have warned me, you clever girl."

After the event closes, Taylor picks Cross up from outside the hotel and drives northwest to a restaurant away from downtown Washington. He has had enough of listening to politicians talk nonsense. They are articulate, very convincing and he gives them that much credit. He ignores the topic of what he saw at the bar since it would serve no purpose here.

"That was a good speech for what he wants from the outcome."

"Yes, Daniel. He will be the next speaker."

"I saw Florence with him after the talk." He uses her first name to make her more a real person. "They looked very friendly, and his eyes were lit. I'm sure his wife must be used to this by now."

"They know what they are getting into. Nothing is hidden, except maybe the actual affairs, until it's too late. The political life for the spouse is fulfilled anyway, so who cares."

"Where are we heading?"

"To a quaint place I know."

She pulls up outside Agave Bar and Grill in Palisades. As they walk into the restaurant, Cross sees someone he most certainly wasn't expecting.

"David, this is a surprise." They all hug and shake hands. "How are you doing?"

"Nice to see you both. Come, sit down."

They follow instructions.

"You can't be seen with me in Langley, not just yet anyway. You aren't working for the CIA anymore, Daniel. This may change because it is turning ugly."

"Yes, it is. Did you bring a rope?"

Looking perplexed, "Why?" he asks.

"I listened to another politician today." He grins and then sighs. "They all sound the damn same after a while. Briar will be nominated Speaker for sure."

"Yes, he will. He has the required votes. He can't become president without something drastic happening though. This is a concern President Walkman is aware of and the CIA is all over it too."

Taylor jumps in. "Florence Anderson was talking with Briar afterwards. She must be working for Wu's organisation."

"Yes, this is obvious to us." Granfield agreeing. "It is also a concern."

"David, I have an idea about Anderson. I would like permission to pursue options. I'm optimistic it could work."

"I trust you, Leslie. Do what you believe to be viable and fill me in later."

"Gabrys is still broadcasting in Vilnius, but they are competing against the prime minister's propaganda machine and his deep pockets."

"I saw that too. More incursions last night and soon they will start lobbing a missile or two. NATO will become involved at that point, so we need to stop this.

"What are your ideas beyond Cartwright and Mitchell, Daniel."

"I messaged a secure contact on the flight here. This is what I have asked for," as he explains the information he is requesting.

"Interesting idea, but fraught with many foreseeable obstacles."

"Since when has that prevented us from achieving our goals?"

"That is why I will be expecting you to push this, but please keep me updated, in case I'm legally obligated to defend you." He frowns. "You are proposing activities I can't condone, in principle, because some are on foreign soil without Congress' approval. However, I will protect you, Daniel. I will need to watch the news too for their reaction."

"To hell with the mainstream media. They are part of this too."

"When do you head back to California?"

"Leslie takes me to the airport tomorrow morning."

"You are using a Gulfstream, right?"

"Yes, thank you."

"Have we any idea where Wu is holding out after the loss of his island?"

"I was told somewhere in Europe, but that is rather inconclusive and vague."

"Cause waves and fuck with these people, Daniel. Then we can monitor flight paths more closely. You know how to do that," and he winks. "Your wedding is next weekend so go and prepare for it. Make Parisa proud and happy, provide what she deserves, my friend. This shit isn't going anywhere. When you return, if you even do – I wouldn't blame you - then we start moving on some of these targets. We need to stop this, otherwise we are all in trouble."

After dinner and drinks, Granfield turns to them as they leave the establishment. "Good luck, both of you," and then walks to his car.

"Representative Briar's speech was very good, sir. It got a warm reception from the US media also and their reporting is very positive."

"Excellent." Wu is feeling better. "He will be voted in very soon. Then we can work on the second phase for the US."

"Yes, sir."

"Where is Florence?"

"She has a rendezvous with Briar at the Hyatt tonight."

"She doesn't get paid enough, not with that disgusting specimen."

"I understand."

"Thank you," and Wu hangs up the phone.

There is a faint knock on the door. Briar walks through the large suite and opens it.

"Hello Speaker of the House," whispers the person standing in the Park-Hyatt hallway on the Presidential level.

"Quickly, come inside, Ms. Anderson. Did anyone see you?"

"No, Jason. Only your Secret Service agent who knows me now." She hugs him so tight.

"God, you look gorgeous, dear. I love those short dresses."

"Thank you. I know you do." What a dumbass, she thinks. It would be more appropriate if she was modestly dressed, especially if someone sees her. At least she now knows the requirement to wear a long cashmere coat over it.

He kisses her on the mouth, and she reciprocates with passion. She detests this but it is what he expects and desires. Her acting will be in full swing again tonight.

Briar is different to the UK politicians. He has fallen for her despite the millions in cash having been transferred. She has bought him lock, stock and barrel. It always was a business transaction involving money, power and sex, but some men don't recognise the arrangements. She isn't for sale and his jealousy is becoming a serious issue. He wants money, power *and* her, but that isn't going to happen. Not in her lifetime.

"Go make yourself comfortable," she says.

He turns his back and as he commences the removal of clothing, she walks into the bedroom and carefully hides a tiny micro-camera on the dresser, facing the bed.

Once the camera is set up, she walks into the bathroom and removes her cosmetics pouch from her night bag. Inside are the pharmaceutical drugs required to help her get through the night.

18

The Wedding, Lake Tahoe California

Cross has a week to prepare for their wedding. He messages Moore Jr.

'Everything ready?'

'Yes. The wedding gift was completed some time ago.'

'Your schedule the same?'

'My family and I arrive in Tahoe in four days.'

'I will be proud to have you as my best man.'

Cross has ordered something special for his wedding and wants to surprise Sadeghi: something from his native country.

Wu is on his plane flying to Lithuania. He needs to ensure plans for the pending war are in place and wishes to discuss them with the prime minister. The cross-border incursions have continued, and people are dying. NATO is sitting back and waiting to be involved but citizens in the Baltics are restless as Latvia's government has warned Lithuania of war.

A call comes in from Handcock.

"Hello, Wilfred. What do you have for me?"

"We found something of interest in Lake Tahoe's local paper. There is a wedding planned this coming Saturday. It doesn't use specific names, but they describe the occasion as a matrimonial affair between a British and Iranian couple who have chosen Tahoe as their home."

"This is short notice, but I am giving you the green light. Do it."

"Done, sir."

It is the day of their wedding and Cross is nervous. He is confident Sadeghi is also. He has conferred with her all week to commit to a set schedule. The ceremony will be simple, with only Moore Jr. and his wife as witnesses. Granfield has arranged a dozen Secret Service agents because he trusts no one.

It is early October, and the skies are clear blue. A frosty night will soon be replaced with high-altitude warmth once the sun gets a chance to escape the mountains' obstruction.

Cross had made the arrangements through a close friend, and she assures him everything is ready.

"Daniel, it is all prepared. The white Rolls Royce arrives at eleven. The flowers are on the beach already. Graeme's gift is boxed. The photographer is my friend. The ordained minister has the marriage certificate done and awaiting your signatures after the ceremony." She understands his apprehension. "You asked me to help, so I did. It is all ready to go."

"Sorry, Christine. I'm nervous."

"I'm sure you are," and they both laugh. "I will message when the car is about to arrive."

Cross had arranged the wedding on a local beach but one that is enclosed by pine trees on three sides. He knows the owner of the restaurant right on the lake, so he booked the whole place for the ceremony and reception. It is a spectacular setting. The trees will provide ample cover and an area for the agents to be discrete. There will be live Iranian music softly serenading in the background. It was a special request from Sadeghi.

They get ready for the ceremony. Sadeghi is wearing a beautiful, laced silk Dolce & Gabbana dress with a short train. Cross has on a white Italian Tuxedo.

A text comes in from Christine. 'Car arrives in ten minutes.'

Everyone is prepared as it arrives at Cross' home. An agent is in the front passenger seat and another is driving. They too are dressed in white. How romantic, Cross thinks. How did his life turn into this charade? Moore Jr. is using Cross' Rover and will follow.

They head out on route 89 toward Emerald Bay and then turn right. The restaurant is in view as the car approaches. It pulls up and tourists are mulling around as the wedding party exits the two vehicles. They all begin to clap and cheer: a warm and telling reminder that romance is still prevalent, even in a sometimes-dystopian world of power and dominance.

Sadeghi and Cross walk around the building and onto the beach. The Moore's are close behind them. A white arch has been erected at the end of a short red Persian carpet and a few wooden chairs sit either side. Floral arrangements in autumn colours sit in large vases carefully positioned around the setting. The minister is standing under it and in the background plays Iranian music. It is romantic, at least the best Cross could achieve under the circumstances. Sadeghi has a glow. The photographer is off to the side and carefully snapping digitals. The couple face the lake with the breathtaking beauty of early-season snow-capped mountains as a backdrop. Tourists are standing on the beach, watching.

Off in the distance, no one sees the drone, nor the person who releases it. It lifts high and off to the east, shielded by the sunlight. It skirts the edge of the lake as it hovers closer. The images from its camera are projected halfway around the world, where the viewing party sees a couple walking up to a white archway on a beach. Someone zooms in to verify who they are.

"That is Cross."

Standing in front of the minister, it is time.

"Two people stand here before God, in acknowledgement of their eternal love for each other. With the sanctity of marriage, acceptance of their own vows, which I will administer on behalf of our beloved Lord Jesus…"

Just then bullets reign down and are military precision. Sadeghi drops on the beach which immediately turns red. Cross is next as he falls beside her, having never had the time to react.

The Secret Service personnel run from tree cover and head for the fallen victims. They see a drone off in the distance and start firing. More bullets are fired, and particles splash up as they hit the sand. Their bodies rebound as Sadeghi and Cross are repeatedly hit. Tourists and restaurant employees are heard screaming in the background and there is no more music playing.

One of the agents has a direct hit and the drone explodes, dropping into the calm water, leaving behind an earie silence.

The minister is unhurt and had scampered for cover behind a tree. Now, he feels safe to emerge. He walks over to Sadeghi and Cross. Surrounding them is blood-tainted sand. There are no movement, no sound, no breathing. He drops to his knees and holds his hands up to the Heavens.

"Why God, why?" as he weeps.

In the forest stands a subject with binoculars, who has witnessed the whole event.

"Cross is confirmed dead, sir, along with his wife."
"Excellent work."
Wu lifts his tumbler and empties the content down his throat. Now he can implement his plans more effectively.

19

Arranging His Own Death

"Daniel is dead, along with Parisa."

Granfield sits in stunned silence as a tear rolls down his face. Even for someone who has seen everything, he can't comprehend what one of his field agents is telling him.

"A drone hovered from out of nowhere and over the lake. By the time we saw it, it was over."

He doesn't even answer, and gently replaces the receiver. He calls Taylor, and she doesn't pick up the phone. Next is Jennings and he can hardly talk. This is devastating and will have serious consequences on morale in the intelligence services.

Gabrys had sent a congratulatory message but nothing. Cross always returns messages, but it is his wedding. Perhaps he is preoccupied, she thinks. At least she hopes he is.

Jennings messages her. She immediately collapses on the floor exactly where she is standing and sobs in the apartment kitchen.

20

Planned Immortality

Granfield is sitting at the bar at his local, drowning his sorrows. He can't talk. The news on a TV sitting above the bar shows the pristine sand adjacent to one of the world's largest alpine lakes, covered in pools of dried blood. The area is swarming with paramedics and police. A photographer had obviously given up their digitals and some of those are being broadcast. The bodies of Sadeghi and Cross have been covered with blue tarps on some shots.

"The deaths of newlyweds Daniel Cross and his wife, Parisa Sadeghi, have been confirmed. In a brazen…"

Granfield picks up his shot glass and tosses it at the screen.

His phone's ringer is switched off so it vibrates, but he ignores it. It vibrates again, then silence. Five minutes later it vibrates again, but only once. This time he looks over and it is from an unknown number. Someone has tried to call twice but decided to text instead: 'pick up, dammit'.

Granfield studies it for a while and then stares at the monitor whilst downing another shot the bartender had brought him. Another message: 'pick up, David'.

Five minutes later the same caller tries again, only this time he elects to answer it.

"Now I am ready."

Granfield freezes and doesn't know how to react. He is speechless.

"Hello," comes the voice on the other end.

He recognises it but is in shock.

"Daniel?" in a subdued, pained but surprising elevated tone.

"Of course, David. Who were you expecting?"

"What the hell is going on?"

"Wu thinks we are stupid and now he will believe I'm dead. I'm sorry, David. I had to do it this way. You know why."

"Is Parisa ok?"

"Yes, of course."

"Fill me in."

"Simple. I put a story in the local paper about a Brit marrying an Iranian. I know Wu is watching everything."

"Go on."

"When the robots were terminated, I asked Moore Jr. for a favour. I shamelessly sensed he owed me one, so I asked him to develop clones of me, Parisa, himself and his wife. That was easy since Wu had already developed them. He was going to use mine to infiltrate CIA and MI6 once they took over the White House."

Granfield is silent, but not through choice: he is numb and can't articulate words.

"I requested some modification though. I needed blood splatter to enhance the effect so they developed packets of fake blood the bullets would rupture when the clones were penetrated. Hence, the blood on the sand. He did a magical job, don't you think? Even shots to the head produced blood." He is giddy about his plan but needs self-control.

"I asked Graeme to be my best man so that he could fly the clones in from England on a private jet, but also so he could manage them. He installed a WiFi system in my car so that the clones would always be close. This negated the need for satellite which would have been too elaborate."

Granfield is still silent but feels Cross' energy level.

"Hello."

"I'm head of CIA but speechless. How did you come up with this stuff?"

"I already know they are foolish. The first responders were arranged by the Secret Service. The scene was staged for the cameras, but this story is leak-tight because only the intelligence services know what is going on, and so few of our people were involved. The media reporting is real since we told them who the victims are and what to say. Afterall, clones can't get married, that I am aware of. Perhaps they can now, in this faltering world." He is digressing so gets back on point. "In any event, it is better for Wu to think we died as a married couple: it feeds his ego. The deception game is in full swing."

He can't believe what he is hearing. "Is Parisa with you?" is all he can muster.

"You are an incredible man and I appreciate the question. I could tell she was changing and becoming more scared as I returned from each mission. She knew I was involved in Cartwright and Mitchell's deaths, but true to who she is, she never told me. She kept her mouth shut in fear of distracting my work. David, I can't tell you where she is. You understand this?"

"Yes."

"She is in hiding now until this ends, but she will be safe."

"What are you asking from me?"

"I want to implement the plan I briefly discussed in Palisades, David. With your help, and protection, I am going rogue."

"Go on."

"This is my new number," and verbally passes it to him. "I tossed CIA's phone, so no one has this number. The less people know, the better."

"Ok."

"I know what Leslie is up to, but she doesn't know I know. She is brilliant. I will work with her and Nick. Nick has a plan for Janina too. Together we can do this."

"Ok." Granfield is lost for words.

"No one else needs to know, except on a need-to-know basis. I am dead, remember? However, I will need your support." He corrects himself. "We will need your support. You will see when it happens what I'm doing and why. The Moore's have insider information but will need intelligence and military support when times require either, or both. Please promise me this. I intend to keep you abreast of everything you need to know. You know who I'm going after so the government must stay out of it. They can't be seen condoning this. I am done with these morons."

"I guarantee support, Daniel."

"My three minutes are up so must run. I will be in contact and thank you."

"Thank God you are still alive. The whole morale in Intelligence died with the news of your murders."

"Thank you for trusting me, my friend."

Granfield orders a double shot. "Who the hell is this guy?"

21

Survivor's Repercussions

Cross calls Taylor, and this time she does pick up.

"Dammit, Daniel. We were all shattered after hearing the news. You are one crazy dude. David called me a few hours ago. He was a broken man until hearing your voice. He was ready to resign but you energised him again and he passed on your new number."

"No, not crazy. Our lives were in danger, Leslie. I am done with this crap and now I am dead, it is time to move forward and end it. Wu will not be expecting this, and he will be pre-occupied with his dumb mission." Clearly, he upset his people, but has no regrets. He had to do something outrageous.

Calming down, Cross needs to focus again. "How are you getting on in your part of the world?"

"I have been communicating with Florence, but you know this already. I asked the Hyatt bartender, a friend, to watch for you and then he notified me discretely when you showed, by bringing me a drink. You demonstrated tremendous character by not asking me after we left the hotel."

"Oh. Not my business but you are a brilliant lady." It is Cross' turn to be surprised.

"Florence has recorded videos of every encounter with these

political figures. She is a smart and courageous young woman. She doesn't know yet who I am. Briar is the weakest link here. He is in love with her and wants to divorce his long-time wife when he becomes speaker. She passes money to them, now totaling millions, at every rendezvous, all recorded. He is jealous and doesn't want her seeing others. It could get messy, but it might present an opportunity for us to take advantage of this tidbit of information."

"Yes, indeed, but he doesn't love her. He needs the control aspect which is all these morons want."

"Absolutely. She has loyalty to her employer but understands she is just another spoke in his wheel. She hasn't told me yet who he is but she knows too much, which is never a good thing. However, he is paying her a lot of money. I am making progress and she is beginning to trust me. That part is tricky understanding her background.

"She doesn't share her private life so will not notify Wu of her liaisons with a dark lady who resembles Leslie Taylor." She laughs. "I find it fascinating that this subject hasn't come up with them. You and I were on top of his death list not so long ago. Why hasn't he got her looking? He surely must suspect we are at these political events."

"This is all good but don't know how to answer the last point. Perhaps she does know who you are and wants to switch sides. I don't mean men to women." He chuckles. "This might be the message she is sending by not saying anything."

"You are just jealous," as they both laugh. "That is a fair argument you are making."

"She needs an out and you might be an option. However, be careful since she might be a double agent. Let me get back to you. I must start making plans for my next mission."

"Ok. Briar's confirmation hearing is coming up next week."

"Granfield told me. Let's discuss this later."

"Don't play like that again. Now you are dead, play dead." She chuckles.

"Now I'm dead, I can watch you and Florence," and laughs but ends the call before Taylor can respond.

Whilst he was conversing with Taylor, Jennings had messaged so he calls him.

"Daniel, you sick son of a bitch. That was brilliant, but man you had people here crying. The whole morale dropped like a tonne of bricks. I was so relieved when David called me."

"Sorry, Nick. They were watching Parisa. She told me, finally. I was sick of this. Graeme was brilliant. He didn't even know they had clones of himself and his wife."

"Thank God you are both alive."

"Where are we in the Baltics?" Needing to change subjects and stay on track.

"You should connect with Janina after this call. The incursions continue but the rhetoric is escalating, and war is imminent. What is on your mind?"

Cross fills him in on what he wants to do. It is a mammoth undertaking with serious potential for downfalls, divergences and volatile repercussions."

"Oh my." He pauses to think. "We can arrange some of these over on this side of the pond. If you come here, we can discuss what I want Janina to do with her media. We can meet off-site."

"Ok. Give me a few days. I have things I need to do here and plan for. Briar's confirmation hearing is next week too, and Leslie has information that may help us."

"Get back to me and very happy you called, my friend."

The connection goes dead.

It is late but Cross messages Gabrys who then immediately picks up the phone and calls.

"Sorry, Janina. It is early morning and I wasn't expecting you to call me."

"Damn, Daniel, are you kidding me? Once Nick called to confirm you had staged your own deaths, no way I could sleep. You didn't even know me when you risked your life to save mine. I honestly couldn't breathe when Nick told me, and I saw the news. That is one impressive stunt. How did you come up with that?"

"Wu wanted me dead, so I obliged. Now I am, I'm at liberty to do what I want. How are you doing?"

"I'm doing ok in London. My kids are fine and we are still broadcasting the real news. Oh, I heard through the grapevine that Wu flew into Vilnius a few days ago and met with Lutkus. A friend then confirmed this which was the reason for extra security around the airport and Palace."

"That is interesting. I fly to England in a few days and we can meet. Nick wishes to work on something with you."

"Ok. Just let me know. He has been good with us on the two occasions we were allowed to meet, and my children like him. They released the security protocols a little. We couldn't be locked away."

"I understand that part. He is a good man, Janina, if a little crazy."

"You Brits are all the same, it seems. He said the same about you." They both laugh, but it is made awkward by sapped emotions.

"Ok, must go. I will let you sleep."

"Thank you. Relieved beyond measure you and Parisa are alive. Loved hearing your voice again, Daniel."

He needs sleep now, but not before he puts his head in his hands and weeps like a baby… The psychological toll is amplifying.

22

Driving the Media's Disinformation

The morning after their mock deaths, Cross is awake. He didn't sleep much. He couldn't. The coffee made with beans extracted from defecated coffee cherries by wild Asian palm civets is helping his energy level.

"David doesn't know what he is missing."

He had some fresh doughnuts delivered by one of the Secret Service agents. They will remain posted for a few days as part of the façade, until the news of his death subsides. He needs the carbs and sugar.

After the nutritional intake, he walks into the meditation room and strips off. In the mirror he notices the scars healing. They are no longer bright red, but a lighter shade of red. "Progress," as he shrugs. He faces the padded wall and starts punching, and punching, and punching. Left, right, left, right. Sometimes right, right or left, left to avoid monotony. He yells and screams like never before with tears rolling down his face. No one can hear him: his home is devoid of life, except his own.

After he finishes and has meditated on the mat for half an hour, he steps into the shower. As he is drying himself off, Moore Jr. messages.

'Parisa arrived and is safe.'

'Thank you. I can sleep now.' He is so relieved, and happy. He couldn't continue and remain afraid for her life.

'Great wedding, lol.' Adds Moore Jr.

'Better than I ever imagined it would be, lol.'

'Did you try the cake?'

'Not yet. I understand it is on ice waiting for us.'

'I will have some info for you shortly.'

'Great. I'm heading to England tomorrow.'

'Safe travels.'

"Thank you, Graeme.'

Granfield had arranged for Cross to utilize their Dassault 6X, only it wasn't theirs anymore, and never was. He can't be caught using anything aligned with the US government. Registration had already been legally transferred, and it was about to be delivered to a major corporation after they bid and won a government seized-asset liquidation auction. Fortunately, they hadn't taken possession yet. Granfield found this out, made a few calls and tendered an arrangement with the leasing company to use it for an indeterminant period, without any records being signed or recorded. It was a plea and approved with a handshake based on mutual respect, since Granfield was school friends with their CEO. Now, if anyone tracks or traces the registration, it will not be tied to any government entity. Cross had used this plane previously and it will aid his rogue missions.

"Don't scratch it," is all Granfield had said.

Cross arrives at East Midlands Airport outside of Castle Donington, England, where Jennings and Gabrys meet him. Jennings had commandeered a non-descript mode of transportation from some rental company in London using fake ID. Their rendezvous was purposely downplayed to remove any unwanted public attention, despite obvious elation at seeing Cross alive. After picking him up, they head over to a country pub outside of Sutton Bonington. There is a university campus in the area which helps conceal themselves and blend in.

It is almost noon and raining hard. They step inside and order beer and food before finding a table in the corner. They remove their wet coats and hang them behind the table before parking themselves on the wooden chairs.

Their self-levied restraint on emotions is finally waning. "Good to see you, Daniel. Brilliant deception," Jennings says, rigorously shaking his hand across the table.

"Good to see both of you, too. I wasn't sure how it would turn out, but Parisa's life was in danger, and it was time to protect her. How are you doing, Janina? You look good too, considering." He is focused but leans over and hugs her.

"I'm doing ok, now." She has a tear rolling down her face. "I never thought disruption of a non-violent protest in my country would be the beginnings of all this."

"It wasn't the beginnings. Nick and I have been involved for months. This is just an inconvenient extension."

"Yes. Nick has been filling in the details. He was particularly amused with your behaviour in Grand Cayman." She smiles at Cross, attempting to relax herself.

They have been through this rigmarole and are familiar, but Gabrys hasn't. She is a news anchor, not a secret agent and is extremely fearful of her capacity to avert a war that could have severe consequences. She is visibly concerned about their expectations and Cross recognises the predicament.

"I'm easily provoked. I admit Nick's face was something special that morning." He places a hand on her shoulder and shifts gears.

"Janina, we can only do what we can do. This applies to you too. Nick here is going to ask you to lie, which goes against all your journalistic morals, ethics and integrity. If it makes it easier, pretend you work for mainstream media or something." All three burst out laughing. "They might offer you a lucrative position after this is over."

Nick jumps in. "I would have missed your humour, mate."

He removes his hand away and continues, being more serious. "Don't look at us but analyse the big picture. We don't know yet if what we want to do will work. We need to find Wu in the end. However, they are going to need to change their underwear many times before this is over. I assure you of that."

"You have this unique ability to see through people and read them."

"No, Janina. I was in your position earlier this year. I sat in a conference room in California listening to the CIA Director, David Granfield, give a presentation. He looked at me when he finished and said we are contracting with you, Daniel, to now go and find these people. I wanted to run but didn't. I saw it as a new vocation, but damn I miss my science," and smiles.

"Thank you for building me up." Now a little more relaxed, she continues. "I go on air later today. Lutkus has been pushing the Lithuanian government's propaganda machine and more people have been killed. He brought up your death, claiming he had proof of your involvement in the political uprising. His media group reported you were one of the assassins in Vilnius and are employed by the US government. They even showed a picture of you on the streets holding a Russian assault rifle. It was a compelling broadcast. Their aim is to empower Lutkus by forcing Lithuanians to dislike the West, then bring in Deep State and replace Ozolins in Latvia. He is doing a commendable job so far."

"Interesting. I have to think if I've ever held a Russian rifle."

Cross sees Jennings stirring so he sits back and listens. "We are going to ask you to continue this persecutory narrative of Daniel and the US."

"What?" replies Gabrys, in a rather disturbed and frustrated manner.

"Yes. We will provide you some falsified information and you will go on air with this today."

"I am confused."

"Don't be."

"What do you mean?"

"While you are on air repeatedly berating our mutual friend here, we will be working on Latvia. Your aim is to calm Lutkus down." He then lays out what their intentions are.

"Are you two crazy?"

"Possibly certifiable," comes Cross' reply as he emits a deep breath. "But you know this already."

23

Going Rogue

Cross is dropped off at an undisclosed location and Jennings with Gabrys head into London for her broadcast. Jennings had provided instructions on how to access her newsroom from the internet. Cross had a drink at the hotel bar before heading back to his room. He hooked up his laptop, accessed the local WiFi and dialed in TV5's network. He is now ready.

"Good evening. This is Janina Gabrys still on location, bringing you the evening news.

"The death of Daniel Cross and his wife Parisa Sadeghi last Saturday is still reverberating around Intelligence and political worlds. The person, or persons, responsible in the audacious slayings on the edge of a pristine alpine lake bordering California and Nevada in the US are still being pursued." A panoramic ariel video of the lake is imaged as Gabrys reads the prepared script. "Details of what authorities know are not being released at this time. However, TV5 has some new developments.

"We confirm that Cross worked for the CIA and was in Vilnius at the time of the shootings during the organised and peaceful protestations."

An alleged picture of Cross carrying a gun in Old Town Vilnius is portrayed on the screen. Gabrys had argued against this insertion but was overruled by Jennings. However, he had photoshopped the facial features in the bogus image so it didn't quite look like Cross. Also, the image captured shows a crowd so could be anyone.

"Wu and Lutkus won't care," Jennings had argued. "They care only about the story, not the specifics."

Gabrys continues. "It is evident he had clearance from the US government and carried authorisation from President Walkman's administration to utilise force on Lithuanian soil. This is, of course, an affront against Lithuanian sovereignty and a clear UN violation of international law."

He had assured her they had been given permission by Granfield to insert these false accusations. He hadn't, but it didn't matter.

Cross continues to watch but isn't really listening anymore. His phone pings.

'Are you ready?'

'Yes.'

Over the next fifteen minutes a series of detailed messages transmit to Cross' phone. He waits until reception is complete and then reads them.

He responds. 'Got them.'

'Good. Get some rest. The window of opportunity resides tomorrow evening.'

'I will message in the morning before I leave.'

'Excellent.'

24

Casino de Monte Carlo

'I am awake.'

'The packages have been loaded onto the plane.'

'Great. I leave in an hour.'

'Message when ready.'

'I will.'

Cross' adrenaline is pumping. He has been preparing psychologically for this all morning.

After showering and then digesting a good English breakfast at a hotel restaurant, he orders a taxi.

A cabin crew member sees Cross walking across the tarmac so drops the cabin door. He climbs the stairs and enters the Dassault. Scouring the boxes that have been delivered, he smiles and takes a seat.

The jet is given takeoff clearance and rapidly gains speed down the runway.

Dressed in one of his finest European-cloth suits and wearing a fedora, Cross is sitting at a bar in the Casino de Monte Carlo. It is late afternoon with still some light outside. He has used materials to alter his appearance that Moore Jr. had included in the packages.

They worked on the clones, so why not on me, he had enquired. A quick photo installed into a passport and diplomatic papers, and he was a new man.

"Another drink, Mr. Horseman?" asks the bartender.

"Yes, please, my friend."

He has been conversing with the bartender for an hour or so, gathering as much information as possible. Cash, the standard currency for agents around the globe, is working.

As predicted, a large party enters the ornate and decadent room and seat themselves away from the bar.

"They have just arrived, Mr. Horseman."

Cross waits ten minutes before he delicately swivels and takes a quick gander. Over on the other side of the room, looking beyond the crowded large high-limit gaming tables in the middle, a big party seems to be in a celebratory mood. Expensive champagne and imported aged whiskey bottles litter their table. The accompanying beer glasses show various stages of consumption. He gathers enough data to confirm the patrons he is anticipating and returns his gaze toward the bartender.

"Thank you, Daren," and drops a Benjamin Franklin on the bar.

"I don't like them either."

"Yes, not many people do. Arrogance and ignorance trump their inheritance, always."

While he has been occupied with discussions accompanied by alcohol, a beautiful, elegant lady sitting alone at a table has been admiring him from a distance. He has seen her and obviously foreseen such an occurrence. He came prepared. A man sitting alone displaying affluence in a high-end casino in Monte Carlos, it was assured and will help distract from his intent. He is also aware security cameras are watching and will be reviewed later.

She walks over after Cross acknowledges her. He stands and courteously pulls away a chair. She accepts it and sits down.

"Thank you. I am Madelaine." Said in a French accent.

"Nice to meet you, Madelaine. I am Michael," as they shake hands.

"I love your accent."

"Thank you. You are French?"

"Yes, of course." She smiles.

"Well, I will not hold it against you." They both chuckle.

"Sorry, I will bore you, but I'm into politics and work in London."

"I am fine with this topic. We are becoming scared with the upcoming election, so politics is front and centre."

"This Marchant character is not a good fit." He stops himself. "Wait, so sorry, Madelaine." He gently places a hand on her lower arm. "What would you like to drink?"

"You are interesting already and I had forgotten, too. Gin and tonic, please, made with Engraved Hendricks Gin."

"Do they even have that brand?"

"I work here, Michael," and smiles at him again, attracting his admiration.

"Of course," purposely being flustered with her comment. "You are beautiful, by the way." Nervously feigning he's-new-at-this-gig.

The bartender brings over the drink and places it in front of her.

"Thank you, Daren," she responds.

She lifts her glass. "Cheers."

"Salut."

"So, about this Philippe Marchant gentleman, what can you tell me."

"He is controlled by the billionaires and doesn't care about the French people. I see it reading between the lines."

Cross is fascinated as he glances over to keep a bearing on the party. "I agree with you."

"So do many citizens. However, it is irrelevant what the people want. The voting will be rigged."

Cross is mesmerised by Madelaine's knowledge of French politics.

"Why are you working here?" he asks.

"Michael, there is huge amount of money down here. All the billionaires have property in this fictitious enclave to help them hide assets and avoid taxes. I come down here two nights most weeks to help them spend their ill-gotten cash. We have our own agenda."

Cross is momentarily stunned by the last comment.

"Who is this 'we'?"

"We have never met before but you know what I am. I'm not at liberty to release information that tells you who I am. You seem a nice gentleman and I want to spend the night with you, but I'm just openly talking."

He digests the latest data before responding.

"What would it amount to if I were to partake and accept such a wonderful invitation?"

She tells him.

"I tell you what I will do." He reaches into his jacket pocket and pulls out cash. He carefully places a few thousand British pounds on the marble counter in front of her. "I left my Euros in the room, unfortunately, but this is so we can talk. I'm not interested in sleeping with you tonight, but I remain overly interested in talking politics."

A few more hours pass, and he has grown tired of the noise emanating from across the room but the conversation with Madelaine has been enlightening. One of the waitresses serving the raucous group walks behind Cross and puts their bill on the counter for the bartender. He looks over and his eyebrows rise when he sees the exorbitant near-seven-figure tab in francs.

"They must be celebrating something important," Cross says to the lady.

"They have an account with the casino and are here often. Most people in this room hate them, sir."

"They must be preparing to leave."

"Yes, sir."

Cross stuffs a Benjamin in her pocket and returns to the conversation with his guest.

"I must go, and I advise you leave with me and don't return tonight."

"Please, here is my number." She hands him a business card as they are exiting the casino. "I have enjoyed our conversation too. You are extremely knowledgeable about our French problems."

He looks at her card. Underneath the name and number is written 'Unforgettable Liaisons'. "Marchant is a dangerous man, Ms. Couton, and so are the people supporting him. It isn't just the French who are in trouble."

"I hope to see you again, Michael."

"You just might." They shake hands and then Cross leaves in a different direction.

25

Spoiling a Party

Moore Jr. had allowed Cross to use their apartment in Monte Carlo. It is hidden with easy access but away from traffic, tourists and other unwanted distractions. He returns there after an interesting evening in the casino bar.

He opens one of the boxes that accompanied him from England and finds a black wetsuit. He removes it and underneath are flippers, a full-face leather balaclava, face mask, waterproof gloves and other required tools.

In another box he finds additional items imperative to fulfill this mission. Across from the apartment is a marina. After slipping into the amphibious gear, he walks over carrying his desired equipment. He opens the security gate and follows instructions to the correct slip number.

"What the hell is wrong with people?" as he stares at the luxurious 39-foot Riviera. "Why isn't a twenty-footer sufficient?"

He walks onto the yacht carrying his stuff and confirms there is a small dingy with paddles. Cross looks around to survey the area and finds this boat might be the smallest there.

Avoiding irrelevant details, he releases the forward line securing it to the dock and tosses the end onto the bow. The rear one he unties but leaves it loosely attached. He then inserts the key and powers up the twin Volvo-Penta engines. They purr into life, but he leaves it in neutral and heads to the stern to untether the remaining line. The relative quietness of the yacht Cross finds astonishing.

Standing at the helm, he looks for the fuel gauge and finds it. At three-quarters full, he is happy.

"Thank you, Graeme."

Cross turns on the forward and navigation lights so he can see, and then moves the throttle to adjust forward motion to a nominal three knots. The Riviera glides through the water and escapes the slip as he navigates out of the marina, being careful not to hit other vessels close to him.

He had been given instructions on where to find what he is looking for so heads in that direction. It is another marina but slightly southwest of where he is at. He maintains low speed to avoid drawing attention.

As he approaches the pertinent marina, he is slightly disturbed by the huge and numerous mega yachts in this facility. A few have helipads on.

"This has to be it."

It is a different world here as he gently guides the Riviera through the entrance in his quest. The target yacht is easy to locate because of the noise originating from it. He finds a slip area he can attach to without too much attention. It is void of any aquatic vessels and he will not be long. He deems himself fortunate since the slip is at the end of a dock which facilitates an effortless escape.

After blacking out his face and putting on the balaclava, he unties the dingy from the deck and drops it into the water, whilst still hanging onto the rope. Using his free hand, he gently throws a bag into the dingy and climbs in after it. Cross now uses a paddle to draw closer to the party boat. It is very dark outside and his cover is perfect. Removing the binoculars, he looks at the huge yacht across the marina. The same people who were in the casino are now on their yacht, continuing in the same party vein. They are even more drunk and others have joined the frivolous activities. He looks for security but can only see a couple of them. Loud music is playing and wonders why no one is complaining. Perhaps they are but no one cares.

He paddles across to a yacht in an adjacent slip. He attaches the dingy with one line and puts on the flippers and mask, before strapping the bag to his back, and then inserts his firearm inside the wetsuit. Gently, he drops into the water and swims over to the party yacht.

"Shit."

As he pulls up the guard on the rear is tossing a cigarette into the water and sees him. Not expecting any altercations, the guard is startled. Cross unzips the wetsuit, removes his gun with silencer and fires two quick shots. The guard falls and rolls into the water. Luckily, the music derails the splash.

Now he must move swiftly. He opens the bag, removes four explosive devices and switches them on. Moore Jr. had made them waterproof and some special compound allows them to affix to fiberglass. He has twenty minutes.

The yacht is so large the deck overhangs help conceal his movements as he swims just under the waterline, occasionally coming up for air, to attach each of the devices conveniently spaced along the hull.

Once finished, he quickly swims across the marina and makes it back to the Riviera. After removing the flippers, he climbs up the ladder used for swimmers, releases the ties and runs to the cockpit whilst tossing his mask. The Volvo-Pentas fire up only this time Cross uses more speed to exit through the entrance breakers and once out into open water, he fully opens the throttles. As he does so, explosions abruptly end the party, with the yacht disintegrating into small fragments and its partygoers shredded to pieces.

"Neighbours can't complain about loud music anymore."

He doesn't look back but instead heads for the rendezvous point, where someone will take him back to the waiting Dassault.

26

Abrams and Blue Ocean Media

Cross is relaxing in a luxurious leather seat watching the news. Outside is black except for the occasional farmhouses and villages, thirty-two thousand feet below.

The hostess, Melanie, had served him an aged whiskey with some snacks. He wasn't hungry at the time.

BBC International is broadcasting the devastation in Monte Carlo that happened an hour and half ago. It has quickly escalated into a major global news event, but Cross knew it would.

"...the huge yacht is registered to the mogul Carl Abrams, who owns the conglomerate Blue Ocean Media. Their empire controls most of the mainstream media outlets throughout the world.

"There is no news yet on who was on board at the time, but witnesses have come forward claiming there was a big party with perhaps at least one hundred people there."

Television monitors behind the studio presenter are showing overhead footage taken from a helicopter of flames still active in the marina. Cross sees at least three more yachts on fire.

"No details either on the cause of the explosion. This is devastating breaking news…"

Cross mutes the volume. Now he is hungry.

27

Death of Target Confirmed

'One down.'

'Brilliant job.' Replies Moore Jr.

'They are reporting a hundred or more people on board though.'

'Yes. This is a massive story so stay low.'

'I soon arrive at the airport discussed.'

'Excellent mission.'

'Thank you, Nick.'

'The death count will be high. No news reported on who was on board.'

'I confirmed many targets, but party bigger than expected.'

'See you in US next week.' Is all Granfield messages.

'Yes.'

It is early morning and Wu is pacing in his office. He is awaiting confirmation but the news from Monaco doesn't look good. Handcock walks in.

"They are confirming Carl Abrams' death, but there were many other media CEOs from his empire on the yacht in unofficial celebration of Cross' assassination."

"Are these people that stupid?"

"I guess they are. Or were. They will not do that anymore." Handcock shrugs since there isn't much he can say.

"This may be calamitous from a financial standpoint and will impact the global media companies he owns too."

"I imagine once the stock market opens, share values will tumble."

"What evidence have they come up with?"

"Nothing yet but it was more than one explosion."

"What about security footage within the city's boundaries?"

"We are looking into that. Nice' Cote d'Azur airport was full of private jets and their group partied loudly at the Casino de Monte Carlo last night. We are checking the tapes."

Wu stands up and leaves his office, walking over to the conference room. A red X is already on Abrams' photo.

"This isn't spontaneous or random and looks like an architecturally structured attack." He looks at Handcock, who had followed him. "Cross is dead, so who else do they have?"

"I will get back to you with information as soon as we review tapes from last night, sir." He departs the room.

Wu stares at the layout on the wall and ponders.

"Cross, what did you do?"

Cross slept on the jet after returning from France and Jennings meets him in the morning hours. He finds a service area near Humberside Airport and stops. As they walk inside, Moore Jr. is there to meet them. They all shake hands and find a quiet booth, after grabbing coffee and breakfast sandwiches; Cross is famished.

"Well executed, Daniel."

"Your layout of Monte Carlo and the use of yacht and apartment worked really well, Graeme."

"I am in the wrong business," pipes in Jennings and they all chuckle. "I get an office with a view," as he shrugs his shoulders.

"I am concerned about collateral damage. I confirmed the targets but there were a lot of additional people at the party. I mean more than we anticipated. I am…"

Jennings leaps back in. "Stop right there. Unfortunately, that's the price of war, my friend. Remember too, we didn't start this." He is resolute. "That was the price they paid for the entrance ticket - whoever they turn out to be — and who cares anyway? They should have read the fine print. They are arranging a coup of the world's economies by controlling what we see, hear and read. Fuck 'em."

"Good point," and sheepishly shuts up.

"Abrams' death has been confirmed. Other members of Blue Ocean Media were there also. It seems CEOs of his media empire had flown in from around the world. Get this though, Daniel. They were privately celebrating your assassination, ironically enough." Moore Jr. smiles.

"That's insanity. Are these people nuts?"

"Yeah, well, I think they already answered that question," as Jennings sips his coffee. "These people have no remorse and care only about money."

"No news on explosive forensics either, I am guessing," Cross adds.

"They will have a coronary when that information gets revealed. Be ready." Cross and Jennings look at Moore Jr. who has a beaming smile on his face.

Cross continues. "Where are we with Lithuania?"

"Janina is making limited progress. We, you, me, somebody, must head to Latvia and meet with Prime Minister Ozolins. The conflict is percolating, and we must pressure him into simmering down.

There are still altercations and border skirmishes. BOM, sorry Blue Ocean Media, is funding Lutkus' media group too. The ramifications from events that transpired last night will be far-reaching. It may take some time for them to identify all the dead, too, and the stock market doesn't like uncertainty."

"We have elections in UK and France coming up. Briar will be confirmed next week which Leslie is following."

"It is undoubtedly very complex."

"Oh, I met a French lady in the casino last night. She was very interesting." Cross discusses what he learnt from his conversation with Couton. "I tried researching her name, but nothing came up, except a known escort in Monaco. Obviously, she is not going to use her real name, but she did provide me a business card."

"Did you try calling her?" Moore Jr. asks. "There are a lot of ladies running around those casinos. Interesting you found one aligned in politics. Did it strike you as odd?"

"Not really, Graeme. I was masquerading as Michael Horseman. Your makeup was brilliant and I looked like him. He is even a real MP in Parliament." He looks at Jennings and grins, before turning back to Moore Jr. "Cameras will have picked him up, but I wore the cologne you provided in the package. Does it really give off interfering signals that foils security images?"

"Yes. No aroma but it blurs digital photography, so they are hard to filter."

Jennings' eyebrows rise.

"What does it do to my body?"

"We haven't finished the research on that yet," and he grins. "Our subjects don't live long enough."

"Hilarious," as he chuckles. "The French don't like Marchant. This is evident when you read the real news down there. The rallies are staged, and his followers are paid. The crowds are also fake. They like their current president, but Marchant is feeding off negatives disseminated by Abrams' media outlets. You see where this is all going?

"Madelaine was speaking the voices of French people so certain she wasn't planted."

"Try calling when you get the chance."

"Oh, I will. If she is real, I have an idea." He beams. "What is next?"

"We will supply Janina more misleading data from the news last night. We will toss in a few possibilities including names of people who may have been behind the explosions."

"I have some things in Nick's car, Graeme. Best we don't keep them lying around."

28

A Falling Stock Market

The following morning Jennings calls Cross.

"Did you see the news last night?" he asks.

"Yes."

"Almost the entire Abrams's family was on the yacht. They haven't confirmed DNA samples yet – we are still waiting on that – but heads of news media companies in US, UK, Australia, France, Germany, Canada and others were allegedly at the party. That would represent a colossal loss for the industry."

"Indeed."

"You seem in deep thought."

"I seriously doubt they were there for my death, Nick. They were down there to continue the operation. Those plans will be severely impacted but I fear for what the fallout will be. We must keep going, and perhaps speed things up, but we have more work to do, and it will unquestionably get more difficult."

"I know, but Abrams is a step in the right direction."

"Monaco was relatively calm. They evidently weren't expecting trouble. However, that all changed two nights ago."

Wu is looking at the list of people who were expected to attend the party in Monte Carlo.

"This list is astonishing."

"Yes, Mr. Wu," replies Handcock. "We await DNA results but the reaction from the stock markets and their media organisations suggest the people represented on that list are missing, so presumed dead."

"I see the market for Abram's media companies is in rapid free-fall. This will be a problem and we may need to bring forward our plans. He was coming to see me next week too."

"How do we bring forward elections, sir?"

"Leave that to me."

Handcock departs the room.

Wu picks up his phone and pushes a number.

"Everything still in place in US, Florence?"

"Yes, sir. Briar's confirmation is in four days."

"The deaths in south of France move our plans forward. This is what we need to do over there." He fills her in on the objectives once Briar becomes speaker.

Cross' phone pings.

'Media stocks are crashing.'

'Yes, I saw that.'

'When do you arrive here?' asks Taylor.

'In two days.'

'Good. I've got you party tickets.'

'Yippy, lol. Can't wait.'

'Bring your A-game.'

'I always do, lol.'

'Great job, by the way.'

29

Jason Briar, Speaker of the House

Briar has organised a private party at an exclusive hotel in Washington, DC. These parties are typically paid for by sponsors and afford an open bar. Cross walks into the room and immediately spots Anderson sitting at it. She is in expensive European attire and wears a hat. Perhaps so Mrs. Briar doesn't recognise her, he says to himself and grins. Banners, streamers and posters supporting the campaign litter the place. He looks over and sees Taylor at the other side of the room. She doesn't recognise him, so he heads for the bar.

He seats himself next to Anderson.

"May I buy you a drink, ma'am? Order anything. Money is no object."

"It's an open bar, sir?"

"Yes, I know." He smiles at her. "I was just opening a conversation."

"You are very funny."

"I try to be but doesn't always work. I am Michael Horseman, Member of Parliament from London."

"That explains the accent, which I love. I'm Chara Ingles. Nice to meet you, MP Horseman." She extends her hand.

"Nice to make your acquaintance also, Ms. Ingles, and Michael is fine," as he grasps it.

"Oh, you have a strong grip, Michael. I like that." Her infectious smile nearly smothers him. No wonder elite politicians fall for her. "I prefer Chara."

Pretending to be nervous, "Well, thank you." He corrects himself. "May I be permitted to ask what you do?"

"I'm in public relations and liaise with Speaker Briar."

Yes, I know you do. "Very commendable, Chara. I'm impressed. Speaker Briar invited me here so I can meet with him after…"

Just then the crowded room erupts as Briar walks in with his posse of disciples. Next to him is his proud wife and three children. Anderson swivels her chair to face the front but Cross stands.

Briar heads to the corner of the fair-sized room and stands on a make-shift podium. American flags are waving and red, white and blue balloons are filling the air space.

"I just wish to extend my appreciation and gratitude to those who believed in me."

As he talks, Cross scans the room and sees a major sponsor trying to melt into the gathering. Another member of the world's billionaire club. He returns his gaze to Briar.

"…I will be fighting to bring prosperity and peace with my fellow Capitol Hill members."

Cross is reminded of a message Granfield sent before he arrived in the US:

'House bodies exhumed. Analytical data reveals copious amounts of cocaine, enough to induce a heart attack. Third politician had heart attack and got t-boned going through a red light. The other driver's test result was doctored. She wasn't impaired. Needle marks pinpoint injection areas.'

Cross listens to Briar. Three politicians were murdered and

others were coerced so that his party would take over the House majority.

"...today marks a new beginning for us all."

Briar was transitioned into becoming speaker so Deep State could gain control. That part is complete and Cross knows what comes next. He admits Briar is a commanding figure in the room. His size aids that perception but he carries himself well, dresses impeccably and is articulate. People trust what the arrogant prick is saying so he is a perfect choice, his sponsors must believe.

Cross is done listening and turns back to face Anderson.

"You really enjoy these liars, cheats and thieves, Chara?"

"No. I get paid well, MP Horseman." Reverting back to being formal in order to portray her displeasure at his question.

Bollocks, thinks Cross. "So I understand."

She turns and looks at him, but it is his turn to switch on the charm.

"You are stunning, and your natural beauty isolates you from the rest of the women in this room. You look like a model from the fifties when people cared about how they dressed and looked. Honestly, you could be a painting on any American military aircraft used during World War Two."

He knows how these women get their kicks. Now she is aware her physical attributes have turned on Mr. Horseman, she rotates her chair around and Cross moves closer.

"You are a quintessential English gentleman, it appears. You have this parliamentary swagger which I like."

Out of the corner of his eye, and behind Anderson, he sees Briar looking at them from across the room. His jealous gaze resonates and leaves Cross amused. This guy is the third most powerful person in America so what the hell is wrong with him? Knowing how to push buttons, he looks at Anderson.

"Can I get you another drink?"

"Yes, please. I wish to discuss British politics."

He gently places a hand on her arm, not in a suggestive way, which pleases her. "My favourite topic."

Taylor is looking over at Anderson and doesn't recognise the guy with whom she is talking. "Is this MP Horseman?" she asks herself. Her eyes venture over to Briar's corner, and she can see him staring and seething inside whilst still trying to recite his prepared speech. "What a moron." He is worse than Anderson described, she thinks, and chuckles to herself. "Cross, the magician. You animal, you."

Taylor can't be seen with Cross so she waits until he leaves, half an hour later. Now it's her turn to walk over and chat to Anderson, leaving Briar to have a premature heart attack. "It would make things easier, and the world a better place, if he does."

30

Wu's Weakest Link

Cross is with Granfield in Palisades, across the Potomac River from Langley.

"That was an impressive mission in Monaco."

"Thank you."

"Blue Ocean Media is essentially done. Eleven family members are dead and they were the heirs to a media dynasty. As the stock value tumbles, people will run. We need to see who will be lining up to buy it. CEOs and partners of subsidiaries around the world have also been named. There are of course innocent people who were the employees just trying to make a living. The total count so far is one-hundred and seven.

"They did find a guard who had been shot twice. The new gun we supplied can't be traced and the bullets are unique. Nothing will exist in any database so those forensics go nowhere.

"The interesting findings are the explosive devices. They have traced the manufacturer to a company in Israel, but the material is from North Korea, they believe. This is confusing, to us as well as anyone else. That combination doesn't exist and quite a challenge for those who need to know." He smiles. "Well done."

"This is a big setback for Wu, and they have to counter these deaths."

"Yes, of course."

"They have Briar shoehorned into position. That can only work if they eliminate the two more important US citizens in front of him."

"Correct. President Walkman has been made aware or is aware. What's next?"

"I saw another sponsor at Briar's private party. He was attempting to be discrete."

Just then Taylor calls. "This is Leslie, I need to answer."

"Go ahead, Daniel."

"Hello, Leslie."

"Daniel, we have a slight problem. Briar arranged to meet Florence in a motel after his party. He arrived with two of his own men and they raped and beat her. She called me this morning crying but she needs to be in a hospital. Briar has threatened her to keep her mouth shut. They performed some security assessments and checked you out."

"How is she? I hope ok. However, MP Michael Horseman does exist."

"This has traumatized her, obviously. Yes. They called his office and the secretary told them he was in the US."

Jennings covered his backside. Brilliant man.

"Where are you?"

"I'm with David. I knew that prick was jealous, but Jesus."

"Tell him he needs to get Florence to a hospital. I don't know how he does it and hides the fact they are CIA."

"I will let David worry about that."

He hands the phone over and Taylor fills him in. Granfield then ends the call and hands it back.

"I must run. He is Speaker of the House for fuck's sake. These people are all morons. What the hell is he thinking?"

"He evidently isn't." Cross shrugs his shoulders.

"He doesn't need to be carrying a scandal like this, not at this stage." Granfield is shaking his head as he gets up to leave. "What a prized dick."

"Keep me posted," as they shake hands.

"Hang around a day or two. I will call you later."

31

Making of a Double Agent

"Sir, we retrieved copies of security tapes from the casino."

"And?"

"There is a man in the same bar as the Abrams family who talked to a known escort for over two hours. Nothing seems spurious or suspicious. He gave her money and they are eventually seen leaving together. There appears to be no security risk."

"And?"

"We traced him to a politician from London and even called his office. The lady who answered confirmed he was in Monaco."

"And?"

"We can't get an image of his face, sir. The cameras all show distortion that we have been unsuccessful at filtering out, made worse because he was wearing a fedora. We continue to look for other potential leads."

"What about the explosive devices? What info do we have?"

"Insider information reveals the fragments are indicative of a device fabricated in Israeli and the tests show explosive materials coming from Korea. None of this makes any sense. Those combinations don't exist."

"Israel attacking Jews."

Wu already knows he is dealing with incredibly smart people and he slams the phone down.

Cross is waiting outside the facility Anderson has been brought to. He can't venture inside. He sees Taylor walking over after having just visited her.

"She will be ok but is shaken up. This was meant to be a warning, but she is a strong, determined lady and this seems normal behaviour to her," Taylor looks sad. "Briar was careful not to have his clowns damage her facial area."

"He is in a powerful position. I don't understand why he wishes to play this futile game. He really doesn't need this attention."

"These men, and women, control. They think they have power over everybody. Briar has exposed a serious weakness in his personality. Haven't we seen this before, Daniel? The strength of any component is compromised by its weakest link."

"Yes."

"We can use this to our advantage."

"Is she going to be ok though?"

"Yes. They questioned her first, asking about you and me. You don't know this but I am a real lawyer in this town and I do work for people on Capitol Hill. When they research the fake name I gave Florence, it will be legitimate. They did their research and asked how she knew us."

Cross laughs. "Fake and legitimate are a contradiction in terms."

"Not in politics."

"I only met her last night and already there is Shakespearian drama. She seems my kind of normal to me," and laughs his head off.

Taylor slaps him on his arm. "You are incorrigible, Dr. Cross. She told Briar what you just said, except for the drama part." She rolls her eyes.

"How did David arrange this?"

"She doesn't know anything. He had a couple of ladies he knows show up and they brought her here. He has stationed three agents in the hospital, wearing lab coats. Briar will not know she is here."

"Politicians have access to everything. There is a café around the corner. I saw it coming here."

They head on over and get seated.

"Where do you stand with her trusting you?"

"This incident will make her situation less tenable. She will be afraid now and I don't understand any of it. She works for Wu so why did Briar do it?"

"Stop trying to make sense of this. I analyse things but I gave up with the 'why' a while ago. He must be envious of Wu as well, which just gets better and better." It is Cross' turn to roll his eyes.

"I can switch her. I see that as being even more feasible after last night. As you said, a double agent."

"What happens now? Death of Abrams will have spooked Wu. Surely Florence has been given instructions on what to do with Briar."

"She will be kept overnight for observation but I pick her up tomorrow. I will know more then."

32

Madelaine Couton

"Daniel, where are you?"

"Still in Washington, DC."

"I picked Florence up this morning and took her back to the same motel. She just called me. Briar is meeting her there in about an hour."

"Give the directions or pick me up. This guy doesn't give up."

Taylor provides the directions and said she would meet him there, since they can't be seen traveling together.

When Cross arrives at the motel via taxi, it is dark outside but he sees a black Lincoln Town Car already there. Standing by the side of it are two, presumably, Secret Service agents. He doesn't know, doesn't bother asking and doesn't care.

He asks the taxi driver to keep driving and he stops at the adjacent property. Cross climbs out and then doubles back. The gun is drawn as he edges closer. The motel parking lot is full which allows him to scamper between vehicles. Why Speaker of the House wants to meet Anderson here in a sleazy area of town is anybody's guess. Even his heart is pounding.

The agents are looking around but are not prepared. Cross runs behind the first one and swings violently at his left kidney section.

As he drops down Cross kicks him in the mouth. His teeth shatter and fly in different directions, along with the agent's blood. The second hears the commotion, pulls his gun and runs around the front of the Lincoln. Cross is ready and fires one round to the forehead.

"I'm done with these people."

Wearing a baseball cap, he looks for the room number Taylor had given him and runs up the stairs to the second-floor balcony. He doesn't bother knocking on the door and just shoots the lock to pieces and barges in. Briar is ripping Anderson's clothes off and is about to climb on top.

"I don't know what the fuck you are into, Speaker Briar, but we are done here," he says, in his best Irish accent, and with venom.

The surprise on Briar's face is eclipsed by the left, right, left, right punches Cross has perfected in meditation. He keeps going and going. Eventually Briar is on the verge of passing out as he loses his ability to function, rolls off Anderson and onto the floor.

Blood from his face being pummeled has splashed against the headrest and wall. Cross could have gone the rest of his life without seeing the image of the third most powerful person in the country with his briefs around his ankles.

Taylor arrives as Briar is leaving, being ushered out of the motel room by Cross. She just stares at him and they don't say a word, as she then looks at Briar's face covered in blood. Cross is too angry and doesn't even acknowledge her.

He gets him onto the balcony and then closes the room door behind them. He looks at the pathetic specimen, as Briar leans over the railing groaning in pain. "We have documented accounts of you taking bribes. We have videos of you cheating on your wife. We also know you are conspiring against the American government and its people. You watched Ms. Anderson being assaulted by your men, so I suggest you drive your Town Car home because I don't believe your agents are able to.

"You will act normal and behave consistent with your position. When the time comes, we will notify you. Your political career is over, and likely your marriage. How soon those will be, is up to you." Damn, he must sound convincing, because they don't have any of that material, yet. "I also suggest you head to the hospital and have that gash checked."

Anderson is covering herself up when Taylor enters and the door closes.

"What happened?"

"Briar turned possessive and bizarre once he became speaker. He just isn't the same anymore, not that he was much better before. He's just more violent, more damaging and more weird. He wants to divorce his wife which is insane.

"The Irish guy who just left came into the room and beat the shit out of him. He knew exactly who Briar is, but who the hell was he?"

The Irish guy? Taylor is inwardly amused. "We should let all this calm down. Gather your things, and I will move you to a different hotel. Why this area of town and this shithole?"

"It is out of his neighbourhood and discrete. I gather the elites use this place a lot, for child sex trafficking mostly."

Taylor's internal amusement is over as she almost throws up.

Cross is alone in his middling motel room close to Washington National Airport. He can hear the planes landing and taking off. His meditation squatting on the floor is over. He doesn't have a padded room so was left to take it out on Briar instead. "What a dumbass," he mutters.

He snatches his wallet and a business card falls out. Upon picking it up, he glances at the number and decides to call it.

"Hello, this is Madelaine."

"Madelaine, this is Michael. We met in Monte Carlo."

"Oh, hello, my dear. I wasn't expecting you to call so soon." She giggles, with aid from alcohol consumption Cross suspects.

"The night I paid for is due," and laughs.

"Ha-ha. That verbal contract ended as soon as you walked away. Nice to hear your voice though. You must have heard about the explosions on the yacht soon after we left the bar?"

"Yes, it made the headlines."

"The people partying behind us were on it."

"I know."

"You knew who they were?" Couton is surprised.

"Yes."

"I was invited on that yacht but saw you instead. You looked far more interesting than a bunch of inebriated Jewish billionaires."

"Well, thank you but you knew who they were too?" In a rather surprised tone also.

"Of course. It is my job to know so I can work the casinos."

"My, oh my. Now I can tell people that I saved a woman's life because she wanted to talk to me. That is sad you could have been on it."

"Are you back in town?"

"No. I am in the US for a few days."

"Damn, you get around."

"Yes."

"For what do I owe this pleasure?"

"Can I call you next time I'm in town? I would like to chat more?"

"Is that all you want?" She giggles again. "I was joking about the contract but yes, just call me."

He chuckles. "Thank you, Madelaine."

33

UK Prime Minister, Assassinated

UK's Prime Minister Clark is on the campaign trail. She has been touring Yorkshire and given speeches in Wakefield and Barnsley. The final stop before flying back to London is Sheffield. Clark arrives in the city centre via motorcade after taking an RAF helicopter from her last presentation.

Sheffield used to be world famous for exceptional stainless steel produced from its mills, but those years died a long time ago as deficient, sub-standard stainless from China was much cheaper and strangley preferred. The city fell into decline but has risen over the last decade into a major industrial powerhouse in South Yorkshire. Clark sees this as a bulwark because of other derived technologies. Unfortunately, this contradicts with what Deep State wants.

The motorcade incorporating the prime minister's Range Rover is heading to University of Sheffield's Student Union where it is set up for her speech. As it approaches up Brook Hill and turns onto the campus, the Rover explodes sending pieces of it flying into the air.

A significantly sized crowd had already gathered in anticipation of Clark's arrival but now they are screaming and running in arbitrary directions. The impact of the explosion blows out windows in nearby buildings, but a voluminous number of spectators are injured, dying or already dead. Police on motorcycles escorting the prime minister are impacted and have been blown off. Other security vehicles in the procession are also severely damaged. Debris is everywhere and screams now punctuate the eclectic atmosphere.

Excitement generated from the VIP visit has been derailed. Sections of the crowd not supporting Clark's favouritism toward policies endorsing big corporations and capitalism have been vocally silenced. Panic and shock have enveloped the entire area.

In the background sirens are bellowing as police try to establish some sort of perimeter but even they are in tears. The Range Rover that had Clark sitting in the rear only a few seconds ago has been blown to smithereens; the remnants of which rest smoldering in a large crater.

The explosion created a fireball generating smoke the wind has drifted toward downtown and the lingering acrid smell of mortality is palpable. It is a stark reminder to the people of Britain already familiar with a violent past that politically-motivated instability is never too far away.

Police cars had already lined Brook Hill blocking the road at both ends to traffic for the scheduled state visit. Now the police guide Ambulances, fire engines and paramedics onto the campus as medical staff are pushing and dragging gurneys toward the injured and dying in an effort to assist doctors tending to their needs. Once death had been determined, the mortally wounded are left covered but unattended since the damage had already been done.

The crowd is being filtered through security checkpoints to allow removal and dispersion from the area. Security and media helicopters flying overhead just add to the cacophony of chaos and bedlam.

Prime Minister Clark is dead...

34

Another Deep State Sponsor, Dead

Jennings is on the phone with someone at MI5.

"Where the fuck was security?"

"Someone made changes at the last minute. They used the correct reference code for authorisation."

"I don't give a flying fuck. This is pure insanity." Anger doesn't adequately describe Jennings' current disposition. "She was our Prime Minister and needed protection for fuck's sake. This is standard protocol which had been heightened since Mitchell's assassination. Jesus Christ, she was murdered on our watch. Get me the person who made those changes?"

"Yes, sir."

"Now." Jennings is going ballistic and screaming through the phone.

Cross had remained in Washington at Granfield's request. He was also waiting on news from Taylor and walking downtown when a message comes in.

'PM Clark has been assassinated.'

Cross finds and enters the nearest bar, and stares as the horrific scenes are being played out on a corner TV. People around him are gasping and horrified.

Someone had it playing on CNN. "The news of the murder of British Prime Minister Clark has outraged the world. Expressions of shock and anger are pouring in along with messages of condolences. Buckingham Palace has lowered their flags to half-mast."

"What the hell is going on." Cross is asking anybody in the bar as his eyes water over.

Recognising Cross' accent, someone answers. "Your prime minister was due to give a speech at a student union hall in Sheffield when someone blew up the car she was traveling in. At least thirty-two dead so far, with eighty-six injured. Those numbers are tentative and will climb, we are told." The guy looks at Cross who has tears rolling down his face. "I'm so sorry, sir."

Cross is stunned and his legs are shaking. The images being portrayed are devastating. What remains of some vehicle is sitting in a crater created by the blast. As the camera scans the area, buildings in the vicinity also show severe damage. People are lying on the ground, some covered in blue tarps and blood-soaked concrete is everywhere. Police and Parliament security vehicles are also seen in the destruction and motorcycles are laying on their sides, obviously blown with force from the blast.

The news anchor continues. "…explosion occurred on the University of Sheffield campus. No word yet on who is responsible and no one is claiming any."

Cross steps outside the bar and removes his phone.

"Nick, what happened?"

"Some security was removed from duty. Apparently, a call came in using coded authorisation asking they be sent to a different location because of a breach of security in that area. I have requested the person who received the message call me." He is emotional and hyperventilating as he struggles to slow the words.

"This is someone working on the inside."

"Yes. That is my conclusion also," as he tries to calm down.

"Shit."

"Something of that ilk." Jennings is clearly distraught.

He next calls Granfield.

"David, I'm watching the news. This is devastating and Charles Davenport is going to jump all over it."

"What the hell was Intelligence doing over there?"

"It was aided by someone from the inside."

"Removing security details is insanity no matter who requested it. This is problematic and I agree with you. Davenport will politicise this to the full extent which is going to help Wu's cause."

"UK has different protocols to the US regarding the death of a prime minister. They are not strict or defined so it would be up to the party in power to quickly elect someone, in this case the Liberal Unionists. The Chancellor is the likely person. However, in the event they can't do it fast enough, the Queen elects someone."

"Interesting. Let's hope she isn't buddy-buddy with our friend."

Cross half snickers. "There is that. Either way, elections are planned and will be happening soon. Davenport will use this incompetent and blatant security failure of the current party in power for his own agenda. I have no doubt this will advance his endeavors."

"More incendiary material tossed onto an already-raging inferno."

"Something like that."

"I heard through sources our illustrious Briar had sought medical attention. Allegedly, he had an altercation with someone last night, and one of his security guards was killed."

"Interesting."

"It always is when you are around, Daniel." He laughs, kind of.

"What next?"

"Good I keep you entertained, at least. I am back to the UK and then the Baltics."

"Daniel, did you see the news this morning?" asks Taylor.

"Yes. Fascinating development. Perhaps Wu is pissed his sponsors keep dying. How is Florence?"

"Doing better. I put her into a much better hotel last night and she seems more relaxed and calmer. Briar called and apologised too."

"He has no choice, unfortunately. How's the double-agent proposal fairing?"

"It is delicate, but she was impressed last night. Some Irish guy, she said."

Cross chuckles. "Damn Irish crop up everywhere," he adds in an Irish accent.

"You never told me how talented you are."

"You never asked but thought that side of me was inferred."

"I see her again later today. I want her to bring up what Briar's next moves are. Where are you heading?"

"UK and then the Baltics."

Wu has his monitor turned on and is watching the news being broadcast out of England. He is staring at the smoldering ruins of what once was a fine automobile hosting the British prime minister.

He slams the PC screen shut and hastily exits his office.

That lunchtime Cross had decided on a detour and flies down to the New York City area. Events across the pond have changed things. Now down on 5th Avenue, he has located the building he had researched the night before. He wanted to verify and confirm Briar's sponsor at his party a few days ago. He did. It is Ethan Jankowski, CEO of one of the largest wealth management companies in the world – TrustCorp Investments. Jankowski is a rather diminutive, introvert and reclusive character, which are the most dangerous ones, and another Jewish sponsor.

Cross enters the vast building, then through security and a metal detector. TrustCorp occupies all the top forty floors of a sixty-five-storey building. He walks around, surveying the area to get a feel for the environment. The marble, granite and expensive furnishings and paintings certainly portray an image of wealth. The people walking around are wearing expensive cloth and carry confidence.

During his research, Cross had found Jankowski's company owns nineteen percent of Blue Ocean Media, which was interesting to him. It appears all these billionaires own portions of each other's companies, so once the first one falls, the rest will surely cascade like a house of cards: the whole house having been built on molten sand. They are all managed and leveraged it seems using identical blueprints, perhaps produced on Jekyll Island in 1910 when a secret meeting had taken place to form the foundation of what is now known as the Federal Reserve, he ponders. Cross had done his research scratching his head. "The great OPM denominator; Other People's Money," he had said to himself. To him, it is all bollocks. The massive stock market devaluation of the media conglomerate since Abrams' death will cause havoc on these leveraged enterprises. He can only hope.

Cross smiles. "Now, let me see if I can cause more trouble."

He steps across the street and locates a café in which to blend, wishing to observe the passage of people in and out of TrustCorp's building. He takes a seat, orders tea and waits.

When Cross looks at his Rolex, it displays two-thirty p.m. He had done some digging in special places and found Jankowski would be in New York today and tomorrow.

A little over an hour of waiting is rewarded as he notices a hive of activity at the entrance. Three black Lincoln Navigators had pulled up outside the building. Cross sees Jankowski run and climb into the middle one as his entourage accompanying him split up in each of the three executive vehicles. They then speed off.

Cross exits the café and flags down a taxi. "Follow the three Navigators, sir."

With a smile, the eastern-bloc cab driver responds. "Sure."

What is it with cab drivers, Cross wonders? Once he realises the direction they are heading, his instincts kick in.

"Head over to the east side of Central Park," he commands the driver, and verbally passes on an address of a high-end luxury home off Park Avenue.

The taxi pulls up across from the building but Cross isn't given long to prepare, because he sees the three Lincolns coming. He climbs out and points. "Wait for me down that side-street, please," as he tosses a few hundred dollars onto the seat.

Cross runs across the wide avenue and median, hiding behind a vendor selling food. He releases his gun, ready.

Focused on the middle Lincoln, they pull up and doors fling open. Cross sees Jankowski climb out, but he is surrounded by bodyguards. He doesn't care and pops the first one, who immediately drops, exposing Jankowski in the process. Cross fires two more shots and watches him start to fall as he turns and sprints to the taxi waiting around the corner.

As he slams the door shut he yells, "Go, anywhere."

The taxi merges into the frenzied afternoon traffic and escapes the area. As he does so, they pass an entrance stairwell to the subway so Cross orders the driver to pull over. He obliges.

"Thank you." He tosses a few more hundred-dollar bills onto the front passenger seat and runs.

"No. Thank you, sir," the cab driver bellows through the driver's open window, still with a smile on his face.

Cross runs down the subway stairwell and disappears into the underground mayhem, ripping off his disguise in the process.

35

House of Cards

Wu is losing it and is livid. News of Jankowski being gunned down on the streets of New York City is filtering in and reverberating around his office.

"Why aren't these people putting two and two together?"

"He had assigned extra bodyguards, sir." Handcock's attempt at reasoning failed.

"What the hell is wrong with you? He is dead. Who the hell cares how many people he had protecting him?"

Handcock looks at him and surely his blood vessels will soon lose their ability to perform as God had intended: Wu's head is about to explode.

Rapidly changing subjects. "Death of Clark will aid Davenport. It formed part of our predictive model, remember? Their election has been brought forward, sir."

Getting irritated. "I see that, and I know, dumbass. Now find out more about what happened in New York," as he picks up his laptop and launches it across the office.

Cross is back on the Dassault and had left New York via a private airstrip. He was feeling satisfied after another perfunctory operation and is getting good at this. Melanie had just brought him a cocktail when Granfield calls.

"Where are you?"

"Heading to Europe."

"You will know about the CEO of TrustCorp Investments being murdered?"

"Jankowski? I saw the news, yes. However, the use of the word 'murder' may be a tad premature."

Ignoring him, Granfield continues. "He was another of Wu's sponsors and a member of Deep State."

"Indeed, he was."

"His company owns shares in Blue Ocean Media. This appears to be a house of cards."

Granfield knows Cross participated in his death but isn't going to say anything. He is seeing what he's doing and why. These massive conglomerates were manoeuvring to control vast swaths of the West's real estate market and, hence, the people. They also want to control everything including energy and what they eat, buy, wear, drive and breathe. Cross is identifying targets in an orchestrated, methodical fashion that will enable destruction of these companies financially, and Granfield is impressed. Now he is aware of the pattern, he can better help and protect him. However, he is aware Cross is playing a dangerous game because these entities only care about their vast wealth as it impacts their ability to control politicians without it. As this implodes Granfield fears for Cross' life, even though he is supposedly dead already. After all, one can only live twice.

"When one of them falls, they all fall. These people built their fortunes off the rest of us. Now it is time we took it all back."

"How are *you* doing?" with emphasis on him personally.

"Actually, considering everything, I'm good, but appreciate you asking, David."

"This is going to get increasingly nasty. Losing family members, they don't care but, on the other hand, losing their fortune is vastly different. Cartwright's death didn't spook investors or the market. Loss of Abrams and now Jankowski, they will be seeing a pattern of activity. The markets tomorrow morning will be interesting. Take care of yourself and be safe."

"I know, and I will."

Cross calls Taylor

"Daniel, how are you and where are you? Did you see the news?"

"I'm good and yes but heading to Europe."

"Jankowski was at Briar's party."

"Yes. He was another of Wu's sponsors."

"I called Florence and she told me Briar is pissed."

"Fuck him too."

"There is going to be less money to control these politicians."

"Absolutely. Nevertheless, there is still enough of it to worry about, even if they are leveraged. The question will be how leveraged are they? The answer to that we will find out soon enough, eh?"

"Be careful."

"Thanks. How is Florence?"

"Recovering and calming. Briar behaves differently now, she said. I don't know what you said to him."

He smiles. "Whatever I said was enough evidently, but is she turning?"

"Yes. I am getting there."

"I knew you could do it," and puts the phone down.

36

Norfolk Farmhouse, England

Cross arrives in the early hours at an airfield just north of London. Jennings and Gabrys meet him and then head off to a secluded farmhouse in Norfolk.

"How many people do you know, Nick?" and laughs.

"It's good to know people in low places. It comes in handy, on occasions, especially when you are in town."

"Janina, it is so nice to see you again. How are you doing?"

"I have been worried about you, what with all the intensive activity of late."

"That has nothing to do with me," and grins.

"I'm fine, for now, but looking forward to going home. I need to get home, in fact."

Cross sees Jennings' reaction and puts a consoling hand on his leg. "I understand that."

"But otherwise we are all ok. Nick is looking after us."

Jennings gets going to distract his immediate attention. "No one noticed Cartwright's death. By no one, I mean the markets. It was seen as an anomaly because there was nothing to link his death. The demise of Western media moguls and now with Jankowski tossed in, this is a different story. I feel this is where we can alter our narrative and have Janina start revealing connections through the back door.

"The death of Prime Minister Clark is of course significant. Killing oligarchs spooks a select few and, generally speaking, the public doesn't embrace them anyway. Assassinating a head of state sets a dangerous precedent because it is meaningful to infinitely more people. The impact is considerable so now all bets are off. Death of Clark is symbolic since not many leaders in recent history in the West have been assassinated. US' John F Kennedy in 1963 comes to mind, but that was an internal conflict."

Cross interrupts. "Sorry, Nick, but did you find the person who authorised the security changes?"

"No. We are still working on that." He continues. "Anyway, the Liberal Unionist Party reacted swiftly to limit the consequences. They were smart there. However, again I feel the impact has been minimised to some extent because it was anticipated Mitchell would win the forthcoming election. His death brought out the illustrious Davenport who is an even bigger wanker. Clark's approval rating had dropped precipitously because she touts democracy, freedoms and free enterprise. Deep State isn't particularly fond of any of those things. A good portion of the populace want free money tossed at them. They want redistribution of wealth which is ironic since the politicians they prefer and who promote this garbage are funded by Deep State's billionaires."

Jennings pauses and as he does so the lady of the house brings in a tray with teapot, condiments and mugs.

"Perfect timing, Rebecca. Thank you."

"What are you seeing in the markets?" asks Cross. "Sorry, I have been pre-occupied the last twenty-four hours."

"The London Stock Exchange opens in an hour or so. At that time we should expect to see significant changes. Blue Ocean Media, as a holding company for its other media tools, has lost forty percent. We saw a flutter in TrustCorp's activity in after-hours trading. However, people will be connecting Cartwright's death so his company, CW Holdings, should see activity today. At least it is a move we anticipate. As you know that company has pieces in almost every pie."

Gabrys is intrigued by all this but decides to pour the tea, as a break, and slides the filled mugs across the antique table lined with a cotton tablecloth.

"Thank you." Cross smiles at her. "I bet when you decided to meet me in a bar, you weren't anticipating all this?"

"This is mind-boggling. I can't grasp it all and I work in the media."

Cross continues. "I did some research into all these companies owned by the oligarchs. They all own a piece of each other."

"This is how they keep control of most of the wealth, Daniel. It is quite remarkable when one analyses it." Jennings takes a sip of his tea.

"So, as I visualise it then - bear in mind I am a novice in this arena – if one should fail, it would be like dominoes lined up. It is all dependent on how leveraged these companies are as to how quickly or easily they tumble."

"That is a simplistic view for all to understand, but yes, this is an accurate analogy. These people obtain loans from major lending institutions based on their assets. Cash is irrelevant. The banks place liens against their stock holdings and corporate values. Billionaires don't use their own money for anything."

"OPM," Cross injects.

Gabrys looks confused.

"Other People's Money."

Jennings is impressed. Cross has been studying and doing his homework. He has certainly educated himself on the people they are dealing with. Granfield had filled him in a little so Jennings is also obligated to protect him.

"They take these loans and buy other assets. So, those new assets are now already leveraged." He rolls his eyes.

"If the markets crash, the bank managers start looking at their own loan portfolios and how far they are extended." Jennings has a captive audience fascinated by all this. "They are legally compromised and must have enough assets to support the loans; at least in theory anyway. When the market crashed in 2008, financial institutions were over-extended because the assets they tied questionable loans to essentially disappeared when the housing market crashed.

"When banks' clients start having financial issues, they will review the assets to which they have structured their loans against. They will be aware stocks are crashing and will re-evaluate their risks. In some cases, if the numbers don't match and the bank's risk is too great, they will request early termination and immediately mature their loans. The client will then have to pay them back. At which time the billionaires will be in trouble."

"We will have to wait and see how leveraged Cartwright, Abrams and Jankowski were," says Cross.

"They all live on the edge and they all play the same financial games. This is going to be interesting for sure."

"Ok. That's one of many issues here. Where are we with Ozolins in Latvia, Janina?"

"My repeated condemnation of the US' involvement in the parade massacre calmed Lutkus in Lithuania. That was Nick's aim, although I disagreed with his logic."

"We all did," answers Cross, as he looks over and grins at him.

"War is still looming and people are still dying across borders." Gabrys injects.

"Prime Minister Lutkus is insane. He is being paid by the Western oligarchs to push their agenda. We had to curtail his immediate aggression after you rescued Janina by killing two of his security folk. These idiots react on impulse and emotions. Janina's broadcasts helped to achieve this. Rightly or wrongly, it is immaterial."

Jennings shrugs his shoulders and sighs, attempting to matter-of-factly justify his logic.

Gabrys continues. "His popularity noticeably gained points because of this and nationalism increased. His media group is pushing both EU and NATO negativity which are also acquiring momentum."

"Both France and Germany harbour reservations about the EU, but their governments keep quiet," Cross injecting his acquired knowledge. "People resent highly paid moronic, uneducated and self-elected politicians showing up from Brussels with their hands out and back pockets open telling them what to do without even comprehending their history or culture. Britain's exit from the EU shows it can be done, although teething issues persist."

"Sources inside the Kremlin are watching this very carefully. They are aware Deep State is pushing for world domination, power and, ultimately, control. The New World Order rhetoric is beginning to show its ugly face in conversations there, and they want nothing to do with it," Jennings adds.

Cross' turn to jump in again. "Wait, I thought NATO will be involved in any war in the Baltic region?"

"Of course, Daniel. But if Lutkus secures the region, be assured he will be pushing to abstain from it."

"This is messed up," and Cross' turn to sigh.

Jennings looks at Gabrys. "What are the rumblings in the media world after the demise of the Abrams family and other important figures?"

"Of course, there were outrage and condemnations. However, the reality is far different from that which is being reported." She shifts forward and places her arms on the table. "Blue Ocean Media had increased their fake-news reporting. The amount of disinformation started to escalate globally. The industry noticed this early in the year, which coincided with the clandestine development of the virus and it continued during the supply-chain fiasco. We were seeing this happen in real time and it was beginning to be a problem. These are major news outlets and their activists disguised as journalists are well known so people believe them. They host prime-time news hours in most western countries and for some it is their only source of information. Abrams knew this and, of course, Wu also."

"Disinformation is an endemic problem. Social media sites have this issue too." Cross finishes his tea and pours another. "The question is what happens now their funding sources will diminish? Also, who is going to purchase the conglomerate?"

"We will find the answers to these questions shortly but someone needs to head to Latvia or we arrange to meet Ozolins in a mutually agreeable foreign country," adds Jennings. "We need to make him aware of what is going on. Wu has his replacement campaigning to attack Lithuania."

Cross is angry. "Wu needs to be put to sleep, permanently."

"I'm sure he is on your list, but first things first." Jennings puts a hand on his shoulder. "We have France and UK elections to deal with." Now he grins.

Just then Jennings phone vibrates. He picks it up and reads the message.

"The markets opened with CW Holdings dropping. TrustCorp is also down. Interestingly, Blue Ocean Media's competition show upward trends."

37

Racial Riots Outside Paris, France

Wu is in the conference room with Handcock. They are reviewing the wall now marked with three red Xs on their sponsors.

"We need to step this up before the markets fully crash. These people leveraged everything they own, based on their corporate wealth."

"Yes, sir." Handcock agreeing, because that is what is expected of him.

"I will call Lutkus and get him to start pushing his generals."

"Ok."

"How are Davenport and Marchant's campaigns going?"

"They are both looking good. The death of Clark because of security failings is advancing his polls and he is acting on this lapse of judgment. However, this is what we need to do in France," as he fills Wu in on his idea.

"Is that feasible now?"

"I have already reviewed the plans. All we have to do is implement them, so yes."

"Then do it."

Cross stayed in Norfolk as Jennings and Gabrys headed back to London. It is best he lays low for a day or two whilst a meeting is set up with Ozolins, likely across the border in Belarus, if it can be arranged. The farmhouse owner has an old Land Rover Series II Jennings told him he could borrow, so he does and heads into the village. He found the local pub and is sitting at the bar when the early evening news comes on.

He sits up and asks the bartender to turn up the volume.

"…the riots started in one of the colossal banlieues projects in the suburbs of Paris. These concrete housing facilities are home to a vast number of Muslim immigrants from North African and Arab countries. They were originally built during the decades after World War II and conceived as utopias for Parisian workers. Now, they are incubators for radicalism, violence and social unrest as poverty swells at their doors…"

Scenes of Muslims running the streets brandishing knives, guns, setting fire to cars and burning homes are visually portrayed on the TV monitor. The French police are graphically observed beating them with truncheons. Shots are heard in the background.

The British news reporter continues. "It's unclear what started this but unrest has been brewing for years here as more and more immigrants fill these massive concrete complexes."

The next segment piques Cross' interest as he sees Marchant being interviewed by Sky. "How did he get to the scene so fast and how is he being protected?" he asks himself.

The bartender turns and stares at him.

"I'm here with France's presidential candidate Philippe Marchant. Mr. Marchant, thank you for braving the riots, sir, but what can you tell us." The reporter thrusts her Sky-emblazoned mic towards him.

"This is a direct result of our current president's immigration policies." Just as he says that a car that was set on fire explodes in the background, but off in the distance. Marchant turns around for visual impact and then focuses back on the camera. "The French people don't want Muslims here. What is worse, the EU policies dictate what France does. Muslims have a difficult time assimilating into their changed world. If whites moved to a Muslim country, we would feel the same. These banlieues projects are massive and promote extremism and social isolation. Our socialist system doesn't pay them enough so poverty breeds anger and frustration which is ripe for terrorism, and what we are witnessing tonight." Then he tosses in a campaign remark. "I intend to change all this," which is exactly what Deep State and his supporters want to hear.

Cross steps to a quieter area of the small pub and punches a number into his phone.

"Michael, how are you?"

"I'm good, Madelaine. What can you tell me?"

"You see the news from Paris?"

"Yes, I'm back in the UK."

"This was organised. Someone purposely started these riots."

This comment stuns Cross for a second or two.

"Hello?"

"I'm shocked."

"An armed group driving military-type vehicles drove into this vast neighborhood and started shooting innocent people. This is already a cinder block and doesn't take much to ignite unrest here."

"That's crazy. Does anyone have any idea who they were?"

"No. They disappeared once the riots were stimulated."

"I saw Marchant on the street giving interviews. How did he get there so fast and how does he know he is safe?"

"Michael, you asked the right questions."

"And?"

"You can probably answer them too, sir."

38

We Must Leave

"Where are you, my friend?"

"David, I'm in a farmhouse in Norfolk."

"The crises remain active."

"Yes, only the one outside Paris was purposely aroused. A group went into the complex and started shooting residents, then left. Interesting how Marchant was already there."

"I saw that too. Wall Street opened with some interesting stock movements. It seems the market is catching on to why Cartwright was killed. His company, CW Holdings, has experienced a big decline already and TrustCorp is trading much lower."

"Let's see where this takes us. Wu must be worried about the declining assets of his dead sponsors. His live ones must be scurrying, like rodents that they are."

"What's the plan in the Baltics? The US heads NATO so we are asking."

"I fly there in a day or two."

"Ok, keep me up to date."

"I haven't heard from Leslie in a couple of days. What is Briar doing?"

"He has been quiet, which is of concern."

"I will call her next. What is happening about the dead politicians?"

"I am moving this through the Department of Justice and we will request a private special counsel. It must be hushed, for now. We cannot let the people who did it know that we know."

"I get that."

"Leslie, how are you?"

"Nice to hear from you, Daniel. I'm ok."

"Good. I'm just checking in."

"I watched the news from Paris."

"Instigated by Deep State is my speculation since it was purposely set up. Wu keeps losing his sponsors so he is becoming irritated."

"Briar has been quiet. Florence sees him later tonight after his talk on Capitol Hill."

"What about?"

"Something not related to our cause. Infrastructure spending, I think."

"For their plan to work, he still has to take out the president and vice president."

"But not simultaneously, Daniel. They can arrange that separately."

"Good point. We need to keep vigilant."

"Oh, I agree."

"How is Florence doing otherwise?"

"She is fine. Davenport is at some event soon because she heads to the UK after seeing Briar."

"Interesting. I will make a mental note of that because the election over here is coming up."

"Take care."

Cross puts his phone on the wireless charger on the antique

bedside table and slides into bed, in preparation for another restless night.

His night is short-lived, however. As medication is beginning to kick in, his phone vibrates, and vibrates. He reluctantly stirs and answers it without looking at who it is.

"Hello."

"Daniel." Jennings seems hyper.

"Nick, what's going on?"

"I'm on my way from London and will be there in an hour. The same Cessna will be waiting for us."

He bolts upright in bed. "What the hell is going on?"

"Lithuania started tossing missiles and is making preparations for an invasion force for the shores of Riga."

"Oh, shit. Why the small aircraft?"

"It can land on grass and we can parachute out of it too."

"What?" in a startled tone.

"That woke you up," chuckling. "I'm joking about the parachutes, I hope anyway. Just checking on you, but we can also fly below radar and be more discrete," as he laughs.

"Well, I'm happy you find this all humourous," and chuckles.

"I don't. Not any of it. Best to keep our spirits up. See you in an hour. I will bring coffee and pick you up, then drive to the field close by, where our plane will land. Don't forget your adult nappies."

Then the phone goes dead.

39

Briar is Compromised

Anderson is waiting in a Washington, DC area luxury hotel for Briar to arrive. She has given up listening to his talks. Finally, there is a rap on the door so she walks over and opens it. Looking through the peep hole first, she didn't see the agents either side of the doorway. Once she breaks the door seal, Briar pushes his way in, followed by the two bodyguards. They are all big men and easily overcome her verbal objections and physical resistance.

"What are you doing, Jason?"

They force her through the lounge area of the suite and into the bedroom. The burley agents lay her on the bed and grab each arm. Anderson struggles but cannot do anything. Her silk gown falls open from the kicking legs, her modesty covered only in a tiny lace bra and panties.

"I have some questions for you."

"You can address them normally, not like this."

"I will ask them once I have scanned the room for recording devices."

In his hand is a gadget which he now uses to detect spurious signals emitted from such recorders. He walks around the bedroom but doesn't find any. He then walks into the living area and kitchen, with the same result. His agitation level escalates as he verifies each room, the bathroom being the last place.

"Where are they?" elevating his voice.

"Where are what? I've no idea what you are referring to."

"Yes, you do. Where are the recording devices?"

"Are you crazy?"

"Your Irish friend told me, remember?"

She is surprised at his question. "My Irish friend?"

"Ye…"

"Your agent outside the door needs help but is this what you are looking for, Speaker Briar?" Taylor, using a spare keycard, had entered the suite and quietly walked into the bedroom. He rapidly spins around, in startled horror. She is holding a phone in her left hand. In her right is a 9mm with a Gemtech suppressor attached to the barrel. These powerful men always act big and strong until confronted with violence.

One of the agents lets go of Anderson's arm and tries to retrieve his gun, but Taylor is much quicker. Her first shot penetrates his right upper thigh and pierces the femoral artery. The second hits the right arm going for the gun. He screams and drops to the floor, as blood is being pumped from his body and onto the carpet.

"Are you insane?" asks Briar. "I'm a member of the House and shielded by the US Secret Service."

"You have a couple of minutes to help save the life of one of those Secret Service members you mentioned. I suggest you use this time wisely, Jason."

The other agent lets go and stands upright, before stepping back. Briar is pissed.

"Why don't you stop her?"

"That's a precision shot so few can make, and even less know how to, sir."

"Who cares?"

"Oh, Jason, that's a very cavalier attitude to adopt." Taylor retorts. "Clearly, this isn't a suitable political position you are facing here and could potentially harm your career. I have you on camera assaulting a US citizen. The video is being transmitted and stored as we speak. You have no idea where, but it will not look good if we broadcast it on our media platform."

Anderson climbs off the bed and covers herself before running into the bathroom to grab a towel. She returns and uses it as a tourniquet on the agent's leg, who is still emitting slightly muted sounds of someone in severe pain.

"What do you want?"

Taylor fills him in, but she notices his expression and demeanor change when Wu is mentioned. Energy suddenly depletes his entire body as he steps toward the bed and just slumps on it.

Anderson pulls on jeans and a sweater, before stepping into a pair of white sneakers whilst slipping on a jacket.

As they head for the exit, Taylor turns around. "I will be in touch, but this is the second time we have caught you. I assure you third time isn't a charm, Speaker Briar." and the suite door closes behind them.

40

A Bunker Outside Riga, Latvia

The Cessna lands at a small grassy airstrip east of Riga, Latvia. The long journey had been arduous in the small aircraft, which was flying low for the last two hours to avoid radar detection.

Jennings had pre-emptively made arrangements to have people meet them and as they climb out of the cabin to stand on solid ground, they see military vehicles in proximity.

"Keep your eyes and ears open, Daniel."

"That's the least I will be doing."

A military general approaches them.

"Hello, gentlemen. I am General Berzins. Welcome to Latvia." He sticks out his hand.

Jennings and Cross reciprocate.

"Hello, General. I am Nick Jennings from MI6 and this is Daniel Cross from CIA."

It is early morning and the sun is peaking through cloud cover as it steadily climbs the eastern horizon. Daylight hasn't fully morphed but it is making progress. However, it is cold in this part of the world.

Latvia's army is approximately half the size of Lithuania's but both are comparatively small in numerical size. They are ranked low on the Global Firepower scale. Latvia is being supported with NATO troops stationed in the country. Most are a Canadian contingent at Camp Adazi which has been reinforced in recent days as the conflict escalates. International forces are primarily peacekeeping but fear is growing of their projected involvement.

"Our rendezvous is a few miles away so please walk with me and we will drive there."

They climb into the rear of an armoured vehicle and speed away from the airfield. They approach a non-descript location but it is brick-walled with barbed wire mounted on top. Security shacks with armed military personnel standing around them are posted either side of the barricaded entrance. The general steps out and has a conversation with a foreboding guard, who then walks over to the vehicle and peeps inside.

"Good morning, gentleman." He says in broken English.

After visually confirming the occupants, he steps away and walks into one of the shacks, followed by the general.

"What the hell is going on?" Daniel enquires.

"Relax. Normal protocols, and we are foreign dignitaries visiting the prime minister. He is just checking us out."

The general climbs back in as the barricades are pulled away, allowing them to enter the small complex. Located in the compound are artillery personnel and anti-aircraft battalions. Cross sees a building but that isn't where they are heading. Off to the side is a three-feet thick steel doorway to a concrete bunker lined with mounds of soil and vegetative camouflage. The vehicle grinds to a halt.

"Follow me," as the general steps out and walks toward the bunker.

They step inside, walk past armed guards and through another door. Now they take a stairway down which Cross estimates at three floors underground. As the bottom step is reached, they follow the general into a chamber bored into rock and hosting many military personnel. Off to the side is a room and they veer off in that direction, and then enter.

A large conference table is occupied by the prime minister and his important ministers and military advisors.

The general walks over and introduces Prime Minister Ozolins.

"Good morning, Mr. Jennings and Dr. Cross. Welcome to my country, gentlemen." They all shake hands. "Please, take a seat," as he invites them to sit down.

Ozolins is tall but of perfect build. He has short greying hair and wears glasses. His suit is European and cut from the finest cloth to custom fit his athletic frame. He too has this air of imposing quality and confidence but Cross notes it is different from the American and UK political arrogance.

Jennings starts the conversation. "Good morning, Prime Minister Ozolins. Nice to meet you although under rather adverse and forced circumstances. Thank you for considering the time to meet in this manner on such short notice."

"The death of Prime Minister Clark has upset a lot of people, Mr. Jennings. It was rather unfortunate but pre-meditated. Western heads-of-state are not normally massacred in such fashion."

"Indeed, Prime Minister."

"It is a pleasure to also meet Dr. Cross, who has been involved in recent world events. Your names keep cropping up so it was agreed we should meet."

Ozolins introduces the rest of his important ministers and military leaders. He also invited a beautiful interpreter who talks at the same time.

"You have flown a long way which we appreciate. Please, there are coffee, tea, drinks and food on a table over there, so please indulge." He points. "I doubt you were served a hearty breakfast on the way over." He chuckles.

"Our flight attendant refused to fly with us." Cross adds, grinning.

There are chuckles around the room but a palpable, silent relief is felt by Cross as tensions are eased. A server brings them coffee, as requested.

"This is a mess."

"Yes, Prime Minister," agrees Jennings.

"People have died already and yesterday Prime Minister Lutkus launched his first two missiles from Lithuania. Satellite images also show a landing force being assembled in anticipation of an invasion we believe off Riga. Already several battalions are parked at our borders. My opposition leader is supporting a military-infused altercation."

Cross' turn to lead the conversation and Jennings obliges.

"Prime Minister, sir, Lutkus and your opposition leader are being sponsored by Western oligarchs."

Ozolins goes silent for a few minutes as he digests the information Cross is presenting. One of his ministers leans over and confers in his ear.

"Dr. Cross, it was brought to our attention you were seen at the recent protest massacre in Vilnius. You were part of that parade, were you not, and media coverage out of Lithuania points to your involvement?"

"I was there, yes. However, I killed two assassins and one of them came from Spain." There is some subdued shuffling around the table as his wording gets translated. "We purposely infiltrated the media broadcasts from TV5 to make it look like the West was involved. Gabrys' is broadcasting 'on location' but she has been conditioned by our Intelligence on what to say. It was Mr. Jennings here who determined, correctly as it turned out," he looks over at him, "it would be much better if we falsified the US' involvement to aid in the appeasement of Prime Minister Lutkus. He had to be calmed down otherwise he would be lobbing more missiles across the border by now."

Cross watches Ozolins as he consults with people close to him at the table.

"I see," looking thankful and impressed.

"The West doesn't want war, Prime Minister. I assure you we had nothing to do with the massacre in Vilnius. Deep State is pushing for war."

Now the noise and commotion are elevated and cease to be neutered.

"To what end?" Ozolins asks, through the disturbance.

"Lutkus is paid for. Your opposition leader is paid for. Marchant in France and Davenport in the UK are paid for. Clark's death was orchestrated. Blue Ocean Media has been spreading propaganda and disinformation throughout its global empire. Deep State wants control, Prime Minister. This is their drive to implement the New World Order."

Part of Ozolins entourage stand and start gesturing in Latvian. Arms are waving and people are leaving their seats to form their own discussion groups.

Ozolins attempts to restore some parity. "Gentlemen, please. We haven't finished." He pauses to think. "Actually, on the contrary, I believe we may have only just begun." He turns to face Cross and Jennings as some restoration of order is established. "There are vast regions in the world that aren't part of this movement?"

"Yes."

"I know for certain Russia wants nothing to do with the West's global political aspirations and corporate greed. The West's entitled and political figures even use some poorer countries for their money laundering."

"We are aware of Russia's allegiance, Prime Minister, and of the West's monetary indiscretions."

"What you are preaching isn't totally a surprise to us in Latvia."

"You are pro-Russian?"

"Absolutely."

"And yet you are part of NATO."

"That was before my time, Dr. Cross."

"Sorry, Prime Minister, but please call me Daniel."

"Thank you, Daniel. We joined along with six other countries in 2004. At that time we had a modern military although comparatively small."

"Lithuania was one of those six although their forces are numerically twice the size of yours."

Ozolins is impressed with his knowledge of their military. "You have been doing your homework?"

"Best to be equipped with pertinent information."

"You will be surprised how many aren't."

"I get surprised once in a while," and laughs.

"I bet you do, Daniel." Joining in the banter and laughing with him. "The Latvian people are pro-Russian. We are seeing how the Kremlin has grown and developed its nation since 1990."

"Where does Estonia fit in here?"

"They remain neutral but, as you know, are also part of NATO. They are a smaller nation and do not wish to participate in this regional conflict. Unfortunately, that doesn't necessarily mean it will stay that way but I will add their government is becoming increasingly concerned."

"I can understand that and something we may need to address at some stage."

"Absolutely."

"However, getting back to the more pressing issue, Lutkus and Deep State want to terminate your friendship with your favoured neighbour, Prime Minister." Cross adds, with some inflection in his voice.

"I see. So, how do we stop this, my friends?"

41

Missiles Hit Kekava, Latvia

Discussions during the day had been vociferous, contentious and politically motivated at times. Cross and Jennings are both extremely tired. General Berzins escorts them back to the military vehicle and heads to a hotel in Kekava, a small town located seventeen kilometres southeast of Riga's city centre.

He drops them off at Park Hotel. "You will be safe here, and outside of Riga where discretion is the better part of valour. Here is my number should you need anything." He hands them a card. "I have people stationed around the vicinity."

"Thank you, General." Jennings shakes his hand.

"Rooms are booked and paid for. Your pilot and first officer are in a different hotel, for security reasons. Discussions were very fruitful today and the prime minister will be working tonight, after what you disclosed. See you in the morning. Oh, there is a bar down the street."

They watch as the general's vehicle takes off and disappears.

"Fascinating," says Cross. "This region is a dichotomy of opposing ideologies but seemingly under the same NATO canopy."

"Yes," Jennings agreeing. "Sooner or later some cohesive force has to buckle under the pressure of hypocrisy."

The hotel is small but fairly modern, surrounded by centuries-old architectural and historical structures, including churches with spires and domes.

They grab their hotel keycards and take a shower before heading over to an antiquated bar for dinner.

It is early morning hours when Cross is disturbed by an apparent explosion outside that shakes the hotel.

"What the fuck was that?" he spits out under his breath.

Before he can react, the next one is much closer and louder as the errant force blows out the windows. Luckily, the heavy drapes prevent the shattered glass from flying all over the rooms, shredding the occupants in the process.

He leaps out of bed but not before he finds his shoes. Walking gingerly over to the drapes, he pulls them aside and observes the destruction from two short-range ballistic missiles that hit properties across the street. There is a bang on his door so walks over. He opens it and Jennings is standing there in the hallway dressed and holding his bag.

"Get your stuff and let's leave, quickly."

"What's going on? I was beginning to like this place," he sarcastically announces.

"I believe they are trying to shell the hydroelectric plant three kilometres northeast of here. These are stray missiles."

"Can't they fucking aim properly?"

Just as Cross grabs his bag, another missile removes one side of the hotel, the force from which knocks both to the floor covering them in dust and debris. Then complete silence fortifies the exception of the sound of burning buildings.

In the background some faint screaming is heard and then sirens from first responders hit the airwaves.

Cross makes sure he is still alive but feels fresh blood on the floor. Using his hand, he locates a gash on the side of the face.

"Fuck. Now I'm pissed."

Jennings is stirring too and he has minor skin lacerations from flying debris. "You mean you weren't before?"

Cross' phone goes off so he stands, brushing himself down as he searches for it.

"This is General Berzins. Are you both ok?"

"I believe so."

"Do either of you know how to fly a plane?"

"Umm, pretty sure we can handle one." Surprised at the question.

"Good. Your pilots are dead."

"Shit."

"I will pick you up. I'm on my way to bring you back to Parliament's protection."

"The shelling has stopped."

"Looks like they were aiming for Riga's hydroelectric plant. They missed, fortunately."

Sirens are getting louder as rescue vehicles approach the bombed areas.

"I can't hear you, nor see anything except flashing lights on fire trucks and glow from burning structures. See you when you get here," and ends the call.

"I heard some screams earlier." Cross says to Jennings.

"Me too."

Jennings gets up and they survey the damage to the hotel as their eyes adjust to the darkness. The structure is only three floors but debris is everywhere. One of the sides is mostly windows which have all been shattered. Another side is obliterated. Instead of finding the stairs, they toss their bags and then jump down from the second floor onto the grass.

Cross' gash is pouring blood down his face and he can feel the warm flow. He searches in his bag for the first aid kit and retrieves some Steri-Strips along with rubbing alcohol.

"Can you oblige, Nick?"

"That requires stitching."

"Well, these will have to do for now. I do have a needle and thread though, if you prefer?"

He pours the alcohol on and cleanses the wound with sterile gauze pads. He then applies six butterfly stitches before wrapping a bandage around.

"Cheers, mate. You look ok."

"A few lacerations from flying glass but not too bad. Just enough to beautify me."

"You may need more for that," and laughs, but it's seriously compromised.

Now the sirens have been turned off, they can hear some faint cries and sobbing. They run over to one of the collapsed rooms where the noise is radiating from and turn on their phones' flashlights.

They cautiously remove wooden beams and flooring, some furniture and finally locate a trapped family. Behind are the firefighters so they wave them over to assist. The firefighters pat the two heroes on their backs and some minutes later are able to extract the four damaged, but alive, bodies.

"Nick, Daniel, over here."

They turn around and see Berzins waving at them, so jog over and climb into his Mercedes.

"Are you two ok?" He looks over at Cross. "That needs medical attention, Daniel."

"I'm fine, really."

"I am taking you to the parliament building, known as Latvijas Republikas Saeima. It is in Old Town Riga and very secure. Prime Minister Ozolins has been informed and will meet us there. He is pretty animated and wants to act on one of your recommendations, with your help of course. Then I will take you to your plane. We had it prepared last night and it is ready."

"With our help, General?" sounding perplexed.

"In a legitimate democracy, he can't unilaterally discard an opposition leader without serious legal consequences. However, with foreign mercenaries at his disposal, he sees an opportunity to recalculate the state's objectives and will authorise the flexing of rules to tailor to prevailing circumstances. Afterall, he has legal and civic obligations to protect his people in time of war."

Cross' eyes open wide. "What the hell does that mean exactly."

"Let's find out, shall we?"

Berzins, with a big grin on his face, rotates his body back around and presses the start button. The Mercedes rumbles into life and he drives away.

Cross looks over as Jennings shrugs and grins too, clearly trying not to laugh hard.

42

Parliament Building, Riga

Cross' phone pings.

'Are you two ok?' asks Granfield's text. 'Shelling made news in US.'

'The stray missiles hit our hotel but ok.'

'Jesus.'

'Something like that. Our pilots are dead.'

'What?'

'We stayed in different hotels and will learn to fly on the way home.'

'That isn't funny, Daniel.'

'Nothing much is funny anymore. Heading to Latvia's parliament building.'

'Leslie compromised Briar. Anderson on the way to UK.'

'Damn, Briar's a moron and I forgot about Davenport's thing.'

'Riots calming down in France but many dead.'

'How about the stock market?'

'The right stocks continue to fall.'

'Good. Running out of words to describe these people.'

'Update me later.'

Cross neglected to tell him how they really are.

Inside the parliament building is a medical facility. However, Cross hasn't made it there yet. He is admiring the short tour Ozolins is taking them on before the doctor shows up. The Louis XVI-inspired styling is majestic in the Yellow Room and the Gothic style in the Dining Room is regal. Cross and Jennings are quiet as they walk through, the historical turmoil of the building being relayed as they do so.

The doctor is just about finished stitching up Cross.

"The last one, number nine, sir."

"Thank you, doctor."

It is five in the morning and Cross is very tired. While he is receiving medical attention, Jennings sits with Ozolins, his ministers of foreign affairs and defense, Berzins and two other high-ranking military people discussing the missile attack.

"Those were errant missiles, Prime Minister."

"Yes, we believe so. The hydroelectric plant spanning the Western Dvina River is a critical piece of infrastructure. Our guess, because we don't fully know, is they were trying to scare us into submission, and intentionally missed their alleged target."

"Ok."

"Our military is smaller. So, unless we have an outstanding clandestine plan, it would be exceedingly difficult to win a war. Lutkus understands his superior position very well."

"We would require help from others who would benefit from keeping your country safe."

"NATO is reluctant to participate, although they have sent eight-hundred soldiers already. They are here to prevent a war, not to participate in one," the defense minister adds.

"Daniel expressed our thoughts yesterday. I can also add to that," and explains what he wants to do.

Ozolins thinks for a few seconds. "Let me make some calls. You would fly there if this dialogue could be arranged?"

"Yes, but only across the border," and points out a possible location. "But we prefer meeting face to face."

"Let me see if this is feasible." He looks at Jennings who is also very tired. War does that to people. "We have rooms here. You and Daniel need to sleep for a few hours at least. I suggest you do that, otherwise you will be needing recreational drugs to stay awake, and we don't dispense those. Well, not legally anyway." He laughs. "We need your strength and cognizant abilities intact."

Jennings is enamoured with Ozolins, who seems to care about his country and people. He can't say the same thing about some other purported world leaders.

"Thank you, Prime Minister," as he shakes his hand.

Just then Cross walks in, with his head partly bandaged.

"Go get some rest. You need it." Ozolins adds. "We can discuss our reaction to Lutkus when you wake up. I'm sure he will still be with us," and smiles.

He looks at his watch. "It is five-thirty. How about we re-convene around eight-thirty?"

"Ok," Jennings answers.

"I will have someone take you to the guest quarters. I also hope to have an update on what we just discussed."

43

Opposition Leader Crushed

Cross is sitting next to Jennings, who are sitting across from Ozolins, Berzins and their two prominent ministers in the parliament café.

"You two look a little better after some sleep."

Cross responds. "Thank you, Prime Minister. I don't know about looking better, but we feel better."

Ozolins smiles. "Looks are subjective." He turns toward Jennings and continues. "The meeting is set up. They will meet you at the airport and head to an undisclosed location."

"Excellent. When?"

"We will notify them when our next course of business is complete."

"Thank you."

"Daniel, here is a name of someone we want you to look into," and hands him a piece of paper. "We are seeing Western oligarchs coming to untimely deaths. However, I guarantee this name isn't on any of your lists."

Cross opens the paper and looks at the name scribbled on it.

"It isn't, Prime Minister. Who is she?"

"Do your research and get back to me. After what you disclosed yesterday, we are confident within the confines of this room that she is Deep State also. She has vast resources to fund anything."

"I will get back to you." He smiles. "Thank you."

"Now, this next topic is delicate, as you both understand it to be. I am about to divulge information that is going to help us. We need this predicament resolved, permanently, gentlemen. Daniel brought this up yesterday in our discussions. However, the legalities of what we are conspiring to initiate are politically life-threatening."

"Ok," answers Cross, inwardly a tad bemused at the drama. He isn't sure either what he brought up, so is intrigued.

Ozolins lays out details of what he wants them to do next. As he picks through the technicalities, Cross and Jennings just sit and listen. Cross wants to shake his head but can't. Then he runs through how they are going to do it.

"The situation is fluid. Last night's bombing was not forecast. Success will not be predicated on following a set plan, but on how we are able to adapt to unforeseen diversions and alterations, if there are any. General Berzins will be your driver and he will have military personnel to support him. However, when the time comes, you will be on your own."

Ozolins was correct, thinks Cross: this borders on political suicide, if not carried out properly. He must really trust the invitees to this party, but he still cannot remember using these words yesterday.

"There he is."

Berzins points to Edgars Kalnins, who is a cabinet minister and self-imposed leader of Ozolins opposition party.

It is midday and the streets of Riga's Old Town district are packed with demonstrators, protestors and/or supporters, some carrying banners, remonstrating the Lithuanian missile attacks in the early hours. People are angry as news of deaths are being reported.

Kalnins had organised parts of the rally in support of action against the people across its southern border. The crowd is boisterous and wild as they head in the direction of a large park situated across from the University of Latvia.

"See that building across the other side of the park?" as Berzins points.

"Yes," confirms Jennings.

"There is roof access and a convenient viewing area for where he will give his speech. We gave you instructions, so will meet you at the rendezvous point."

Cross and Jennings climb out of the automobile. Jennings peers through the driver's open window before they depart.

"See you shortly."

"Good luck," are his last words before he drives away.

They walk across the street and head towards the assigned building, trying to avoid the mass of people. It is anarchy with emotions running high. The building belongs to a different university organisation but has no security, and so they enter. They locate the stairwell and climb to the fourth floor where roof-access is permitted, if authorised and they had keys. They don't have either, so shoot the lock instead. The rally is a convenient distraction and very few people are around. The door is opened and they bolt onto the roof. Cross wanders around taking in the environment. Jennings follows suit but on the other side of the roof.

Hiding behind a heating and cooling exchanger, Cross looks out over at the park. The crowd is vast, the noise amplified and he sees Kalnins talking to supporters in preparation for his anticipated talk. He is expected to rile up emotions and restore the need for nationalistic pride requiring a retaliative response. He will intentionally provoke the crowd from either side of the war debate.

Jennings is done surveying and is happy. He sticks his thumb up at Cross.

Cross pulls out his silenced high-caliber firearm and ensures the modified carriers are there. This from his nerves playing havoc. He should be used to this by now, but it still gets to him.

Hiding behind the exchanger, he waits for the opportune moment. Kalnins is getting ready to climb a few stairs and onto the removable platform. He is now set behind a small lectern and three microphones mounted to floor stands: the crowd screams. The noise is deafening and he attempts to talk above it.

Cross aims through a small scope and trigger-pumps twice. From this angle, he is easily able to find his target aligned through trees. He sees the pants momentarily ruffle as the darts penetrate his leg. Kalnins has no idea what has happened so keeps on talking.

Cross turns around and runs toward Jennings.

"We have ten minutes."

The building has an adjoining structure that is at a lower height, so they jump down on that roof and sprint. At the side of that is a dumpster with mattresses as planned and they leap into it, their falls being cushioned by the soft bedding. With impeccable timing, two police cars arrive. Cross and Jennings climb into the back of the rear just as it pulls away with its lights now blazing.

The crowd is getting agitated and stirred by Kalnins' speech. The use of provocative and libel words, his perpetual drone and assertions that Ozolins needs to use military force in retaliation are stoking and inciting the people.

"Our current prime minister doesn't have the balls to take on Prime Minister Lutkus in Lithuania. I do. I will take him on. We need a military response to unprovoked Latvian deaths from missile strikes early this morning. This situation is unacceptable and can't continue. We must act now." The crescendo increases in pitch with the last sentence being yelled into the mic.

His followers are turning emotional and violent. The security is becoming overwhelmed as the crowd surges forward.

The police arrive with sirens on. They step out of the vehicles and climb onto the stage, removing Kalnins just as his security have been overpowered.

Kalnins is beginning to fade and has no idea what is going on. Two police officers push him into the back of one of their cars. Cross and Jennings make way for his lapsing hulk.

"Hello, Mr. Kalnins," says Cross, but he is already comatose. "I didn't want to listen to anything you have to say anyway." He turns his head and grins at Jennings.

The police escape the surging mayhem, navigate through the crowd as it spills onto the streets, and fly across the river, where they meet Berzins at the rendezvous point. Cross steps out and brusquely walks over.

"Everything set at the site?"

"Yes, Daniel. Let's go."

They arrive outside one of the homes in Kekava destroyed by the missiles earlier that morning. The rubble is still smoldering but the site is surrounded by blue tarp attached to stands so no one can view the destruction behind it. Someone sees the police vehicles approaching and pulls away one of the tarps just enough for the convoy to enter the property. Two of Ozolins' security people open the rear door and remove Kalnins.

Cross and Jennings, their task now successfully executed, transfer to Berzins' vehicle. Once seated, he puts his foot down and heads out of town to where their mode of transportation is parked, fifteen kilometres away.

44

Surprise in Pskov, Russia

Cross has a private pilot's license for single engine but, luckily, Jennings has a multi-engine one, or so he informed him. As they approach the Cessna, it is already being prepped for their next journey. Ozolins had a couple of military pilots be ready and Berzins had informed them they are on their way.

The engines are idling and safety checks have been administered. Both climb out of the Mercedes as soon as it comes to a halt. They shake Berzins' hand before climbing on board the aircraft, and Cross secures the cabin door once the military pilot disembarks.

Jennings sits himself in the left pilot's seat and prepares whilst Cross dials in coordinates to Pskov, Russia. They both put on their headsets.

"Here we go, Nick."

The flaps are dialed in and Jennings pushes the throttles forward. He sets it at the end of the cropped airfield and then pushes full throttle. The plane barrels down the bumpy strip and a few seconds after it reaches V1, Jennings lifts the nose. Once the aircraft is off the ground and clear, Cross moves a lever up and the landing gear retracts. As it gains speed, he retracts the flaps and selects autopilot as the plane heads east northeast on an approximately one-hour flight to Russia.

"Well, that was easy."

"Just like everything else we have done, Nick."

"I meant the takeoff procedure." They both laugh, as best they can.

Ozolins had been informed of their successful mission and assured them he would contact the Kremlin. A message comes in on Cross' phone.

'Russian representatives are in Pskov already and await your arrival.'

'Thank you,' Cross responds.

'Safe travels.'

"I like Ozolins. He seems like a leader who cares about his people."

"How about that." Jennings turns his head. "There has to be one in the world."

Cross stares out across the nose of the plane. The sun is setting in the west behind them so they are flying towards darkness. They will maintain a low altitude until they reach their destination.

As they approach, Cross is looking out over the horizon and Pskov's runway lights are coming into view. The airport's Instrument Landing System locks onto tracking electronics installed on the Cessna and guides it down. They had been given instructions on where to park the plane once they had landed so Jennings follows those. Multiple vehicular lights are present as he slows and sets throttle to idle. Finally, after running through the checklist, fuel is cut off and the engines are powered down. Cross looks over and to the right of them is a Russian corporate jet with the hammer and sickle insignia painted on it.

"Here we go, Daniel."

Cross looks at Jennings. "Again."

They climb out of the plane and are met by a representative from the Kremlin. He is a big man and well dressed.

"Hello, gentlemen. Welcome to cold Pskov. I am Sergey Rostov, the Kremlin's advisor on military legal matters." He has a strong Russian accent but his English is good.

"Hello, Mr. Rostov. I am Nick Jennings from MI6 and this is Daniel Cross representing the CIA." They all stand and shake hands warmly.

"Please, call me Sergey." He smiles. "Follow me. We have a small local government office in town that we will use for the purpose of this meeting. Two rooms are reserved at a local hotel."

"Thank you, Sergey." Jennings responds, hiding some nerves.

They walk around the side of the plane and as they head toward their transportation, Cross can't believe who he sees as she runs up and hugs him so hard, kissing him gently.

"Daniel, I have missed you."

"Alexandria!" He is almost lost for words and doesn't know what to say through the emotion, which has hit him hard.

"These are very delicate times, Mr. Cross." Rostov adds. "We thought bringing Alexandria along would help you feel more comfortable."

"Wow, I'm lost for..." as he grapples with holding back tears. "I can't speak."

She walks over to Jennings holding her hand out. "I am Alexandria Fedorova, Mr. Jennings. Daniel and I worked together on the virus scandal in Moscow. It is a pleasure meeting you."

Jennings grabs her hand and speaks a little Russian which pleases her.

Cross is overcome.

They climb into a military vehicle which whisks them away from the airport. Fedorova sits in the middle as they verbally communicate in Russian heading into town.

"We are here." Rostov announces from the front passenger seat.

Whoa. Cross hadn't noticed them driving into town. His own self-imposed vigilante mandates went out of the window talking with Fedorova and he let his guard down.

They follow Rostov into a modern-looking government building, which isn't small at all, and into a conference room. Seated at the table are local government figures and military personnel waiting for them. They are introduced before sitting down.

Someone brings over a couple of bottles of the finest Beluga Gold Line vodka and they pour shots.

"This should warm you up, gentleman."

Cross lifts his glass. "Вашему здоровью."

"To your health," Rostov copies in English.

"My favourite vodka, Sergey."

Fedorova takes a seat next to Cross as they prepare for discussions.

Jennings opens the conversation.

"First, we asked Prime Minister Ozolins to arrange this meeting, so I want to express appreciation on behalf of our respective governments for doing so, Sergey."

"My pleasure."

"These are rather troubling times." Jennings goes into a monologue about what is going on. Fedorova is the translator for those who can't speak English. This slows him down but also makes him more methodical in his presentation. As he talks, there is stunned silence from the others. He stops on occasion to allow questions.

"Deep State wants to control under the New World Order doctrine?" asks Rostov.

"Yes, sir."

"We have no intentions of giving up our sovereignty to the West. You understand this of course?" he forcefully states.

"Perfectly. We know this already." He smiles at Rostov as the rest listen, dumbfounded.

"The West' major corporations want to also control?"

"This is part of Deep State. The Western oligarchs fund and, consequently, control the politicians."

"I see. The globalists," said in a mocking tone.

Jennings explains some of what they know but doesn't reveal everything. He can't do that. He mentions Davenport and Marchant.

"Davenport replaced Mitchell who was assassinated on the London streets."

"Yes." Jennings more aware they know what is going on.

"We are sorry Prime Minister Clark was murdered. She was a good lady and admired behind the Kremlin walls."

"Thank you, Sergey." A touching moment from an adversary he realises. "Murdered by Deep State, I will add."

Jennings goes into detail about Lutkus in Lithuania.

"He strikes me as a dangerous man, Mr. Jennings."

"That is because he is. We had to fabricate US involvement in the massacre on the streets of Vilnius in hopes of calming him down."

Rostov studies what he hears. "Now that makes more sense. The Kremlin couldn't understand why the US was involved."

"The Baltic region is a simmering powder keg ready to explode. Have you seen the news today, Sergey?"

"Yes. Prime Minister Ozolins' popular opposition leader in Latvia was apparently crushed this afternoon by falling debris at a property that had been targeted by Lithuanian missiles. He was surveying firsthand the damage but we regarded him as another dangerous animal."

Jennings looks at Cross with surprise written on his face but continues. "And paid for by Western oligarchs."

"You are painting an extremely disturbing picture."

"We didn't know what colours to use, Sergey," Cross injects.

"So, we elected the real colours."

"You just came from Riga. You obviously had nothing to do with this turn of events?" Rostov has a cheeky grin.

Cross tries to look shocked at this assertion but fails miserably. "We aren't at liberty to discuss how we are handling this crisis."

"Oh my, you Western mercenaries." He stops and pours more shots of Beluga. "This one is on me," as they all down them.

Jennings turns serious. "We require Russia's help, Sergey."

"This is what our comrade in Latvia told us."

"Latvia has a problem. Lithuania wants to start a war to empower Prime Minister Lutkus and endear his citizens. He wants to control them. The illustrious Kalnins wanted to stop the pro-Russia stance of Ozolins and convert Latvia's government to pro-Western. Lutkus was helping him, so Deep State could then infiltrate the Baltics and take over the people."

"Like the West did during the Orange Revolution in Ukraine in late 2013?"

"Yes," but avoids that topic. "However, there is a problem. Latvia's military is half the size of Lithuania's. There is little chance, barring a miracle, of the government in Riga winning a war with its neighbour."

"We agree with your Intelligence."

"Nick and I escaped one of the hotels that was shelled."

Rostov stands up and backs away from the table. "Ozolins told me this morning."

Fedorova stops translating and looks at Cross, grabbing his hand.

"This is why we don't look too good today." He laughs and the rest of the room obliges. It was a good moment to deflect direction away from this grim conversation, thinks Jennings.

"I didn't know how to broach the subject. We didn't know how you looked before the blasts." The whole room cracks up. "We thought it was Hollywood makeup."

Jennings stands, walks over and shakes Rostov's hand.

"We will provide medical attention before we eat dinner. However, let's continue. What do you want from Russia?"

Jennings steps back to answer. "Lutkus needs to stop sending missiles into his neighbouring country. They also have two battalions on the border and have amassed what looks to be a precursor to a landing party for invasion. We need your help to stop these incursions."

"We don't border Lithuania."

"We are aware. However, Belarus is an extremely close ally so we thought some battalions on the border of Belarus and Lithuania would do the trick." Jennings is smiling but knows what he is asking.

"That will be a very sensitive political subject, Nick."

Jennings paces the floor and then he looks over at Rostov. "It already is. The current riots outside Paris were planned and instigated by Deep State. Davenport is giving a speech, tomorrow I believe, in London. We need help in the Baltics, sir." Elevating his voice just a touch to force the last sentence.

"I see that." Rostov turns and takes a few steps away from the table as he formats his wording. The other Russians in the room are now just fixtures. All eyes are on him as he turns around to face Jennings. "If we put Russian troops on the border of a NATO country, this could be construed by some as provocation and tantamount to war."

"Lutkus isn't dumb enough to attack Russia, is he?" He raises his eyebrows.

"We may find this out. If he does, NATO would be obligated to defend Lithuania."

Jennings calms down as he sees a sway in his nemesis. "We have some latitude so leave that to us. I assure you NATO doesn't want to partake in a war with anybody, never mind Russia."

Rostov excuses himself from proceedings and steps outside the room with his phone in hand. Silence now penetrates the space. A few minutes later his mind returns.

"This has been a fascinating discussion, but you and Daniel look very tired and I promised more medical attention." He gestures and acknowledges Fedorova. "Alexandria will take you to the hospital, then the hotel and after that to a fine restaurant by the river. Daniel knows her tastes." He returns his gaze to Jennings. "I have been ordered to fly back to Moscow and present your findings. I will return in the morning before you leave."

Jennings slides him a business card. "Here is my number. We will likely sleep well tonight because last night was shit." He chuckles, and then sighs.

Rostov empathises with his demeanor. "I can only imagine. We are putting you under no pressure to leave here, other than your own commitments. Rest, enjoy the city and we will reconvene in the morning, perhaps around ten. You are our guests so thank you for flying here."

"Our pilots were killed in another hotel so we had to fly ourselves. I didn't tell Daniel I am only certified on single engines."

"Hey, me too, but I didn't tell you my certification lapsed when I was in the South China Sea," Cross chimes in. "Between the two of us, we can operate two engines."

The room erupts into laughter: a welcome interruption by all in attendance.

"You gentlemen are insane."

"There is a case to be made for that, but insanity is a pre-requisite. Trust us, it helps," Cross replies, shrugging his shoulders.

"Alexandria, please take these two gentlemen to our local medical facility and have them checked out. Don't have the clinic perform psychological evaluations though since there isn't enough time." He chuckles. "Then please take care of them."

"Of course, Sergey. Daniel looked after me earlier this year. These are good men."

Oh, God. Now Cross remembers her tangible smile.

Jennings turns to Rostov and smiles. "I am under the illusion Russians are supposed to be bad people."

"We are. Wait until tomorrow comes if you are still alive." The whole room laughs out loud, again. "See you tomorrow. It has been a pleasure, gentlemen."

With that, they shake hands and Rostov hastily departs the room with others who flew in to attend the meeting.

45

Perfect Hospitality, Russian Style

There was huge reluctance in Handcock's desire to feed Wu the next news story impacting their mission, but he has no choice. He had suppressed it from Latvia's media circles but eventually extracted it. It has taken several hours to bring himself to do the inevitable. Finally, the medication is working so he strides with purpose into Wu's office delivering what will undoubtedly be a violent reaction.

His prediction was notable for its accuracy.

Handcock ducks as Wu grabs whatever he can from his desk and launches it across the room. He had never seen this crazed motherfucker so wickedly angry.

"How did our man in Latvia die?"

"Kalnins was crushed by falling debris whilst surveying a bombed structure."

"Sounds suspicious. You mean to stand there and tell me Lithuania is responsible for killing our own man?"

"We are working on accessing clarity from circumstantial details, sir. He gave a raucous speech outside the university and then was hurried away by police as the crowd became violent. That is the information we have."

"Cross is alive. This is his work. I sense it." The sentences are separated by brief time-lapses as he seethes.

"No. We verified their deaths, sir. We had someone on the ground observing the proceedings. He also had a funeral we physically verified week before last."

"Bodies?"

"Cremated. He wasn't Catholic and Sadeghi's body was returned to her homeland."

Handcock is sure he sees steam coming out of Wu's orifices in his head.

"This is all too clinical and awfully convenient."

"No unverifiable aircraft entered or left Latvian airspace. No names were entered into hotel registries."

"Of course not. He isn't going to fly a flag announcing himself. He's a very clever man."

Cross is awakened by the sound of his door closing. He looks over at the digital clock in the room.

"Three-forty a.m. Shit," he says to himself.

His head is pounding after the Baltika beers and vodka shots. The bed displays use by a second body but he can't recover his memories fast enough.

His wound was cleaned up by medical staff. He was supposed to rest after the stitches were first administered but there was a fat chance of that happening. The exertions of the day tore three of the sutures and they had to be re-worked. More Novocain and pain meds along with cauterisation of a blood vessel.

The hotel isn't a hotel per se, but a large private residence on the banks of the Velikaya River. Whoever owns it employs staff to take care of guests.

They then had dinner at Restoran Pokrovskiy, which is a five-star restaurant close to the river. He remembers entering it with Fedorova and Jennings, enjoying remarkable local corn-fed beef with organic vegetables.

The combination of beer, vodka and pain meds did some damage.

Cross sits up and can smell Fedorova. Oh God, what did he just do. Memories of the night in Hotel Metropol in Moscow do not excuse his behaviour, but she is still gorgeous and desirable. The short dark blue woolen dress, black leggings and high heels last night had him turned on for sure and had the rest of the government staff salivating. When she sat next to him in the conference room and touched him under the table, he almost completely lost his focus.

He gets up and heads to the bathroom. After he pees and washes himself, he searches for Advil in his bag and takes four.

He is somewhat awake half an hour later, showers and heads downstairs. A staff member is taking care of a few things. He communicates in Russian and after showing him where the house computer is, she heads to the kitchen to brew fresh ground coffee.

He visually scans the room for hidden cameras but just because he doesn't find any, doesn't mean they aren't here. Then he scans for listening devices with his CIA gadget. Nothing either. Being very careful to block the monitor, he rotates it toward the curtain-covered window and turns on the computer. Once it powers up, he disengages the local WiFi network. He then ties into his phone's satellite system and links to his favoured private search engine.

He types in the name Ozolins had given him and watches as he hits 'enter'. After clicking on a link that looks interesting, his eyes nearly pop out. He never knew that was her. He sits and reads the data.

"Holy crap," he mumbles.

Out of curiosity, he exits that search engine and enters Google. Nothing comes up. He tries several other known sites and nothing, except when he uses her real name. He enters MI6's encrypted database and is shocked when nothing comes up.

"How did Ozolins retrieve this information?" he asks.

The young hotel worker knocks and enters the small room carrying his coffee. On a plate in her other hand are local chocolate delicacies.

"Большое спасибо." Big thank you, he says. Her early morning smile is radiant and she shyly returns to the kitchen.

He clicks back to his private internet engine and reads more about who this person really is. He remains curious why Ozolins passed this information to him.

Cross is still at the computer when Jennings shows up around six a.m.

"Don't you ever sleep, Daniel?"

"Too much in my head." He looks disheveled, even after his shower, careful not to wet the bandage.

"I understand that too, but I was tired."

"I am also, but very restless."

He smiles. "Alexandria is stunning. Wow, and so interesting too."

"Indeed, she is, Nick. I almost lost it and wasn't expecting to see her walking towards me."

"She has a thing for you, and I don't mean sexually. I mean she admires you." He grabs a chair and pushes it over to Cross, then sits on it. "I can tell from the way she stares at you. It is acutely heartwarming and adorable."

"Thank you. She has attributes superficial men like me crave but she is also accurate with a gun too, so be careful," and he laughs.

"I wouldn't mess with her for sure," shaking his head.

"Katerina is about somewhere. She made some coffee for me earlier. Let me check."

He leaves the room and then returns a few minutes later.

"She is making some fresh. Let me show you something."

As he accesses Google and searches the real name, he continues.

"I was impressed how you handled the meeting last night."

"We made some headway since it was critically important we did. I saw their body language and visual cues are imperative in international diplomacy. Isolate egos, add levity and one can talk rationally."

Cross points to the screen. "Look at this."

Jennings leans nearer the monitor. "She used to be famous, but only for a short period of time."

"Now watch this."

He switches search engine and types in a different name. "This is the name Ozolins gave us yesterday."

Jennings stares at the screen as he reads the info and observes the profile pictures. "This is crazy. How can that be?"

"I don't know yet. She's one of the richest ladies in the world but no one knows that. She has never portrayed this image, ever."

"The quiet ones are always the people to watch out for," as he sits back in the chair.

"We know this to be true already. It makes me wonder why Ozolins provided her name."

"He must believe she is funding Deep State, Daniel, and this new world order nonsense."

"That is my thought also. It makes me also realise we may have only scratched the surface in eliminating a few of Wu's sponsors. I wonder if she is his majority stake holder." Cross leans back in exasperation.

"I think we need to turn the computer off. Remove all our transgressions on there and let's have breakfast."

"I'm using my private cloud-encrypted window and the network from my phone's portal."

Jennings' phone pings so he picks it up.

"This is Sergey. He leaves Moscow around eight-thirty which will put him in Pskov around ten."

"Good. Let me reach Alexandria and see if she is up for breakfast."

The defense minister had taken his time to enter Lutkus' office in the Palace and is aware of his temperament.

"Prime Minister Lutkus, missile strikes confirmed southwest of the target we elected to miss."

"This is a day late and a dollar short. We hit hotels and homes in Kekava. Civilians have been confirmed dead." Lutkus is livid at the minister.

"Yes, Prime Minister."

"Even in war, Minister, dropping bombs on civilians in the middle of the night is perceived as an act of cowardice." He waits for his comment to sink in. "Well?"

"Three missiles strayed from our intended targets, targets that would not have caused consequential casualties."

Lutkus doesn't ordinarily have a restraining mechanism to control his emotions. These actions and the manner in which they are being presented make him even more furious.

"What do you envisage killing Latvian civilians will do? Our plan was to scare them into submission. We wanted Ozolins to consider the ramifications of not complying."

"I'm fully versed on what the intentions of this mission were, Prime Minister."

Leaving that subject, Lutkus changes the angle of attack.

"What is the update on Kalnins?"

"The evidence remains the same: crushed by a building collapse."

"I don't' believe that account for one second, Minister. It is too

methodical and convenient. Leaving that aside, we are implementing our contingency backup plan?"

"Yes, Prime Minister. We have a live body in Riga working on
this."

"Keep me appraised of developments, and next time verify missile coordinates, for fuck's sake. Do I have to tell you everything?
Now get out."

The defense minister abruptly turns and exits.

They are all at the same conference table in the same government building with the same representatives. After greeting each
other, they seat themselves. Again, Fedorova sits herself next to
Cross, dressed as impeccably as last night.

Rostov commences this morning's revised talks.

"I have spoken with people within the Kremlin. Discussions
were heated but with remarkable clarity." He takes a short breather.
"We are forced to take some things into consideration, gentlemen.
Foremost is protection of our sovereignty. I don't need to explain
this to two incredibly sharp people."

"No, you don't," interrupts Cross.

Rostov looks at him. "You saved our country earlier this year.
The death of Romanov released energy in the citizens we have not
seen in decades." Fedorova squeezes Cross' thigh in appreciation.
"The information you provided last night was disturbing. However,
we wish to help you but there must be some reassurances in return."

He has the floor, and everybody's attention. "You flew here with
no recourse. No expectations were implied in your frank approach
to the world's predicament. We at the Kremlin respect this in words
I can't translate.

"Our objectives are to protect Russia and its allies. Deep State
is troubling, and we have no interest in being controlled by the West

and their massive corporations imposing their own globalistic will on our people. We wish to remain autonomous and you are smart enough to understand this.

"We are prepared to help with the crisis in the Baltics. Lutkus is a serious flaw who needs to be addressed."

Rostov lays out conditions on which they will cooperate. Cross and Jennings listen intently.

"Russia has formulated a tentative, binding agreement to get this process moving forwards, gentlemen." One of the attendees passes across the table some documents. "Time is of the essence, we understand. This needs to substantively move rapidly in its execution, otherwise the Baltic states will be imperiled, which will ultimately impact other regions.

"I'm aware you don't have the legal authority to agree to terms, so we kindly ask for these documents to be presented to your prime minister and president. They must be reviewed by your people from political, legal and military perspectives. We get that. However, we agree: Deep State's threat needs to be eradicated and we need our borders secured and protected. It takes time and effort to organise and implement a workable plan but we don't have that time."

Cross and Jennings take deep breaths, but this is Jennings' territory now.

"Sergey, thank you for those kind words. If you can provide a private room for half an hour, equipped with a fax machine, we can process these documents and get them sent to the right people. This is an easy way to expedite the process.

"Thank you also for the hospitality last night and this morning. We both needed urgent medical attention and you somehow figured that out without asking."

"You arrived in our country without knowing what to expect. You were experiencing severe medical issues and yet still flew here. I saw Mr. Cross…" He stops himself. "Sorry for my ignorant error;

let me rephrase that. I saw Dr. Cross' reaction when Alexandria hugged him. I can tell you, Nick, we know when people are being disingenuous. Russian culture doesn't allow grown men to shed tears but that was moving, even for me. The sincerity was genuine. No one can fake that."

Cross wants to speak but Rostov prevents him with an index finger gesture.

"Our local government secretary will come in and show you to a private room." Just as he says that one of the people sitting at the table stands up and exits the room.

"Daniel taught me a Russian phrase recently: Большое спасибо."

"You are both good men."

A secretary walks into the room and motions over to Jennings and Cross.

"Please follow Olga. We will convene in thirty minutes but take your time."

Thirty-five minutes pass when Cross and Jennings return.

"Done, Sergey. They did a cursory scan of the terms and have some questions, but those will be addressed by others."

"Indeed. We left contact information on the documents so they can work directly."

"We don't wish to offend your lavish hospitality, but Daniel and I need to urgently return to London."

"Of course, I pre-empted this. Your aircraft is filled with fuel and ready. Alexandria will drive you to the airport."

They defiantly shake hands.

46

Emergence of Formidable Foes

After departure from Pskov, Cross sets the autopilot in a linear direction for London, via the Baltic Sea to avoid errant missiles. A couple of hours into the flight, Granfield calls so Cross puts him on speakerphone.

"Good work."

"It gets crazier."

"The document isn't that outlandish and has a couple of issues but nothing we can't handle. Russia needs to halt Lutkus."

"Agreed. Nick tells me the UK government has only a couple of issues too."

"Yes. We're coordinating and expediting this because it will take effort to organise battalions at Belarus' border. We are aware who Sergey Rostov is and he is highly respected."

"He was good to us, David."

"You handled Kalnins remarkably well. The media reports his death as accidental."

Cross hasn't disclosed the full story. He can't. "It was Rostov who disclosed how he had died so, as far as we know, the media is accurate. Of course, we trust the media."

"It wasn't BOM," and they both laugh. "A shelled home apparently collapsed and crushed him."

"This is what we were led to believe."

"What's your itinerary?"

"Davenport gives a talk tonight in London and Leslie told me Florence is there already. What is the deal with Briar?"

"Leslie caught him assaulting Florence."

"There is something amiss there. He can't be that stupid so who is behind the facade to make him believe he's God?" He doesn't wait for an answer because he thinks he has one. "We hope to arrive in London for Davenport's talk."

"Oh, Blue Ocean Media crashed and looking at a potential bankruptcy filing. However, we believe they will be rescued. Not sure by who yet."

"Does this mean other pertinent stocks are falling?"

"The simple answer is yes. Safe travels and well done."

Cross' turn to sit at the controls whilst Jennings takes a breather. He removes his headset and heads to a lounge seat at the rear of the cabin. He puts his feet up and calls Ozolins.

"Prime Minister, thank you for organising the meeting with the Russian dignitaries. Mr. Rostov was very gracious and kind."

"You are welcome, Mr. Jennings. Sergey called me after you left and was extremely happy and grateful you visited."

"We are formulating an agreement that will benefit all parties. He wants to help."

"Yes, he does. An unstable border is not a sustainable environment for Russia."

"Sorry to hear about Kalnins' death."

"Ah, yes. An unfortunate mishap. He stepped where he shouldn't have stepped. We threw in a few of our own people into the crowd, just to keep the atmosphere going and encourage unrest. Thank you for everything. We had heard a lot about you and Dr. Cross before your arrival. The visit just solidified what we had been told."

"Thank you. I will update you when we have one, Prime Minister."

"Safe travels, Mr. Jennings."

"Oh, by the way, we researched the name you provided us. Very interesting findings."

"You have the resources my small country doesn't but I suggest you dig deeper. I believe there is something there."

"How did you find her?"

"My source will be exposed soon enough."

"I will get back to you."

After an hour break, Jennings heads back to the cockpit and sits down.

"Ozolins wouldn't explain how Kalnins died."

"He can't, Nick. He can't say on a device that can record what they did. He used foreign dignitaries – meaning you and me – to trap his opposing leader. Now his hands are clean. Very simple, and cleaver, but I knew what he was doing."

"Yes."

Cross messages Moore Jr.

'On our way to London.'

'Ok. Good work. Everything is good on our end.'

Cross is happy now, kind of. That was code for Sadeghi is fine but his heart aches for her.

He messages Taylor. 'Leslie, how are you?'

'Daniel, nice to hear from you. I'm fine.'

'We arrive in London in a few hours.'

'Good work in Latvia, sounds like.'

'Very interesting circumstance.'

'Ok. Tell me when you get here.'

Gabrys is next.

'Kalnins was an existential problem for Ozolins,' she replies.

'Not anymore.'

'The media in London reported a partially bombed building collapsed, crushing him, which is almost identical wording used by Latvia's media. Lithuania talked of a conspiracy and Ozolins' involvement.'

'Let's go with Latvia's description.'

'I wonder what Wu's reaction will be?'

'Time will tell. We land in London shortly.'

'Ok.'

47

Losing Patience

Cross is tired of listening to politicians. They all seem to play the same notes and spew the same verbiage. He scours the room at the hotel's conference venue in London's Mayfair and sees Anderson, so ventures over.

"Ms. Ingles, you seem to like these political events."

She turns around with a surprised expression. "MP Horseman, you seem to get around also. How nice to see you again."

"I must keep track of adversaries as they scale the political ladder. However, in my defense, this is my home turf."

She chuckles. "Your aspirations include being prime minister?"

"Anything is possible," and he smiles at her.

He had been standing on his good side but as he shuffles, he exposes the side of his face with the laceration.

Displaying concern, "Oh my, MP Horseman, what happened?" She gently touches his face and he absorbs her soft, smooth skin.

"The last lady didn't like my answer. I think she is a Davenport voter." He laughs. "Please call me Michael."

"Seriously, Michael. That looks nasty."

"It looks worse than it is but thank you."

"Let's go find a bar. I think you offered to buy me a drink last time we met. I presume that offer is still on the table." She smiles. "It's boisterous and loud in this room anyway."

"The offer could be still open. However, you will miss the script being played out."

"They all play the same record."

They leave the conference area, avoiding security, media and cameras, and head up the escalator to locate the bar. Once found, Cross pulls out a chair and Anderson obliges. She is dressed modestly but still in expensive body-hugging attire and so professionally plays the part of a politician's wet dream.

Cross orders the expensive whiskey she had asked for and sits himself down. He watches the barmaid prepare it and then she brings two tumblers over.

"Thank you." He picks his glass up and they clink them together. "So, Chara, what is it with these powerful men you find fascinating?"

"I work in public relations, for MP Davenport also."

"Does he beat you, too?"

Anderson has a shocked expression on her face when she turns to face him.

"What are you talking about? He is a highly respected political figure in the UK." She is a little miffed, but Cross saw it as a fair question to ask.

"I also work in politics, Chara. I can access any information I please."

"I ensure their image and persona are not tainted. I search for past transgressions that could be deemed harmful in their quest to seek a fruitful government career in public office." Clearly, he has spooked her.

"I'm aware what public relations are all about. Let me ask you, who is Speaker Briar working for?"

This question physically rocks her and she hesitates, not sure where Cross is leading her. He observes her body language, but before she answers, he continues.

"Briar has a history. I did some background checks and data has been purposely covered up or removed. His Auntie is, or was, famous, but only for a short period. Now she languishes in a seemingly benign lifestyle and off the radar." He lies; no, she doesn't.

It took some effort to research this information. The long flight from Pskov gave him time to look further into what Ozolins had insisted to Jennings they do. He seriously doubts Wu has told her who Briar's Auntie is. Cross grew suspicious of his aggressive and volatile nature because assaulting Anderson was pure insanity. For a man now in an incredibly powerful position for what Wu wants him to do next, he had to know he is protected with impunity. This is the only conclusion Cross could manage. Wu requires the White House. Absolutely nothing moves forward without it and Briar's behaviour casts critical questions.

"I have no idea who his relatives are, Michael."

He analyses her in a way only he knows how. He believes this is a factual statement, even for someone with her impeccable abilities to forage lies and manipulate people. It is also information she will never be able to ascertain herself.

"When do you see him again?"

"I feel this is my business." She has become noticeably very uncomfortable.

He looks at his Breitling and swallows the remnants of his whiskey. "I must go. MP Davenport will be finishing soon so you will be required to attend to his needs."

"Yes."

He stands up but before leaving, he whispers in her ear. "Please be careful, Chara. These men are vicious animals. You should see what I'm doing to the people who are trying to kill me."

His best Irish accent throws her off guard. As he exits the bar, she turns and stares.

48

Another Sponsor of War Appears

"Leslie, I handed Davenport another two-million cash tonight."

"Where are you?"

"In my hotel."

"Ok. How was Davenport's behaviour?"

"A little kinky but not anything disturbing. I mean this line of work is ripe with creative disgust which just dives further into a cesspit of depravity and satanism, especially with the rich and powerful. He isn't turning like Briar though.

"I met who is serenading as MP Michael Horseman tonight too. He showed up at Davenport's talk but, interestingly, wanted nothing to do with his speech." She fills Taylor in on what happened. "Whomever he is warned me. He also has a recent laceration to his face."

Bloody Cross, almost snickering out loud, but composes herself. "That's interesting. When do you return?"

"In a couple of days. Wu wants me to visit him before heading back to the US."

"Be careful. Does he suspect anything?"

"Not at all and there is no reason for him to, that I'm aware of. He will fly a plane into London but I will not know the destination because it will be dark and I'm never told."

Cross finally slept and is waking up to his phone being inundated with messages. He even turned off the ringer last night, before bumping into Anderson. He ignores them whilst undergoing his need for medically imposed meditation.

An hour later he elects to call Granfield first. The five-hour time difference means it is early morning hours on the east coast, and he is bound to be awake. Cross is beginning to dislike his predictive clairvoyant powers as Granfield answers.

"We have a tentative agreement with the Kremlin. Lithuanian tossed a few more missiles into Riga's region last night."

"I saw the news and the hydroelectric facility is a concern. I'm impressed governments moved so quickly on an agreement, but there is something much bigger and alarming going on," and Cross fills him in.

"What the f…"

"Ozolins provided a name for us to research, so I did."

"Who was his source?"

"He wouldn't disclose that, for obvious reasons."

"Just asking."

"Anderson looked visibly shaken last night. We know she is in tremendous peril if she continues seeing Briar."

"We are making progress but need to refrain from doing something stupid just yet. This does explain why Briar believes he is immortal though."

"He is a typical affluent, political dumbass," but quickly changes subjects. "Let me follow up with Rostov since Lithuania needs to be tamed."

"Agreed. Good luck, Daniel, and brilliant work in Latvia."

"Nick, had breakfast yet?"

"No, where are you?"

"Down the street from Vauxhall Cross Houses," and provides the café location.

"How was the Davenport circus train last night?" Jennings asks hosting a big grin, even before getting comfortable.

"I didn't listen to him for very long. I'm done with listening to rich people's bullshit."

"Yes, it gets old."

"I did have an enlightening conversation with our friend Florence Anderson. She isn't aware of Briar's family connection."

"She is a pathological liar."

"She avoids sincerity a lot, yes. However, her body language and the wording she used suggested, in this case, she is being truthful. She looked visibly shaken. I fear for her next appointment with sleezeball. We might need to extract what we can and then protect her."

"These people are all friggin animals. However, we have a war to avert first. Did you see the news?"

"Yes."

The café is quiet, so Jennings makes a call.

"Sergey, how are you?"

"I'm fine, Nick. Hope the trip home was uneventful."

"Yes, thank you. We can fly both engines now." They laugh. "I understand the document is almost complete."

"It is. We are moving on contingency plans we already had in place. We will then adapt as needed."

"Excellent. Looks like Lutkus is losing it."

"He does seem to be heading off a cliff. I will see to it this madness is curtailed since a war in the Baltics benefits no one."

Jennings returns his phone to the table.

"He needs to move fast, Nick."

"He is doing. They are aware of the mounting political turmoil in the area and the problems those are developing. It is yet another cluster-fuck."

"Aren't they all?" Cross physically sighs.

"The scar looks pretty good." Jennings says whilst peeking, trying to inject some positivity into the conversation.

"Thanks. The fragments of the shelling look to be healing on you too."

"They are, yes."

"What do we do with this Amanda Robertson, now we know her real name? The Hollywood name was fake, like most things out of there."

Research revealed Robertson, who originates from Scotland, owns two global banking giants with other investments in petrochemical, oil and gas, retail and manufacturing. However, her name isn't listed anywhere on these companies' charters. They are simply blank. They tried to look at other names listed to perhaps correlate and compare but came up empty. The huge problem: these are all private companies, which leaves Cross and Jennings powerless to some extent. Diving into areas of the internet the average person can't go, they were beginning to elicit some details. At least enough to determine her vested interests. They would have to assign some people to dig much deeper, but they don't have time.

Her personal background seems even more vague. She was married once but the husband walked away. No children but there is uncertainty regarding that statement also. She has older step siblings from her late-father's first marriage and one of the stepbrothers marries and becomes the stepfather to Briar. No wonder they are all maternally screwed up in the head, he thinks, since their DNA map must look like a plate of spaghetti. He wonders how they keep track at Christmas and birthdays.

"We know enough to make knowledgeable conjectures," answers Jennings, "but you are thinking what I'm thinking."

"Absolutely, since it makes sense. The key for Wu is the US. Vast regions hosting the majority of the earth's population, such as Russia, China, India, Middle East aren't going to comply with Deep State's horseshit. So, he needs, they need – being more specific – the US and its military to in effect control the rest of humanity."

"The problem is preventing the war in a sensitive area. The Baltics would likely drag Russia, Ukraine, Belarus, Poland and NATO into conflict. Remember vast energy and food resources emerge from there and the impact would be global. Billionaires don't give a toss. Who cares if price of petrol goes up twenty percent or price of bread doubles? You think these people care? No, they don't and inflation would be a benefit to Wu's political objectives."

Cross is angry. "Indeed. When are the elections here? Soon, I think."

"Yes. The death of Clark moved them forward a week but not even sure how that happened. I believe in ten days' time."

"Have we, I mean you," and chuckles, "researched to see if anyone is behind Davenport? He must have his own team."

"He does, yes. They don't seem as noble or powerful, which is, of course, how control works. He cannot elect men and women of equals to be part of his cabinet. He is the leader and will ultimately and unilaterally lead, without pesky interferences."

"How convenient: the old and proven method of political deception. You know, make the populace believe it is democracy, until it is too late." Cross sits and ponders whilst sipping his tea. "This predicament does lend itself to one major flaw, doesn't it?"

Reading his thoughts. "Mitchell was protected, but it doesn't look like they have another behind Davenport, that we have uncovered," Jennings adds.

"Exactly, although his security detail is now huge, but I doubt impenetrable." He grins.

"They never are."

"Talking of which, what happened to Clark's security? Did you find the insider?"

"No. However, the alleged person never returned to work after her assassination. We researched their background and came to the realisation we need to perform more substantial security checks as part of job candidacy formalities.

"We reviewed security around UK's airports and found him leaving Birmingham, but under a different name. The name never appeared again after that."

"Interesting. Perhaps changed their identity mid-flight."

"Exactly."

"I have never done that." He turns and grins, but this is a serious dilemma.

49

Organising Deep State

Wu tries to avoid bringing his group together but the events over the past several weeks have made it impossible for him to deflect.

Anderson flew in wearing a watch Taylor had provided. Using it she was able to create a rough flight path of the Gulfstream she boarded at Stansted. She noticed it had taken two wide, slow arcs, then had headed east before doubling-back on itself a couple of times to camouflage and protect directional details. However, she mentally graphed it out, so no one would find material evidence.

On the walls of the conference room are additional red Xs placed on the portraits of those who are now deceased. Kalnins is double marked.

"What new information do we have on Kalnins and what is our backup plan for Latvia?"

"Media are reporting Kalnins was crushed. However, Lutkus is accusing Ozolins and his government of a conspiracy without providing any evidence," Kowalski answers.

"Well find some." Wu is interrupting because he is pissed. "Do you know what the difference is between conspiracy theory and reality?"

"No, sir," comes the sheepish reply.

"Six months. We don't have six months, Jan," in Wu's now seemingly common elevated tone.

"At the time of the plan's inception, we were told to hold off on a Kalnins' backup," Kowalski continues, apportioning blame on someone else for this now egregious oversight. "Too many people on payroll as it was to keep this mission privileged and confidential. We harboured legitimate fears."

"As it turns out, the Baltics is a key region."

"We are urgently working on this anomaly. We have a live body active in Riga, sir. It will take a little time to engage and recruit."

"Time is a commodity we severely lack."

Handcock vacates his chair and steps forward. With his tall stature he commands the floor. "The problem isn't Latvia, per se. The problem is the arsehole we have in the US, Mr. Wu." Preferring to be more formal and noticeably angry too since no one is paying attention.

Wu recognises his demeanor. "He isn't the choice I would have made, but we were left with no option."

"I'm aware of the internal politics, sir, but someone needs to neuter this guy's rage and extra curricula activities. A better idea yet is just to neuter him, period." Chuckles break out.

"Go on, Wilfred," toning down Handcock's indignation.

"One of his security men was recently killed and another beaten up outside a seedy motel in a questionable neighbourhood."

"And?"

"The one thing not questionable is why this motel. Elites allegedly use it for child trafficking."

Now shocked, Wu needs to learn more. "Where did this information leak from? You realise what you are implying?"

"Absolutely I do and I'm not implying anything: I am saying it. It is my job to confirm the veracity of material deemed a detriment to our endeavors. This could jeopardise everything we are doing." He remains indignant.

Anderson listens and hides her smile.

"I will investigate it personally. Thank you for bringing it up."

Handcock returns to his chair not happy because this perennial problem demands more attention than it just received.

Wu continues. "Lutkus has started tossing missiles toward Latvia. This must be methodical, rather than random. Let's get our ducks lined up, otherwise Russia will be asked to join in."

"Satellite imagery has already alerted us to Russian forces being mobilised," Schmidt adds. "Their media suggests these are training exercises."

"Keep tabs on what is going on. Sanchez was assassinated in Vilnius so what have we done to correct it?"

"Our replacement is already back in Spain," says Handcock, rather sharply.

Wu turns to face Anderson. "Florence, you heard the comments regarding our illustrious Briar. Is he still on course for the next assignments?"

"I see him when I return. However, I have no disparaging information that contradicts that, Mr. Wu, but will follow up when back in Washington."

Wu smiles, and Anderson wants to throw up.

"How is Marchant's tangential march to the French presidency?"

"The riots were very successful, sir," Schmidt answers. "His numbers have gained as they keep counting the dead. Germans are watching all this play out too."

"Great. Let's keep going. We are almost there."

They all rise and follow Bao, Wu's chief of staff, into the dining area. Anderson is behind Wu and she seats herself next to him. A few minutes later his hand migrates to her leg.

This is nearly over, she thinks, or hopes.

50

Prime Minister Lutkus, Lithuania

Lutkus makes his way through a private entrance into Seimas Palace, home of the Lithuanian Parliament. It was time to assemble the war cabinet to discuss and then enact their next forays into Latvia.

He walks into his personally designed room boasting a large conference facility, set deep within the walls of the parliament compound. Lutkus had it built void of all electronic gadgets, power outlets, TVs, and the like, but lined with sound-deadening materials. It has no windows and only one light switch. Once the main door closes, that is it. Nothing can be heard or electronically transmitted and received.

The war cabinet members were hand-picked and financed by the sponsors. Lithuania was a democratic country, but not anymore. That title was unceremoniously dismantled when Lithuania started launching retaliatory missiles at its northern neighbour. Those strikes being a consequence of the planned massacre on Vilnius' streets that Latvia played no part in.

Lutkus is upbeat and a formidable leader who plays that role exquisitely. He is tall, slender, handsome and portrays the image of a powerful, confident man. His dress code just enforces that. In his mid-fifties, he has plenty of time left to live out his dream once it is fulfilled.

The massacre and Lutkus' subsequent control of state media's portrayal of information depleted his opposition party and their leader. His approval rating skyrocketed to an astonishing seventy-six percent. That plan worked better than anticipated so now he can do what he wants, essentially. So he leads himself to believe anyway. The legalities may beg to differ, but he doesn't worry about those nuances either.

The President of Lithuania has been silenced. The aging figure was paid off and told to shut up. The recent death of his sick wife was questioned but Lutkus shut down the enquiries himself. This enabled the arrangements to function more coherently with less obstruction: no bitching wife to contend with. To ensure his cooperation, Lutkus stationed two senior guards at his residence and monitors everything in and out, including the telecommunications network. Luxuries to keep him quiet and happy are regularly supplied, including Viagra and young ladies.

The backing of his country's citizens has given him carte blanche which makes the noise generated from any conflicting parties opposing the war irrelevant. They are now deemed insignificant in Lutkus' eyes.

He seats himself at the head of the table and all his underlings follow. He is now at liberty to execute military and executive powers at will.

"Where does Ozolins currently stand?"

The foreign affairs minister enters the conversation. "It is clear the death of Kalnins was no accident."

"I think we all agree on that." Lutkus shoots a death-wish look at the defense minister.

"It is not clear yet where Ozolins stands politically because the murder was only two days ago. Even though Kalnins was gaining ground, Ozolins still exhibits considerable clout which should not be underestimated."

"I concur. We have an option though?"

"Yes, Prime Minister. She was groomed a week ago, but we need time. Kalnins' death was not anticipated and he was a rising popular figure."

"Time isn't what we have in abundance, Minister."

"I'm fully aware."

"How was his death received by the citizens?"

"Initially it was devastating. There were marches on the streets of Riga and other major cities which turned into riots and fighting with police. Ozolins brought in the military very quickly, almost too quickly, which suggests it was planned. The uprising was expeditiously quashed, but that was in part due to the overwhelming emotional shock, sadness and horror at such a big loss."

"Janina Gabrys is still broadcasting remotely on TV5. Why hasn't she been intercepted and stopped?"

"We can't even determine which country she is transmitting from. They also keep switching satellites and alternating transmission frequencies."

"TV5 is now being fed into Latvia's channels and, more disturbingly, around parts of Europe. This is a detriment."

"Yes, of course. Originally her broadcasts concurred with our media in that the US was involved. However, the death of Abrams and the demise of his holdings are causing chaos in the global media markets. No one knows who is going to purchase the assets."

"US involvement isn't the narrative being played on TVs now." Lutkus is visually irritated. He sees the demise of Abrams a distraction, rather than inflicting potential harm. He, therefore, avoids commenting.

"No, it isn't," the minister answers.

"We need more energy in resolving this issue."

"Yes, Prime Minister. I'm on it."

"What is happening with Russia's military buildup?"

This is a question knowingly directed at the defense minister, who Lutkus needs for now, but deplores and loathes with passion and vigour.

"Their media is reporting an exercise justifying a battalion heading to Kaliningrad Oblast. Infrared telemetry reports naval vessels around St. Petersburg powering up."

"These are ominous signs. Is there any intelligence suggesting possible cooperation with Latvia?"

"None. No Russian diplomats have met with Latvian counterparts, either in Riga or Moscow."

This piques Lutkus' interest, but he doesn't act on it.

"Keep an eye on these manoeuvres, Minister."

"Yes, sir."

Lutkus dismisses his lack of respect. The minister has it coming to him one day. "We have two battalions on the border. How are the preparations going for the potential invasion force?"

"That scenario is very difficult to predict because Riga is in a cove, and well protected. I'm working with the generals to support this attack."

"Our forces are twice the size as Latvia's. Sometimes size does matter since we have lost the surprise factor." Clearly, he is done with the negativity espoused by this man and needs to handle it. "We are not aiming for the hydroelectric plant on the Western Dvina River yet. Perhaps those plans should be brought forward, Minister."

"Let me analyse and evaluate the political impact this would have. I will get back to you later this afternoon."

Lutkus doesn't want a political analysis performed. He isn't interested in mathematical models and theoretical playbook presentations. Just bomb the fucking thing.

"Yes, you do that. We are going to continue shelling?"

"Yes."

Turning back to his foreign affairs minister, he adds, "Is Estonia still neutral?"

"We see some defensive military positioning after we started lobbing missiles, but they are remaining out of this although alert."

"Good." Lutkus is done. "Thank you, gentlemen. Any questions?"

None are forthcoming, which is precisely what happens when a democracy collapses.

"Good. I will leave you to continue our mission. You all know the end game here."

Lutkus stands up and leaves. His security men, now numerically substantial, surround him as they vacate the premises.

Once the war cabinet meeting concludes, the defense minister heads to his office. He sits in his chair, retrieves the phone and composes a message.

'War cabinet convened. Green light imminent."

He stares at it for a few minutes before hitting 'send'.

51

War is Spreading

Cross is preparing to find the Dassault, hoping it is where he left it, when Jennings calls.

"Where are you, Daniel?"

"I'm still in England but ready to leave."

"Are you still in London?"

"Yes."

An hour later Jennings is sitting across the table sharing his phone message with Cross. He had picked him up from an intersection in Westminster and found a pub down the street.

"Ozolins has a mole inside Lutkus' war cabinet?" Cross asks.

"Yep. He does, apparently."

"Holy shit."

"I didn't use those exact words but the concept was the same."

"This guy is smarter than even we think he is."

"We in the West underestimate other cultures. We have no fucking idea about anything. We stick fingers in our ears and make blubbering noises, pretending we are listening. We haven't a damn clue."

Cross sits back after reading the message for about the tenth time. "So, who do we inform first?"

"My mother, because I'm sick of this shit."

Cross didn't anticipate that answer and bursts out laughing. "Fair point. However, getting back to reality, and I'm not implying your mother isn't." He grins. "Will he have notified Rostov, his political ally, or will he leave that with us, his new-found mercenaries?"

Jennings reaches into his pocket and pulls out a coin. "Let's see," and flicks it.

"I thought we are more analytical than this," and chuckles.

"This will work nicely."

"The more serious aspect, what will be their first targets?" Cross is attempting to keep on topic. "Remember they bombed near the hydroelectric plant which surely must be a collateral priority. I'm not sure Latvia has an anti-missile defense system."

"I'm not sure either. Perhaps NATO installed one."

Cross picks up his phone and messages Granfield.

'A basic one, I believe.' He answers.

"David doesn't really know either. The concern isn't if they have one. The concern is the proximity from the launch platforms to Riga. Lithuania can install the things right on the border, or a few kilometres inside their perimeter. Any defense system will not have the time to react before the missiles land on them."

Jennings ponders this as Cross sends another message.

'We have an agreement in principle with Russia,' answers Granfield.

'Great, David. We will get back to you shortly.'

"We can't wait either for the governments to sign something quickly. Once it reaches the legal branches, the lawyers will be charging by the hour."

"Hold on," as Jennings steps outside.

He returns five minutes later.

"Sergey is galvanising their forces. Their media announced it as a training exercise. They are even looking at sending troops into

Kaliningrad, which is south of Lithuania's border."

"Wow, what will they do? Wave as they fly over or drop some flags?"

"Perhaps." It is Jennings turn to smile. "I asked him about missile defense systems. He said Belarus has some."

"Why don't we just invite everyone to the party?"

"I'm not sure you understand the geographical history in this area of the world."

"I do, Nick. I researched it before all this started. Do you know Lithuania used to be part of Poland? This is so delicate that we must tread very carefully. We are on eggshells here."

"Remember too, these are NATO countries, except the ones that aren't." He grins.

"The West must screw up everything, I guess. We must interfere with everyone's sovereignty, except our own." Cross sighs, again. "What is Sergey going to do?"

"He can't act faster than they are doing. You can't just mobilise military units in a matter of days. It took Margaret Thatcher six weeks to get UK's naval fleet sailing in convoy down to The Falklands."

52

New World Order is Jeopardised

Back in Washington, DC Anderson had arranged to meet Briar. She has some details she needs to pass on after returning from Europe, and more cash. Briar had suggested another low-end motel and she is getting tired of this.

"Ok." Is all she said.

"Around nine."

"Fine."

She is already in the room when a car pulls up outside. She had walked the area to get a grip on where she is staying. The immediate vicinity is disturbingly abandoned and derelict.

The parking area is full, lights are on in most rooms and yet she didn't see anyone around. The hour she had been there, no car had moved either. It all made her nervous.

"Leslie, I'm in the motel room."

"Ok. I'm across the street and watching the curtains. Listening devices have already been implanted. New technology too so even Briar will not be able to detect them. I see his security people walking the motel grounds. Hold tight."

Taylor is concerned but Anderson's involvement must remain. She is Briar's liaison with Wu and they need to keep the pretense active since any deviation from consistency will spook him. They will continue to cultivate his infatuation over her as a weapon, because it has blinded him and guides his ego.

However, Anderson hadn't anticipated at the time that her job of administering support for these mindless political juveniles would be so emotionally intensive and physically exhausting. The games they try to instill are mind-numbing and a detriment to her sanity. She is nearing the end of her mental capacity to remain an active participant, but she never expected their brilliant minds to operate down in the dungeons of moral civility and human depravity. They simply have no empathy for anyone.

From somewhere deep inside, Anderson recaptures a modest amount of enthusiasm to keep going.

She hears footsteps along the balcony, but more than one pair. She gulps when there is a knock.

She opens the door.

"Hello, honey. I have missed you and so nice to see you," as she gives him a big hug.

"Welcome back home, Florence." He kisses her on the lips.

Just as he does someone else walks into the room. Anderson is startled and pushes Briar away, but she recognises him. He is a senator she has seen at his talks but wonders why he is even here.

"What's going on?" she enquires.

"We are not using this motel for tonight's activities. However, we will need to blindfold you so you will not know where we are going."

"No way. I haven't signed up for this, Jason. Let go of me," as the two men secure her. "What is wrong with you?"

Taylor is listening and notifies her Secret Service agents.

She talks into a two-way walkie-talkie. "Keep a safe distance behind them. You know the drill. We have prepared for this eventuality."

"Ok." Is all the other person says.

They watch as Anderson is ushered into the non-descript Chevrolet. She is blindfolded and her hands tied together.

Two security men climb in and drive off, with the Secret Service members following in a vehicle behind.

Briar's two-car convoy goes through an intersection and the one Taylor has following peels off, whilst another turns onto the street to replace it. Taylor is in this second vehicle, but they have no idea where they are heading.

After a three-mile drive, they turn into the driveway of a run-down single-storey commercial building and drive into the back.

Taylor's car pulls over and the occupants run across the street toward where the Chevrolets went. They reach the rear of the property, but they aren't there. Taylor panics until she notices a roll-up door. As she runs over, she hears it locking and grabs her phone.

'They are in the building. Quickly find an opening so we can view inside.'

'Ok,' came the return text.

A few minutes later Taylor's phone vibrates once.

'Found one. Come around the front.'

She follows instructions and locates bodies looking through a peephole. The head Secret Service agent approaches her in a hushed, soft voice.

"I'm going to warn you," and looks for her reaction. "It is your choice if you want to see what we are witnessing."

"I need to know," without hesitation.

"Ok, I did advise you, but be prepared."

She follows the agent, locates the hole and peeps through.

Anderson is seated but tied to a chair. The blindfold has been removed so she can observe what Taylor is now looking at. Off to one side of the room are young children, perhaps eleven, twelve years of age, Taylor doesn't really know. She counts seven; three girls and four boys. They are mostly naked and someone is filming them on a makeshift bed.

Taylor turns around but doesn't make the grassy area. She throws up what she ate the past week, feels like. Her gut spills out with repeated convulsions. Once she is empty, she turns back to the peephole. She can see Briar and another House member, who she vaguely remembers although his name momentarily escapes her.

A plethora of expletives enters her head. "What the fuck," is all she can muster.

"I warned you, Agent Taylor."

"This is a site I could have gone the rest of my life not visualising. What the fuck is it?"

"This is what these precious creeps are into, I'm afraid. Child pornography is a serious crime throughout the world, perpetrated by people like these folks. The word reprehensible doesn't do justice. These are sick bastards and I wish I can just shoot them right here."

"Me too, but we can't. Please take pictures."

The agent moves over and allows another to snap some photos and video them.

"I want to throw up again but I have nothing left." She is bent over attempting to recover.

"Sorry, Agent Taylor. I knew it would affect you."

"This shit will affect anybody."

"Yeah, well, not these sick bastards."

She prepares herself and peers one more time, only this time two boys are fully naked and engrossed in sexual activity, and Anderson has now joined them, but wearing a face mask. Taylor's stomach retches but there is nothing left. Just as she is about to turn away, the bulking House member she can't remember the name of comes into view, naked. She finally must pull herself away, before she explodes with rage.

The overwhelming urge is to move in and hang Briar and the other guy by their scrotum, but she can't. It would blow the whole Deep State case from which they would never recover.

"Oh, God, please help me," she whispers. "Please help me take down these pricks. I beg you and promise to attend church more often."

The agent grabs her arm.

"Your work is done and you need to get away from here." Taylor has tears rolling down her cheeks. "Let me drive you back. We have others who can control it from this point. You are too involved and there is nothing more you can do than you have done already," as he leads her away, but needing effort, because Taylor doesn't want to go.

"But Florence…"

"We have our instructions on what we are being allowed to do. However, I promise you, we will follow this through and if they lay one finger on any of them, Briar and Hislop will never be seen again."

"Shit." Suddenly remembering. "That's him. Jesus. He isn't in the House. He is Senator John Hislop, the Free Socialist from New York. Holy crap. He is such a spiritual person too. Oh God, help me."

She climbs in the back of the agent's Tahoe, curls up and sobs.

A few hours later, Taylor's phone vibrates as she wrestles with the images. She picks it up.

"I'm home, but it was awful."

"Are you ok?"

After a short hesitation. "Physically, yes."

"How about the children?" The phone goes silent. "How about the children, Florence?"

Still silence.

"Please stop all this. Please, please stop them." She can hear Anderson sobbing uncontrollably.

'The children?"

'They paid someone a large sum of money and they were transported away. I have no idea where to. I'm sorry, but I did get a license plate."

"I can come over."

"Yes, please do, Leslie. I need help."

53

Cracks are Appearing

In the morning Taylor calls Cross, as he heads to the airport.

"Hello, Leslie." He is happy to hear her voice but senses something is profoundly wrong.

Cross holds his phone to an ear as she spews into it the events of last night and this morning. He doesn't say anything, but just listens to her troubled voice.

"We need to take these kleptocrats down, Daniel," in a frantic tone. Seconds pass with no answer. "Daniel?"

"I almost threw up myself. What the hell is wrong with these people? They have money. I mean vast resources, but they want *this*?"

"I will never be able to purge what I saw." Her voice now quivering.

"How is Florence?"

"I think she can handle most things, with her history, but not that."

"But a senator, of all people. Holy shit."

"Florence has something else, too."

"Go on."

"I sent her a watch with compass, which she picked up in London. She was able to tentatively map out the flightpath of Wu's

Gulfstream that flew her. We can vaguely map out a location where she meets with Wu and his people."

"Brilliant."

"It looks like the Spanish mountain area. I will send you the info she wrote down and perhaps you can verify."

"This has to be tentative because she will not know speed of the aircraft."

"Yes, true, but she knows the location is at altitude because of the thinner air. And, as you know, a plane can't fly too slow otherwise it will not have aerodynamic lift at thirty thousand feet. There is enough information to narrow it down."

Cross is impressed. "Send it to me."

"What else? I see the war is starting."

"Yes, but we are trying to mitigate it. At least limit the reaction until Russia can get its military in place."

"A cinder block?"

"Oh absolutely, for sure."

"An Irish accent, huh?" she adds with a touch of sarcasm.

Cross laughs.

"You truly spooked her, but she is a smart cookie. She remembered the guy who beat the shit out of Briar in the motel room having an Irish accent. She likes you." She can hear Cross chuckle. "She put two and two together but still doesn't know who you are. Clever, Daniel. I pleaded the Fifth when she asked me."

"She needs to be spooked because these are very dangerous high-level people she is playing games with. It's good that she likes me. At least she will not run next time we meet."

"How is the facial laceration?"

"I had forgotten, so guess it's healing. It improves my looks anyway." They laugh before the conversation is terminated.

Cross sits and deliberates for a while. Why Florence Anderson? Why, out of all the women Wu had access to, why Anderson?

Curiosity is now starting to eat at him. There is more to this than surface evaluation permits. He needs to find the answer, and quickly.

Circumstances now encircling his rogue mission demand that he accelerate it.

54

France's Liberator

Cross arrives outside of Paris, but no one in his world knows this, except for one person and the three flight crew.

The Dassault taxis to a parking area at a private airport. As he climbs down the stairs, Couton is there to meet him.

"Hello, MP Horseman." She smiles. "I mean Michael. That's an interesting corporate jet to be flying around in." Her eyes are falling out of their sockets, "but I love the Savile Row-tailored suit."

"Hello, Madelaine. Thank you." They shake hands. "We meet again. A friend lets me borrow it, from time to time, especially for long trips." He grins.

The cold and rainy afternoon is suddenly warmed with the welcoming presence of Couton. When he first was introduced, his mind was pre-occupied on his deadly crusade. No such objective forestalls today's appointment.

"Justified from London to Paris, Michael?" She winks. "However, your phone call came as a surprise."

"Yes, sorry for the short notice."

"My car is parked over there," as she points to a small car park. "There is a restaurant around here you will enjoy."

They get seated at an antiquated restaurant; the history of Charles

IX's visit in 1572 Cross reads on the wall plaque before entering. The waitress takes their drink order.

"Still on that Engraved Hendricks gin?" he smiles.

"My preferred choice."

She is as beautiful as he remembers her being. Very chic and elegant, very French, and dressed in high-end fabrics.

"So, what is someone like you doing in politics, Madelaine?"

"Someone like me?" She raises an eyebrow.

"Politics is a veritable nest of wasps all trying to sting each other. You seem more of a fashion lady, where you can use your elegance and class to be above everyone else. Your skills would work in a boardroom setting."

"Thank you, Michael. My looks hide my bite," and chuckles. "It can be quite ferocious and toxic, I assure you."

"I will try not to find out, but no promises I can prevent your exasperations from spilling over."

"You are very funny, as I remember you were." The drinks arrive and she takes a sip. "You know, we were lucky to escape Monte Carlo when we did. Why did you ask me to leave with you? That moment likely saved my life."

"You answered your own question." He takes a sip of his own cocktail whilst looking over the top of the tumbler.

Couton thinks before saying anything else. "Who are you, exactly? I did some background research on a Michael Horseman." Cross notices she is now talking about him as a third person. "Very impressive, I must say. I even called his office and spoke with a lady who answered the phone. However, you don't fit the profile of a member of Parliament. You don't have that arrogance or obnoxious personality, and you most certainly aren't bland."

"I'm working on those aspects of my character to further my career." They laugh.

"In my line of work. Sorry, one of my lines of work, men come onto me. Most politicians would have jumped at my offer and taken me back to their bed. No question. It is exceptionally rare in this profession for a man to behave like a gentleman."

"I will take that as a compliment."

"You should, because it is one."

Cross is using his skills to dispel any anxiety Couton has meeting him. The fact he flew to Paris should have quashed any apprehension, but some may still be lingering. He wants her in his court, but she is already questioning who he is.

Their waitress approaches the table.

"I have a question, ma'am," says Cross, with a straight face. "Do you have frog legs?"

"Yes, sir."

"Well, you can't tell in that dress."

The waitress loses control and bursts out laughing whilst Couton stares at him as only a woman can. Other restaurant patrons in the vicinity turn and peer.

"I apologise, ma'am," and grins. "I have always wanted to say that."

He turns to Couton: now he has her in his court.

Afternoon lunch arrives and they enjoy the cultural cuisine that includes escargot whilst basking in the mutual ambience of getting to know a stranger they like. Cross realises too, for her to divulge certain information, she must be comfortable, otherwise this is a waste of time.

Cross orders two brandies and they are brought to their table.

"So, Madelaine, you know why I flew down here?"

"Yes, that was obvious."

"We have a mutual distrust toward a French political figure who is very dangerous."

"Indeed, Michael. The riots were forced on the people. I mean it doesn't take much to stoke violence in those banlieue projects."

"What was the final death count?"

"About twenty-seven, I think. The number kept changing."

"Who do you think started them?"

"Obviously Marchant's camp. He was there very fast, wasn't he?"

"We noticed that, yes."

"His poll numbers have since climbed too." She stops for a moment. "Wait, who is this 'we'?"

"I recall asking you that very same question. So, neither am I at liberty to disclose who I am, yet."

"Ok." She steps away from that topic. "His polling climbed because, he claims, he is going to stop this immigration-derived violence."

"He is going to do that by halting immigration and tossing money at the migrants already in France. It's called control. He may even deport them."

Couton goes silent. She doesn't know who Horseman is anymore because he has got a fixation on the problems facing her own country. But why? He is a UK politician and she is intrigued.

"Why does France interest you, Michael?" Her facial expression reveals a confused look. "Why indulge yourself in politics south of the English Channel?"

"Do you watch the news?"

"I read more than watch, but yes."

"There is a war starting in the Baltics."

"I have been reading about that. Lithuania just launched some missiles that killed many Latvians. They landed on homes and a couple of hotels."

He turns his head. "See this scar? You do, obviously."

"I didn't want to ask, but it looks nasty." She hesitates. "And recent."

"I was in one of those Latvian hotels when the shells hit."

Couton's mouth drops as she noticeably turns a paler shade. The sound of silence pervades the cozy atmosphere found in the sixteenth century restaurant. He can feel the warmth radiating from the real fire they chose to be seated next to.

Cross sits back in the chair and picks up his brandy. He is letting what he just disclosed sink in as he stares into the lucent heat.

"I…" She is lost for words, but he lifts his eyes and sees a tear rolling down her cheek.

He removes a cloth handkerchief from his trouser pocket and wipes it away.

"I…" She can't speak anymore.

"Your reaction speaks volumes, Madelaine. I'm only referencing Marchant because he belongs in a fraternity from an evil society. He can't be president of France. No way on this planet earth do we allow it to happen. It is inconceivable the fallout if he is elected. It. Just. Can't. Happen."

Now her mouth opens and starts making words again. "You use the proverbial we, again."

"MP Horseman is a very powerful man, but his involvement is classified." He chuckles but his facial expression is serious.

"I guess so."

"I believe you can help us. Your organisation," he misspoke, dammit, "or whomever you work for, can help facilitate his demise."

She notices. "We will do anything to help our country, but how do you know who I work for?"

Cross ignores the question. "You have heard of Deep State?"

"Yes, of course."

"Marchant is a billionaire made possible by the untimely death of his father."

"The enquiries into his death were halted by his own son."

"I read that, yes."

She is impressed by his knowledge of facts. "This opened our eyes."

"So it should have. We call it the Billionaire Club, which he is part of, but the reality; it is Deep State."

Couton is silent again, deep in thought, so Cross continues.

"Prime Minister Lutkus in Lithuania, who is also Deep State, is starting a war to get rid of Ozolins in Latvia, who is pro-Russian. Kalnins, sponsored by these morons, was supposed to have been his replacement, but he is no more."

"Crushed by a bombed building that collapsed."

"Yeah, whatever." Being too nonchalant, even for him, but the conversation has energy and he is in his groove. He also has a captivated audience.

She stares at him in partial shock, trying to read his mind. "He wasn't?"

"I never said that. Russia must protect its borders so it is amassing troops."

"I read that too."

"We asked the Russians to help us."

Couton turns away and looks into the fire, trying to figure out who he is by analysing his words. Provisionally giving up, she grabs her brandy and pours the remaining contents down her throat.

"Another glass?" asks Cross.

"I need the whole bottle."

Cross motions the waitress over and orders a bottle.

"I was joking," and laughs.

"No joking allowed."

There is something about his smile that turns her on. In her seductive voice, "So, MP Horseman, I now know it isn't you but will continue to use this name anyway, to keep you sexually aroused." She crosses her arms on the table and leans closer. In a whispered tone she continues, "What do you want our band of French liberators to help you with?"

55

Russia's Military Buildup

Rostov is getting his military officers prepared and mobilised. The people in the Kremlin have passed on instructions. He has been requested to act as a middleman and help facilitate the preparations as they move forward. That way, the West is aware that a non-military person is involved to aid in keeping the pretense of war toned down. Consequently, Rostov isn't actively participating in this military exercise since he isn't qualified: he is just coordinating. Whether Deep State will merit the distinction is questionable and highly unlikely. However, it isn't Deep State that worries Russia, but how NATO reacts to activating military movements that could be perceived as a prelude to war.

Despite the mitigating circumstances and an alleged document that each participating government has agreed to sign, there remains distrust which manifested through the Cold War years and has festered ever since.

US and Russia have cooperated in the past, so conceptually isn't entirely alien to either country. When the space shuttle program was scuttled soon after yet another catastrophic disintegration, this time over Texas, Russia's own space agency flew NASA astronauts to the International Space Station. The governments and intelligence services have high hopes this will work, because the consequences of it failing will be dramatic.

Battalions are being readied to be flown into Belarus using Ilyushin IL-476 transport aircraft. It was deemed a superfluous exercise asking Belarus not to be involved if Russians need to be on their soil, so anti-missile deployment had been requested to protect Latvia's vulnerable infrastructure. They are being quickly moved into positions along the Belarus-Lithuanian border.

Skirmishes and altercations have already been happening across Latvia's border and some deaths amongst civilians and soldiers have occurred. The big concern is the mobile missile regiments which Lutkus has moved closer. Once he directs a major hit, all hell is anticipated to break lose.

Rostov calls Jennings.

"I can't disclose our military orders, you understand this, Nick? But I can tell you we are moving hardware and people into place. We are also commissioning battalions with their approval to move across the border into Belarus via air transporters. This is as quick as we can push."

"Thanks for the update, Sergey. We understand Vilnius will give war the official green light very shortly."

"That is good to know."

This answer makes Jennings suspect that Ozolins didn't pass on the message to Rostov.

"We hope for cooler heads," Jennings adds.

"Good luck with that, because that doesn't happen when money and power are involved."

"History books confirm what you just said. At least the ones not erased. I will update you when we have one."

"Thank you."

Lutkus is angry. "The Russians have moved very fast in two days. What have they been told?"

He suspects a mole or an internal leak in his war cabinet. Those can be the only explanations for Russia's rapid deployment. Nothing else makes sense.

The foreign affairs minister had requested a visit, so Lutkus invited him to the Palace.

"The build-up over the last twenty-four hours has been unprecedented and remarkably swift. What do they know?"

"That is a good question," replies Lutkus.

"Only people within our war cabinet know what is going on. Russians moving a force of this magnitude on speculation is highly provocative and irresponsible, considering the potential consequences. If the West isn't moving hardware to combat this, suggestions of a leak are profound."

Lutkus is comfortable learning what someone else's interpretation is and hasn't questioned the minister's loyalty.

"My thoughts exactly. We need to isolate who it could be, and quickly. I have my suspicions without definitive proof. I do have an idea," and proceeds in offering his suggestion on ferreting out the mole.

"Done, Prime Minister."

He turns and hurriedly departs, ready to implement Lutkus' idea.

Jennings receives another message from Ozolins which doesn't make sense.

Cross had returned from his diversion to France happy and is sitting across from him at a location outside of London.

"What do you make of it, Daniel?"

"Seems very interesting, but you are correct. There is flawed logic to this reasoning."

"So, my thought is this: they realise they have a mole and gave them spurious information knowing it was going to be passed on to their adversaries."

"Got that."

"This simply means we can do one of two things. We can act on this information or ignore it."

"Does this mean we de-activate your coin-tossing formula?" and grins.

"Ok, so there is another option you came up with. We can act on it, ignore it or toss a coin."

"I go with ignore it. This course of non-action will irritate Lutkus even more because then he will need to go digging for another mole that doesn't exist. Now we will have put him in an unenviable position where he must question everybody in his inner circle. That can't be comfortable."

"We will need to confirm with Granfield but I'm in agreement with you."

Jennings calls Granfield and obtains his approval in minutes.

"Daniel, we don't act on it."

"We surely must let Ozolins know what we are thinking."

"It would be prudent but let's stew on it for a day."

Moore Jr. picks up his phone and looks at the message.

'Graeme, I have something for you.'

'Ok.'

Cross forwards the information Taylor had given him regarding the estimated flightpath Anderson had extracted.

'Got it.'

'Can you analyse this and get back to me?'

'Yes. The mountains of Spain sound about right though.'

'Thanks.'

56

Wu's Nerves are Rattled

Wu is monitoring the movements of Russian forces as they spread west. He had foreseen their reaction because of the Ozolins connection, but not at this volume and rate of speed. Of course, they hadn't anticipated the premature death of their man either. The twelve IL-476 troop transporters landing in Belarus has Wu on edge.

"What's going on?" Yelling at Handcock.

"We always knew Russia would react once Lutkus started lobbing missiles at their pro-Russian ally in Riga, sir. We hadn't planned on Kalnins being murdered, that's all."

"It is almost as if they have been tipped off."

"That crossed my mind also. They are amassing at and aiming to protect specific Latvian locations."

"Have we contacted Lutkus to gauge his reaction?"

"No, sir."

"Wait."

Wu picks up his satellite phone and calls.

"Prime Minister Lutkus." Wu knows he must tread lightly with these prima donna arseholes in order not to disrupt their insecure tendencies. He already has Lutkus' replacement lined up, once they are ready.

"Mr. Wu, what can I do for you?"

His reply irritates him. "Your war cabinet must have met at the Kremlin and discussed your movements," he says, intentionally being sarcastic.

Egomaniacal narcissists always miss sarcasm. It is uncanny really. "We have it under control."

"Not from where I'm sitting, you don't."

"We are aware of Russian movements."

"Substantial hardware and foot soldiers are heading to your borders."

"No way Russia will join this war since we are part of NATO."

"This I'm aware of. However, NATO isn't reacting to their buildup. This suggests to me there is military cooperation on a level never seen since World War Two."

"I'm working on it."

"I hope so." He disconnects the call.

Wu returns to the conversation with Handcock.

"Lutkus is an idiot. He has a leak in his cabinet but didn't mention it."

"Of course not."

"Get his replacement ready."

"I already have, sir."

"Good man, Wilfred."

"On another disturbing front, I have some further news on Briar, if you want to hear it." He shifts his demeanor because this isn't going to be well received.

"Go on."

"He abuses children and is allegedly part of a huge child trafficking enterprise in the US."

Wu falls silent. He has done many things in his life he isn't proud of. He is even a sexually abused child himself, so this crosses an invisible line for him.

"This is confirmed?"

"I'm working on it, sir. However, the part about him abusing children is accurate."

Wu flinches at the thought and is visually repulsed.

"Keep me appraised of what you find out. Like I said in the meeting, there are politics involved."

"Yes, sir."

"We must comply until the time comes."

He is enraged, as he watches Handcock leave. They had planned redundant contingencies, but it looks like he may have to implement some of them. He didn't' want to, not yet.

Cross picks up his phone.

"Return to the US as soon as you can, Daniel."

"I haven't finished in Europe."

"You have, for now. Just get on the plane and meet me at my office."

"I'm not supposed to be seen at CIA's headquarters." Cross senses something big is happening.

"Correct. I will review that request while you fly over here. Just message when you are in the air."

"Ok, but Davenport's election is coming up."

"I will get you back in London for that."

"Ok."

Cross puts his phone down. He is back in some hidden digs in Westminster, always a different location, but was preparing for France. He sends a text.

'Ok, Michael. Keep me posted,' is Couton's response.

'I will, Madelaine.'

She knows she isn't dealing with a Michael Horseman anymore, but who is he?

He sits at a desk in the small hotel room and opens his laptop. It is time to find out more about this Amanda Robertson woman. Moore Jr. had provided a different search engine, buried deep in the dark web. I bet the designers of the internet had no idea it would morph into multiple layers, each one getting more grotesque as the depths evolve, Cross thinks. He is appalled and disgusted with all of it.

He types in the name and goes searching. He finds further information and clicks on a link. Reading the data, shock suddenly envelopes him. He recoils against the back of the chair and just sits in silence.

He clicks on a few more buttons, types in a few more words and reads. "What the hell," he says, under his breath. "This can't be."

Additional typing is called for and another layer activates, leaping up on the screen as he stares blankly.

Cross remains comatose. He can't believe any of it. He looks at the photos and compares each one by flicking between layers.

"Jesus wept."

He eventually leans forward, pulls the power plug and closes the screen.

Cross messages Jennings from the Dassault.

'Heading to Langley, short notice. I will be back in two days, I think.'

'Ok. Safe travels. I will keep an eye on Russia and Lithuania.'

'Use both eyes, please. Lol.'

'I need the other eye on you, lol. Safe travels.'

Melanie, the hostess, brings a cocktail, and he downs the whole lot.

"Please save me, Melanie."

"Are you ok, Dr. Cross," as she observes tears rolling down his cheeks.

A thousand air-miles later, Cross informs Granfield he is on his way.

57

Chaos Reigns

"You were right, Daniel."

"I know I was. Nowhere near done with this psychotic madness and I can't be seen in your office. I'm still dead, remember?"

"Sometimes I forget that part." He chuckles.

"I'm getting riled up now and must remain rogue."

"Yes. Understood."

Cross had landed at Washington National Airport, and Taylor picked him up. Palisades, outside of Washington, DC seems to be their location of choice for these meetings.

Granfield loves the man and they had hugged hard.

"Your facial laceration appears to be healing. Next time don't lie about your condition." Granfield was a tad perturbed when Jennings told him. "Good to see. Despite their valiant attempts, you have refused to die."

"Thank you. Yes, it is feeling good too. However, I didn't lie exactly. I just failed to tell you because it wasn't that important a detail." Attempting to justify his discrepancy.

"Of course it was. Your health is my concern."

Cross moves on. "Do you remember how this started? I went to test a diamond. What the hell has happened since?" He drops his head in his hands but checks his emotions. He will reserve those for another day, after he is done.

"It gets worse."

He lifts his head up. "How is that even remotely possible?"

"I was being serious. Briar is part of a huge child sex trafficking racket in the US."

"What?" Cross sits upright but looks stunned. "I didn't think it could get any lower."

Taylor jumps in. "Anderson was alert enough to recall a license plate number of a van loaded with children."

"There is more to this isn't there, and possibly why you dragged me over here?"

"Very astute, Daniel, or perhaps you see the levels of deprivation they have sunk to," Taylor says. "Senator Hislop is involved, but we don't know who else yet."

"Didn't think we could drop any further."

"This is the tip of the iceberg," adds Granfield. "The FBI has been following this trail for over a year, and it's global."

Cross sighs. "So, what now?"

"The van came from out of state. There are tens of thousands of children missing in the US. You really don't want to look at the statistics, but over twenty-two hundred go missing for various reasons."

"A year, a month?"

"No." He hesitates, as his facial expression changes to visually graph the horror. "Each day."

Cross has no answer. He can't fathom this and there is disdain forged into his complexion.

"There are five main reasons but one of those is abduction by a stranger. They just disappear." Granfield looks traumatised.

"So, where do we go from here?"

"We have Briar and Hislop videoed and photographed. That case is open and closed and the damage to their careers is irreparable.

Now, we need to finish with Deep State."

"I'm ready and done with these people. However, what is known about Briar's next move?"

"A very interesting question. He can't now become president because we will release the photos and arrest him. We have enhanced protection on the president and prime minister, but Briar is essentially done. It makes no sense at all."

Granfield fills him in on what the FBI wants to do next. "This has to be coordinated."

"Yes, I understand."

"Nick just called before you arrived. Rostov has most units in place including some warships in the Baltic Sea. Poland is remaining neutral but not mobilising. Estonia is alert and preparing. Finland and Sweden are monitoring and staying active, but they aren't part of NATO."

"All are ready for the ignition source." He laughs, but it is laboured. "Wu can't have foreseen Russia's response, nor our ambivalence to them mobilising their forces. How does he interpret that?"

"We know Lutkus has a mole." Granfield gestures with his hands. "However, we aren't going to be ambivalent. NATO is going to respond, to keep Wu guessing."

"I'm more concerned about what Lutkus will do next. He may go crazy."

"That is a distinct possibility we can't predict, unfortunately, because we simply don't have an answer. We just have to keep monitoring the situation and err on the side of caution. We can't barrel in with both feet."

"You Americans usually do," and laughs.

"What did you do with the flight info I sent you, Daniel?" asks Taylor, wishing to change the subject.

"Graeme has it. He told me it is in the Spanish mountains but waiting for him to pinpoint a location."

"Good."

"Do you have an update on this Robertson lady?" asks Granfield.

Cross wants to spill what he found out about her, likely Wu's major sponsor, but not yet. He hasn't digested its credibility anyway and needs to verify. "No update at this very moment but working on one."

Time for another round of drinks, so he waves the waitress over.

"By the way, Daniel, how is the knee?" Granfield infuses, as they try to enjoy another round of beers whilst clouded in abject revulsion.

"I did the exploratory stem cell injections after I returned from the South China Sea, and it has been immense. I notice, of course, but definitively less pain and more movement."

"Happy to hear that."

"On a different subject, now Cartwright, Abrams and Jankowski have been removed, what is happening to their stock values?"

"They are doing exactly what you had calculated they would do. They are tanking and dragging others down with them. It is fascinating to observe. You have predictive powers, and you knew which ones to go after. Whatever you did, the research is commendable and extraordinary. Even Washington lobbyists who push their agenda are collapsing."

He smiles. "I'm still not done."

"I hoped not." He laughs. "Other media organisations are looking at Blue Ocean Media. The government isn't allowed to manipulate markets and stock values, so we can't interfere. Your friend's TV5 in Vilnius is attracting serious attention and they are being offered affiliate rights. You never know, perhaps mainstream media will change into providing factual and non-misleading news along with termination of their disinformation spread, isolated from political bias. How about that?"

"So, something positive to look forward to then?" He grins.

"I have friends looking into this and they pass on confidential information, that I can use to help us. It is likely any purchase of Blue Ocean Media will not include Jankowski's TrustCorp Investments. That company will be hung out to dry and liquidated or purchased by a hedge fund company for peanuts. In any event, all this impacts Wu."

Cross picks up his beer and finishes it, before ordering the next round.

On the floor lies Lithuania's defense minister with a bullet hole in his forehead. Lutkus had verified a message being transmitted from the minister's office soon after they had finished the war cabinet meeting a couple of days ago.

Lutkus is in the war room with his foreign affairs minister.

"If he is dumb enough to send messages to our adversaries within the confines of the parliament building, then he isn't intelligent enough to be part of Lithuania's new movement. Please have him removed."

"Yes, Prime Minister."

Underlings get scared when they see such blatant violence, which is precisely what Lutkus is doing. It is part of every pariah's playbook.

"Meet me back at the Palace."

The minister walks into the spacious Palace and heads to Lutkus' meeting room. He enters the salacious room and seats himself across from him, and on the other side of the vast mahogany desk.

"It's a go," Lutkus tells him.

"I will arrange the cabinet and move on our plans."

"You are our defense minister now. Congratulations on the lateral promotion."

You are an arrogant dick. "Thank you, Prime Minister," and smiles.

The minister stands and they shake hands before he leaves the room.

"Fire!" Yells the commander.

The officer punches the button and two missiles eject, one after the other, with savage force and brutal disturbance from the mobile launcher on trajectories toward Riga.

"I hope we are in time."

"I hope so too, Commander. Otherwise, this escalates."

The regiment is in Belarus and their system is anti-missile defense. The Russian counterpart had ordered deployment because of active projectiles heading from Lithuania.

"We will know shortly."

Jennings picks up his phone.

"It started, Nick. Two missiles fired from Lithuania: one of those being intercepted by an anti-missile battery based in Belarus."

"Shit, Sergey. So much for mitigating war."

"We are not responsible for the actions of dumb people seeking more power. Trying to predict their thoughts and movements is like pissing into the wind."

"What is the damage?"

"One missile landed in the river, sending a shock wave through the water which forced it to spill over the hydroelectric facility."

"The plant still functioning?"

"Yes."

"Keep me appraised and good work." He nearly puts the phone down. "Oh, NATO is positioning hardware. You know this?"

"Yes, thank you."

Cross receives a text message.

'When are you back in the UK?'

'On my way. I leave in an hour.'

'War has started.'

'Shit.'

'Sergey called me. One missile missed the electric plant and another was intercepted.'

'Collateral damage?'

'Superficial.'

'I'm recalibrating and it is time to implement the next phase.' He doesn't give a damn which prick goes down next.

Cross calls Granfield.

"Lithuania has started tossing missiles."

"Yes, we know. We are moving hardware through the North Sea."

"Russia knows this?"

"Yes, Daniel."

"Just checking. Time to end it."

"Russian built air-defense batteries in Belarus intercepted one of the missiles, sir."

Wu had organised his primary military people and had them assemble at their allocated war room. His pieces are falling into place, despite some unforeseen failures.

"What about the second one?"

"It hit the river," his commander answers.

"And?"

"Plant still functioning."

"What happened to the defense minister, their mole?"

"His body will never be found."

"Good, now our man is in place."

"Yes."

58

Pyrenees Enclave Located

The Dassault is losing altitude in preparation for landing as it approaches the North London area, when Cross' phone vibrates once.

'We have worked out the coordinates.'

'Remarkable turn of events.'

'They are in the Spanish Pyrenees. Here they are.'

Cross receives them and stares.

'Thank you.'

'Let me know what you need, and we will deliver as before.'

'Ok, Graeme. I am changing course.'

'Wait. You are doing what?'

Cross gets up and runs to the cockpit. He instructs the pilots to change their landing destination.

"Ok, strap in, we must lose altitude fast."

He messages Moore Jr.

'We need to do this. Landing sequence activated.'

'We will meet you off the plane.'

'There in about half an hour.'

'Daniel, when does your plane land?'

'It did already. I changed my plans. Can you meet me tomorrow, late afternoon?'

'Shit. The UK polling starts the day after.'

'I know.'

Jennings is exasperated. 'Keep me updated.'

'This is important, Nick.'

'It is all vital. Lutkus showing signs of moving his forces.'

'I hope to end this. Will update you.'

Moore Jr. meets Cross off the plane in Humberside. It is early morning, but cold and damp as North Sea fog pervades the air.

"Hello, Daniel. We have seven hours to prepare you, so must move quickly."

"Good morning, too," shaking hands. "Ok."

He follows Moore Jr. to his car and they speed off to a warehouse somewhere in Hull. After arriving, Cross climbs out and walks into the building. He surveys all the various military hardware and gadgets, wondering what is going on.

"You are dead, Daniel. It must be perceived that way too. You can't go to MI6's storeroom and grab stuff with their badges and markings on them. If this equipment is captured or left behind, it can't be traceable. What you see is unmarked. Where do you think we got the Israeli material from for the Monaco devices?"

"I did wonder." He looks at Moore Jr. and smiles. "So, what are we looking at here?"

"Their facility is at high altitude so it will be cold. It is in the mountains too, so we had to organise a way for you to get there."

He goes into details about the location and what they know, which isn't much.

"Florence gave us some information that is very useful," and explains that too.

"This sounds like a formidable compound. Explosion-proof window shutters should be interesting."

"Nah. We can take care of those."

They head into a small office and sit down, but not before Moore Jr. brings over two shots.

"Thanks, Graeme."

"If this is Wu's compound, it is going to have a lot of security and armed personnel, one would imagine. Interestingly, Florence didn't convey that in her description."

"Then I have to play that one by ear."

"Like everything else we have done so far."

"Nothing ever changes." They both laugh.

Moore Jr. gets out a map of the Pyrenees and points to the location they have roughly determined to be the compound.

"Roughly?" Cross' eyebrows rise.

"Sorry, approximate location, I meant."

"That's better." He grins.

He brings out a drawing composed from information Anderson provided.

"This is pretty much built into the mountain side?" Cross enquires.

"Yes."

"Then it should have ventilation shafts somewhere."

"One would anticipate those, yes."

Moore Jr. reaches over and brings out satellite imageries. Now Cross' eyes open wide.

"What are these?"

"Using the approximate data, we zeroed in employing military satellites in the area."

"You can do that?"

"Technically, yes. We can do anything. Don't ask if it is legal or not."

"That was my next question." He smirks.

He spends an hour explaining the location, the points of entries, possible building layout. Cross is impressed.

After the talk, they go back into the main warehouse and select the gear he will require.

"Jesus."

"You may be past redemption."

"Very likely."

"We will load this onto the plane, as before. Then I have someone meeting you when it lands on the French side of the mountains. They will then drive you from the landing point and rendezvous with an electric vehicle. Like we did before, so you are familiar," he adds, trying to console his disposition.

"How did you arrange this so fast, Graeme?"

"Once Leslie and Florence sent us the information, I knew what was going to happen. This must be taken out."

"Why the Conquest I? I never knew that was yours."

"You will find out."

"Ok." Cross' impressed and his nerves are jangling already. Moore Jr. sees that.

"That is a good emotion, my friend, and keeps the right chemicals fluid. Come on, let's gather this stuff and then there is a small local bar around the corner."

It is dark when the plane touches down somewhere close to the border between France and Spain. The runway is a field and someone laid out flairs for the landing lights. He has already changed into winter mountain gear and other essentials including a balaclava, which is around his neck.

As the cabin door unlatches, there is someone there to meet him.

"Hello, Daniel. I'm Mr. Moore's friend, Julian." The French accent is pronounced but his eyes nearly pop out. "Very fetching attire,

I might add," and chuckles.

The Moores have an interesting list of participatory friends wishing to be complicit, admires Cross. Perhaps they like their freedom too. "Nice to meet you, Julian. Sorry, this is to screw with people's heads," and winks.

"That will do it," and shakes his head.

They transfer several boxes of items to the guy's 4Runner and then leave, heading off up a long, two-lane paved mountain road. Ninety minutes later, Julian pulls off and heads through an even narrower mountain trail, used ostensibly by power company personnel and forestry services. It is rough so progress has slowed. On either side are large pine trees. Occasionally the driver swerves to avoid a power pole.

After another thirty minutes, he starts to slow and then pulls off the trail. Now in front of them is an electric four-wheeler ATV and he stops. He hands Cross night-vision goggles.

"Put these on and follow me."

Julian takes him a hundred or so metres and then they enter an opening in the forest. In front of them is a small valley that has been partly cleared of rock and trees. Cross is staring at a runway built into the mountains and is gob smacked.

"How did they build this without people knowing?"

"That depends on what they are using it for, sir. Pay someone enough money, it can be just a corporate retreat. Mountains are typically owned by federal governments."

Now Cross remembers Sanchez in Latvia, whom he killed. This explains why a political figure from Spain was part of all this.

"Astonishing. I am in awe."

"Across the runway is the structure built into the mountain," as he points.

It is dark with very faint lighting, but Cross sees an outline of a structure.

"You have your instructions, Daniel. We are on a fixed timetable."

"Yes."

"I am also using a satellite phone. Just message or call if there are problems with timing but watch out for lumberjacks."

"Very funny." They both exchange chuckles.

They head back to the 4Runner and transfer boxes to the four-wheeler.

Julian extends his hand. "Good luck. Just follow the trail we walked on which will take you to the edge of the runway."

"Thank you," and shakes his hand.

Cross climbs the electric vehicle, pulls up his balaclava and heads off wearing the goggles. He stops at the perimeter fence and cuts a hole in it, before proceeding around the runway and toward the complex. His heart is pounding.

He takes a visual scan to confirm the layout Moore Jr. presented. All looks good so far.

He approaches what represents covered aircraft parking built into the rock. A corporate jet sits in the corner with a refueling hose still attached, so he goes over and hides his vehicle. A black van and a damaged truck sit next to the compound.

He grabs two rifles already loaded and a few incendiary devices. There are no movements, no sounds, no people, nothing. It is eerily peaceful as the silence deafens his sensors. The metal shutters over windows have been activated and are closed.

According to the diagram, an entrance is just across the tarmac, so he looks over and locates it hiding behind some rock formation. He silently runs over to it. It is a coded entrance, as expected, so removes his electronic device. It starts scanning, but it is having issues tying into the system.

"Damn."

He runs back to the four-wheeler and retrieves another device:

his own. He powers that on and starts scanning for a local network, watching as the digits randomly spit out alphanumerics, numbers, letters. It is also finding difficulty tying into their local system. Cross is losing hope and is about to go looking for a ventilation shaft when the device activates and locks onto a network.

"Finally."

Now he locks onto their WiFi and finds the code. Jumping those hurdles, he enters security and finds the whole compound's layout.

"Got it."

He unlocks the door to the jet parking area and as he does so, he hears a thud. He walks over and grabs the door handle.

As he enters the building, things don't seem kosher. No one is around and there is no noise. Most rooms have their lights turned off and they are void of any lifeforms.

He gingerly walks further in and sees a conference room. Observing the surroundings and ensuring solitude, he enters and flicks the light switch. As the room illuminates, plastered on two walls are the remnants of what were poster-boards with material, details and graphics. What were once pinned to the corks have been removed, except for a few odd pictures. On one wall, under the heading 'Sponsors', Cartwright's portrait, plastered with a large red X, had been left. Next to that is Abrams' portrait similarly violated. Mitchell and Kalnins are there also, their headings removed. Whatever else were pinned has gone. He looks at the floor and notices Jankowski's portrait with a red X.

"How about that. I was right after all."

He takes a closer look. Interestingly, whoever was at the top of the sponsors' board, their portrait has been removed.

On the second board is a world map partially removed. The Baltics is still up there, along with the US. Russia's map has been ripped in half. China's has graffiti provided courtesy of a black marker pen.

On another wall, the board has leftover photographs pinned of Cartwright's plane crash. Cross looks at them for a few seconds, admiring his polished work. Next to those is one photograph of Mitchell's Jaguar after he pumped two rounds through the rear window. He is finished here and turns around.

Across the hallway from the conference room is an office so he heads over. It is a large room with expensive furniture remaining. The drawers, shelving, cabinets are void of anything, but they left in a hurry because inconsequential papers and office items litter the place. He expeditiously rummages through the drawers and cabinets, in search of anything that would provide evidence. He retrieves a few material items of interest and puts them in his pocket. Feeling under the edge of the desk he locates two thumb drives taped to the wood, so takes those.

He's done here and needs to move. This place was abandoned very quickly which leaves him perplexed and frustrated, but also suspicious. Before embarking on his escape, he takes a walk-through of various other rooms that have all been rapidly cleared. There are living quarters too, via a tunnel, including kitchen and dining area.

He ties into the WiFi and signals Julian. 'Time to go.'

Pushing his perceptive limits and feeling the need to get the hell out, he heads for a different exit. As he does so he notices a blinking red light from a security camera mounted to the ceiling in another darkened room. Almost immediately he hears a helicopter and realises it is too soon for his rendezvous to be arriving. Rapid gun fire starts hitting the building. He doesn't show concern because of the window shutters, until they start to open.

"Shit."

The rapid fire begins again but this time no shutters to deflect. The high-caliber artillery from the gunship penetrates the building as Cross dives behind a stone wall. The bullets rip up furniture and send debris and glass flying everywhere. Once a gap appears in the firing, he darts toward the door he came in. He doesn't make it when bullets start raining down once more. He spins around looking for protection and finds an outside building wall framed into the rock, so leaps behind it.

Above it is a blown-out window. He gets his Russian rifle and points it in the direction of the helicopter and starts offloading round after round. The modified bullets leave small tracers which allow him to verify where he is aiming. The liability of which also gives away his position. The pilot sees where they are coming from, but he is too late to swivel the chopper. Cross penetrates the cockpit glass and the glow from the instrument cluster reveals the pilot and co-pilot's bodies shredding, as the chopper crashes into the ground and explodes. He ducks behind his vantage point to avoid flying rotors.

Cross hears another one approaching and runs for the exit, but not before he removes a timed incendiary device and tosses it into the conference room. He exits the structure and navigates for the corporate jet. Using it as a shield, he empties more rounds at the second helicopter. Now he bolts as the machine guns from the Cobra pummel the jet, lighting up the jet fuel into a huge ball of fire.

Off to the side but feeling the heat, he aims at the engines and penetrates the rear rotor. Sparks flash and smoke starts billowing as the pilot loses control and it spins close to the first one, exploding on impact.

The sound of burning wreckage now displaces mountain solace as he heads into the compound and plants more small nuclear incendiaries.

Two minutes later, he hears another chopper approaching but with a different rotor pitch. He runs out onto the runway to find it is his rendezvous, and just in time. Without it even touching down, Cross jumps through the open cabin door with help from someone on board dragging him in.

He screams, "Get out of here."

As the chopper pulls away and takes off, behind them are several huge explosions as the once formidable, hidden mountain enclave is obliterated. The blasts are compressed by the rock formations and forced through the open windows, the flames spreading across the runway and lighting up the mountains.

Cross sits and stares at the burning compound in disbelief.

"The retreat in the Pyrenees has been destroyed, sir."

Hancock is reporting the recent events in Wu's office.

"When?"

"About an hour ago."

"How?"

"An imposter penetrated security and entered the building. The alarm notified our guards."

"And?"

"Two helicopter gunships were destroyed in the process."

"Who was the responsible party?"

"We have them on camera, but they were wearing a balaclava, sir." He is very hesitant in delivering the rest of it.

"Them, they are strange personal pronouns, Wilfred. Come on, spit it out," Wu adds, getting irritated.

"Hair was sticking out and it looks like the outline of a woman, sir."

"How do you know that?" looking bewildered.

"She had a chest, sir," trying to remain impartial.

"Interesting."

Wu knew the end of the mountain enclave would come eventually. They had prepared for that, but the escape was short notice. During their last intimate session, he had Anderson's room searched and they recovered a watch, so knew what was going on. Very little material evidence was ever stored there but that doesn't mean there wasn't any. He does share some concerns.

"Was she killed too?"

"The explosions were large which destroyed our ability to keep recording events."

"I see. That wasn't my question."

"Possibly."

Wu walks away in frustration. He needs to focus on the real events.

59

Wu's Compound Abandoned

Cross is back in the Cessna and on his way to England. He had removed his wig, padded bra and fake breasts but hoped it was the last time he is forced to wear those for His Majesty's Secret Service.

It is early morning, but he calls Jennings anyway. He picks up.

"Nick, I'm on my way back from France and heading to northern England."

"Ok." He sounds tired.

"I just blew up Wu's mountain refuge in the Pyrenees."

Now he is wide awake.

"Wait." Cross hears ruffling in the background, along with the unmistakable sound of Gabrys' voice.

"Tell Janina I say hello."

"I will. You just did what?" in a shocked tone.

"We located his hideout. Got the coordinates, satellite imagery, rough drawings. It was truly a site to see."

"Holy crap. Does that mean this is over? Please tell me it is."

"That is the bizarreness of all this, just to add to everything else. It had been recently abandoned."

"What?" Not comprehending what Cross is saying.

"No one was there, except two gunships that showed up. Likely I set off alarms."

"Which means they have you on camera."

"It's ok. I was prepared and dressed to look like a woman."

"Hang on, mate. I'm not awake enough for this conversation," and laughs.

"It was very impressive and built into the mountain. They had flattened the valley for a runway. However, there was very little left behind when I entered."

"Shit. And more shit. Are you ok?"

"Yes, thanks. A few cuts and bruises from flying debris but nothing more. I found a few items in Wu's office but have no idea what they are yet."

"When do you land and where?"

"Humberside in about two hours, perhaps less. I'm using Graeme's Cessna."

"Get a few hours' sleep and I will meet you up there around ten."

Cross messages Taylor.

'Pyrenees complex blown up. Wu is somewhere else.'

'What do you mean?'

'It was abandoned.'

'This is crazy. Are you ok?'

'Yes, thanks. How is Florence?'

'I have a spare room so she moved in.'

'Ok, good. Let David know. I am too tired to call so will do so in AM.'

'Ok.'

Five minutes later his phone rings.

"You did what?"

"Wu's sanctuary in the Pyrenees is history. I removed some pieces but I have no idea what yet. It had been abandoned."

"Crap," came the sound of frustration. "Perhaps they got tipped off."

"I have no idea, but it was empty."

"Are you heading back to the UK?"

"Yes. Nick meets me at ten. I hope for a few hours of sleep before then."

"Get back to me."

60

Rigged Election

Jennings meets Cross and Moore Jr. south of the Humber. The no-tell motel is some flea-bitten joint but discretion triumphs heroism, especially at this juncture. Jennings even stopped using people he knows for Cross' lodging. Moore Jr. had arrived just ten minutes before he did. Cross was relieved to hear Sadeghi is doing ok and dearly misses him, but they are intimately aware they can't communicate directly.

"Gentlemen, let's venture around the corner to a café and find the cousins of the fleas in your room, Daniel."

"Very bloody funny. I didn't know we are dropping down to Briar's standards."

"These people escaped out of a sewer, but we cannot go that low. Unfortunately, scientific research and methodologies dictate we must be on similar footing, down in the gutter, for our minds to operate the way theirs evidently do."

Everyone chuckles.

"Brilliant mission, Daniel. Wu got spooked and ran. I wonder who did that?"

"Florence wore a rare watch with compass and altimeter capabilities, I was told," Moore Jr. adds. "Perhaps she forgot to remove it."

"That is crazy," Jennings responds, rolling his eyes.

"Hey, we have all done dumb stuff, Nick," says Cross defensively. "It goes with the territory. She has helped getting us this far, so let's refrain from berating her with assumptions not confirmed."

Jennings is worried. "She is going to be a marked woman."

"She is, anyway, Nick," adding empathy. "Her days were numbered long before Leslie got her to trade sides. Wu wasn't going to let her loose and she knew that."

"Fantastic rogue mission though."

"Graeme provided the help I needed." He looks over at him. "Dabs on that plane though. She is a beauty."

"All yours, mate."

Jennings changes subject, dragging their focus to more pressing and immediate needs, such as current events. "Gentlemen, Davenport's election is tomorrow."

"I thought it is known as the general election?"

"It is, but he made it about Davenport, Daniel. It is all about him."

"That figures. Have you implemented what we had discussed?" Cross asks.

"We have the people set up and we are going to do a trial run this afternoon. I will be notified of the results around four. Graeme has designed a software version so we can run a simulation and it will show what changes need to be addressed in real time as we input data. It also has a predictive monitor built in, and it doesn't look very good."

"It has a predictive what and what doesn't?" looking puzzled.

"Davenport knows he is going to win. Can you imagine the consequences of what we are implementing?"

"Yes, well, fuck him. However, this dummy run is cutting it fine."

"With you galivanting off to US and France, we had no choice but we can work around it. It is what it is."

"We already did a simulated run with people we know in various parts of the country. It works," adds Moore Jr., backing up Jennings.

"The other question: what have you prepared for the fallout?" Cross is looking at Nick. "We need to be active for the consequences and that ball is in your court."

"All taken care of. You still have your gun, right?"

"That's your plan?" as he shakes his head.

"Yes," and prophetically giggles.

Cross leaves that aside. "What is happening in Lithuania?"

"Lutkus will invade day after tomorrow, looks like. The British Navy has ships in the Baltic Sea, along with a US aircraft carrier and support vessels."

"How do we stop this? It will escalate if we don't."

"Indeed. Russia has troops to prevent it but even with a signed agreement, there is genuine reluctance for a full-blown war with a NATO country, for obvious reasons."

"How did we ever get here?" Cross sighs before remembering something. "Nick, who do you know at the National Intelligence Centre in Madrid?"

"Umm, why?"

"Irrelevant." He immediately regrets his impetuous behaviour and corrects his flippant remark. "Sorry, I'm on edge and lack of sleep doesn't help." He rubs his eyes. "I don't have an answer yet. It might not be relevant."

"We all are mate. Ok, wait." Jennings thinks for a few seconds. "Garcia. Santiago Garcia."

"I want to know who Sanchez was, the guy I killed in Vilnius. He was masquerading as a member of the Senate, but he wasn't. I don't know if we gain anything from knowing, but who knows. Wu had to have someone paid off in Spain to permit the construction of his mountain facility. He then had to silence them."

"Let me make a call."

Jennings steps away from the café booth and walks outside. A few minutes later he returns and sits down.

"Mr. Garcia is going to find out. The body was returned to Spain, but they just handed it over to the family in a casket, after the state funeral."

"The family never said anything?"

"Evidently not. What are they going to say to Spain's government?"

Moore Jr. jumps in. "Daniel, I told you they swapped bodies, sometimes with real people who look the same. They performed medical procedures, extracting body parts from the donor, transferring them to their surrogate. Particularly on those with noticeable features."

"I'm sick of all this shit, which I am sure I have repeated on a number of occasions."

Jennings' phone pings. He turns to Cross after reading the message.

"Santiago in Spain has been given permission to exhume Sanchez."

"I seem to be responsible for the exhumation of people whom no authorities have bothered to question."

"We don't believe most of what we are seeing, so how can they?"

Cross turns to Jennings. "Yeah, there is that not so insignificant fact."

They had left Moore Jr. and are flying back to London in preparation for the election. Davenport is back in London on the campaign trail, and they need to be close.

Around four, Jennings' phone jingles. After talking for a few minutes, he turns to Cross.

"It looks good. The test was positive and Graeme's software will adjust on-the-fly."

"Well, time will tell." This is a risk and he is extremely nervous.

They are back in Mayfair which seems to be Davenport's preferred campaign spot. Of course it is since he is surrounding himself with affluence. Jennings wanted to be local so booked a suite at a hotel near 45 Park Lane, where Davenport will be. Here they can rest, make calls, confer with Intelligence and organise. Their laptops are open.

"Where are we with Lutkus' ambitions, Nick."

"They simmered a little. He still has his forces aligned along the border and they lob missiles from time to time. However, the missile batteries in Belarus seem to be working, most of the time. Ozolins is restrained too, because his forces are limited, but also because we asked him to be."

"I think the election here will play a big role in what happens next. Once Davenport is elected, it will fuel their egos and away we go."

"That, I believe, is an accurate assessment."

Cross picks up his phone.

"Hello, Madelaine. How are you?"

"Michael, nice to hear from you. I'm good. We are all waiting on the UK election. Presumably you are also."

"Yes, as a member of Parliament, I must comply with rules implicitly demanded of someone in my position. I am, therefore, required to behave."

He can hear her laughing her head off.

"I miss you, MP Horseman," as she continues to giggle. "We are ready, when you are done frolicking up there."

He laughs. "Let's get through the next twenty-four or so hours, and I will be back in contact."

He turns to Jennings. "I'm going to lay down for half an hour."

Cross walks into his room and lays on the pillows he set against the headboard. Rest is required but it isn't on his agenda. Next to him is a small bag. He unzips it and ruffles around looking for the material he had scrounged from Wu's office in the Pyrenees. He starts to pull it out as he finds it.

In a pile on the bed are a few papers and a couple of thumb drives. He flips through the papers but doesn't note anything of importance. At least nothing they don't know already. He picks up the two drives and walks over to his computer.

Sitting on the living room couch and holding his phone, Jennings looks over.

"I thought you wanted rest. You should get some."

"I will get it when this is all over."

He sits at the desk and inserts the first drive into his laptop. Some files come up, but they are encrypted and useless. Most, unfortunately, are empty. He removes that and inserts the next drive.

"Now this looks more interesting."

Jennings hears him muttering. "What does?"

"I found two thumb drives taped under Wu's desk. The first one didn't reveal anything. This second one might have some info."

He clicks on a folder and up pops a series of jpeg files. He opens the first one.

"Take a look at this, Nick."

Jennings gets up and walks over.

"This is a photo of a poster board I found on the walls in their conference room."

Jennings is leaning over Cross' shoulder. "Interesting."

"Yes but look at the first name on the list of sponsors."

"Amanda Robertson."

He is excited now. "This *is* the confirmation we needed. Ozolins gave us this name, but how the hell did he know and who told him?"

Cross clicks on the next series of files and finally brings up Robertson's picture.

"This is her. I remember from researching her. This is what we needed."

"Brilliant. Now what?" asks Jennings.

"I call her up and tell her to stop it." He cheekily grins.

Jennings laughs and slaps him on his shoulder. "If only it's that easy, mate."

"The rest of the data on that poster board is what we know already. However, it does pictorially expose the accuracy of our information."

"Yes. Nice to know we don't have our heads shoved up our own arses."

"Well, it doesn't exactly reveal we don't." He grins a second time.

Cross studies the poster board photo once more.

"Look who's underneath Briar."

"Hislop. Who is Hislop?" enquires Jennings.

"He is part of Briar's child sex trafficking syndicate, only this time he is a US senator."

"Wait, have I missed something here?" and abruptly stands upright. "Come again."

Cross swivels the chair. "Right, I neglected to tell you. Sorry, I got distracted in Spain. David asked me to fly back to Washington because they have exposed a child trafficking ring that has Briar's involvement. In the photos and videos is also this scumbag, Hislop."

"What the hell have we dropped down to?"

"Who knows," and shrugs his shoulders.

"They have videos of these people in the act?" Jennings is now even more shocked and incensed.

"Yes."

"Obviously they couldn't react because of our on-going operation, otherwise the overwhelming urge must have been for agents to string them up by their testicles."

"Precisely. However, this isn't restricted to the US. This is global."

"Oh, shit. Didn't one billionaire get caught recently and he committed suicide in jail?"

"The evidence collected didn't support the suicide theory."

"What? You mean Abrams' media circus covered it up?"

Cross looks at him. "Now you are seeing the real picture and it was categorised as fake news."

Jennings walks over and slumps on the sofa. His mind is in a fog and can't compute this level of depravity and sickness. He doesn't live down there in the gutter, swirling in a cesspool of excrement.

Cross walks over and sits next to him.

"Sick, isn't it?"

"I don't know what words to use, Daniel."

"There aren't any."

He turns on the TV and flicks channels to find Davenport talking.

"This guy is one of them," Cross adds.

Jennings gets up and walks over to the window and pulls back a curtain. Darkness has fully transcended onto London as the sun disappeared hours ago. Unfortunately, it isn't the darkness from lack of sun that he sees. Blackness has fallen on society too as he listens to Davenport in the background.

He blankly stairs out the window as cars and people below scurry through their mundane lives, unaware of what is truly going on.

61

The Domino Effect

It is seven the following morning and some daylight is filtering through the curtains. Cross emerges from his dark bedroom and Jennings has already made coffee, so pours him a cup.

"Good morning. The sun keeps coming up so someone must believe we are worthy of another day," and hands Cross the coffee.

"Thank you. Let's try and justify their belief in humanity."

The TV is already on

"Polling opened; I think."

"Yes, Daniel. A few minutes ago."

Cross walks over and pulls back the curtains. More light now filters into the room, but it is bleak outside with clouds and rain.

"I miss the English weather." He chuckles.

"Sure you do."

"When it rains in California, I stand and watch it."

"Rain at your temperatures is different to the biting cold coming in off the North Sea, English Channel or Irish Sea."

"I can't argue with that."

"It will be a few hours before polling gets interesting. How about breakfast downstairs?"

Wu is back in the war room.

"Polling stations have already opened. Today will be a good day."

"Yes, sir." Handcock is dialed in. "Davenport's speech last night captured the fever and polls show strong support. This should be a formality."

"Keep me posted."

He exits the room and heads to his office. After seating himself, Wu picks up the phone.

"John, very early morning for you but the election is vital."

Hislop is monitoring the election at his Washington, DC dwelling. "Good morning, Mr. Wu. Yes, this is important."

"Are things clear in the US?"

"Yes, sir."

"Is Briar under control?"

"He will do as he is told."

"You are aware of his indiscretions?"

"He is under surveillance from now on. You can be assured I'm controlling him."

"I hope so, John."

Jennings looks at Cross sitting on the other couch in the suite. "The early exit polls are showing Davenport clearly leading."

"Yes. I see that."

The BBC news is playing on the TV and the anchor is reading early numbers surrounded by political experts.

"...as evidenced from pre-election polls, Davenport is clearly leading as he commands support from the British people. The murder of MP Mitchell, still an open case, plus the loss of credibility surrounding ministerial security after Prime Minister Clark's assassination have spooked the electorate."

"The BBC is supposed to be untethered, lack bias and be politically neutral," Cross adds.

"Of course it is. Can't you tell?" and chuckles.

The narrative continues. "A resounding speech last night in Mayfair energised the voters. This is anticipated to be an election with high voter turnout."

Cross gets up and walks over to the minibar. He opens the door whose seal had already been tampered with, and then looks at his watch.

"Is it too early?"

"It is never too early listening to this crap. The only question is do we have enough?"

Early afternoon shows a strong lead for Davenport as initial exit poll numbers are counted and the data released. He is dominating in early reporting with a lead of fifty-nine-point-two percent, which would create a full majority government in which he can operate and manipulate.

"I hope you know what you're doing, Nick."

He turns his head with a big grin. "I hope so too."

By mid-afternoon, that percentage had climbed to sixty-two-point-four. Cross is nervous, but Jennings is not.

"Relax. I got this."

"Ok, if you say so."

Jennings reaches over, grabs his phone and calls Moore Jr.

"What is the data showing, Graeme?"

"We see his strong regions, which are obviously the north. Conservatives, or Liberal Unionists, are inherently southerners where the money always has been."

"Ready for this?"

"Yes."

"Go."

Jennings puts the phone on the coffee table and sits back.

"Daniel, are we ready?"

"Yes, because this is going to get ugly."

"Absolutely it is, so let's be prepared."

Cross feels for his gun. "Ready."

Wu has a big smile on his face as he watches the polling numbers from his desk, which are now at sixty-three-point-one.

Just then, the next series of numbers show a half percent decline in Davenport's vote. He picks up his phone.

"Wilfred, what's going on?"

"Stay calm, this could be just an aberration or the way they round, or just the districts they are counting."

He puts the phone down.

Half an hour later it had now dropped another zero-point-three percent.

"What's going on?" Now yelling down the phone.

"Nothing, sir. Hold on"

One hour later the polls are showing Davenport's lead declining further. Wu hastily exits his office and beelines for the war room.

"Wilfred, what is happening?"

"I don't have an answer. Let me get back to you." He hastily leaves the room.

The BBC news is now reporting Davenport at fifty-seven-point-eight percent.

"...Davenport's decline has been steady over the last few hours." Reports the female anchor, clearly not understanding it.

"Could be the regions reporting in. Independents aren't liked in all quarters of the British Isles."

Jennings looks at Cross. "That guy is a paid political analyst and an expert. What a joke."

"This is incredible. I have seen and done a lot of things lately, but I have never seen this in real-time."

Jennings is smiling. "I told you."

"Yes, you did."

They return to listening to the political bullshitters. "It is now at fifty-seven-point-two. Clearly everyone has misinterpreted the public's reaction to Prime Minister Clark's death. However, the polls can't be this far wrong, James?" as she asks another political analyst, but obviously distraught by what she is witnessing, simply because it has never happened before.

"Yes, this seems unprecedented. All pre-election indicators were clearly defined as poll after poll showed Davenport leading, by a significant margin I might add."

Half an hour later the next set of numbers flash on the bottom right of the screen.

"Davenport now at fifty-five-point-nine. Chancellor Carlisle's numbers are climbing." Jennings is beaming.

After the death of Prime Minister Clark, the Liberal Unionist Party had chosen Carlisle to replace her. He was a veteran of war and an aggressive but smart politician. He is also an amiable character and well-liked by the citizens. His selection, in the British political powerhouse, was a formality and the Queen endorsed him.

Cross receives a text.

'Michael, you must be watching.'

'Yes.'

'This is wild.'

'I will contact you shortly, Madelaine. Be ready.'

Cross messages Granfield.

'Watching, David?'

'Yes.'

'The domino effect.'

'Be careful. You are poking a raging wild animal with a tiny little stick.'

Cross returns his phone to the table.

It is now seven in the evening and the polls are indicating Davenport at fifty-one-point-one. It is a massive political fall that no one outside of Intelligence is even remotely understanding.

Jennings interrupts. "Another three hours before the polling stations close, by which time this will be over. We need to go."

"Yes."

62

MP Davenport's
Night from Hell

The last time Cross and Jennings were at 45 Park Lane, it was like a militarised zone. On the night of a general election, it is no different.

"This is nuts," says Cross.

They walked through a park across the street from the venue, just to hide and blend in, but the crowd was gathering, and was already raucous and animated. The change in polling numbers throughout the afternoon and into the evening hours is beginning to stimulate anger and hate.

Jennings shows his credentials and Cross follows, with his fake MI6 ID. They are waved through a special security entrance and head to the hotel, and through another isolated entrance.

"The military and police are on the government's side, yes?" asks Cross.

"Of course, but admittedly this will not be a safe place to be later. Davenport is now below fifty percent and dropping, and the night isn't over yet."

"I can see that."

Passing through more security, the media and cameras are

everywhere. Cross needs to avoid them as they take the escalator down. He twists and turns as his head swivels looking to see who he knows and who he recognises.

They are downstairs and walk into the heavily fortified room. It is plastered with campaign posters hosting pictures of Davenport. Bunting, banners, flyers, ribbons are everywhere and the carpet is littered. The vast room is packed and the noise deafening. At the front Cross sees Davenport, with the people he recognises from the event several weeks ago. He is talking with sponsors, constituents, government ministers, who the hell knows.

Just then a blonde woman walks past him. He takes a double take to verify and can't believe it. No other woman looks like her. He is floored.

"Florence is here," he shouts above the cacophony of noise.

"What?"

"Florence is here, look," as he gestures using his head.

"What the hell. This is dangerous for her."

"Perhaps Wu doesn't know. Also, Davenport might not know she has switched sides."

"Possible, but here. Why here, tonight?"

"They are business associates that includes a bed, and perhaps he is being paid more cash after he wins. Luckily, she doesn't know who I am, yet."

Cross watches as Anderson walks toward the front of the crowd. Davenport sees her and is obviously smitten. He apologetically relinquishes himself from a conversation and walks down off the small stage to greet her.

"Shit. I'll be back."

Cross walks through the dense madness and approaches the front. As he gets nearer, he sees Davenport give Anderson a big hug, but his eyes widen in disbelief and horror.

Anderson, the syringe hidden, reaches around him and injects the needle into his thick neck. It happens so quickly, Cross can't react. With the noise and chaos along with his adrenaline and excessive weight, Davenport doesn't feel anything. As he releases her from the hug, Anderson whispers in his ear and then turns around and walks away. His lips read 'ok'.

Cross first looks at Davenport, who is none the wiser as he returns to the platform, and then at Anderson, who is now coming in his direction and is about to walk right past him.

"Chara, what a surprise. Don't say a word and follow me," he says in the Irish accent.

Anderson's mouth opens but nothing comes out. Cross grabs her arm and moves swiftly back through the crowd, looking for the exit.

They reach the top of the escalator, and he sees Jennings.

He shouts. "Nick, we are over here."

Jennings looks and strides over. They then head through the hotel, through the bar and out to the other side.

"We need to get out of here, and fast," Cross says.

Jennings waves another agent over and has a brief discussion.

"Quickly, follow me," the agent says as he runs over to parked security vehicles. He climbs into one and Jennings gestures Anderson and Cross to follow. Within minutes they are through security and out into the city streets, away from the mayhem. Jennings must have told him where, because he drives over in their hotel's direction and eventually pulls up outside the rear entrance.

"Thanks, Agent Nichols."

All three climb out and run into the hotel. Once inside the elevator, Jennings punches the floor number. Now in the suite's relative safety, Cross moves Anderson over to a couch and gently pushes her to sit.

"What the fuck is going on, Florence?"

She is stunned and doesn't know how to answer. She looks scared and frightened. The strong woman controlling all these powerful men is fragile, powerless and shaking.

Cross sees her fragility and isn't surprised. Being dragged away by a stranger and then pushed into a hotel room must have brought back some dreadful memories. The lack of protest meant it is something she is used to. He sees tears so takes out a handkerchief and passes it to her.

"Thank you."

He quickly needs to reassure her but discards his rendition of an Irish accent. "You are safe here. This is Nick Jennings from MI6, and I cannot tell you who I am. Not yet."

She looks at him and his heart breaks. Her eyes are wide and yet so angelic. She looks like a very damaged, scared child, which is what society created. Some damaged people try to appear strong on the outside, whilst their insides have been shredded to pieces.

"I knew you weren't MP Horseman, despite me researching him. The fictitious character you had created was fantastic. However, a member of Parliament doesn't behave the way you do. Politicians are mostly arseholes."

"What did you do with Davenport, Florence? I saw you. What was it?"

"He will experience a heart attack tonight, after the election is over. Authorities will believe it is from the shock of losing."

Cross looks at Jennings and walks him over to the kitchen.

In a whispered tone, "Now I'm speechless."

"You told me she is beautiful. I can see why the elites fall for her. You didn't tell me she is smart, though. You failed to pass on that tidbit of valuable information."

"I thought it was implied, but we need to get her out of here, before Davenport has his premature heart attack."

"What's your next plan."

"France."

"Take her with you."

"I wasn't leaving tonight."

"Well, now you are."

Cross walks back to the sofa.

"Where are you staying?"

"Davenport put me in a room in Mayfair. We planned on meeting up tonight, but not after I kept seeing the results change. He is an arsehole at the best of times."

"Who put you up to this caper?"

"My own volition. My life is over, as I know it."

"Did Leslie tell you about the compound in the Pyrenees no longer existing?"

Anderson is silent. The shocked expression tells Cross all he needs to know.

"Who are you?" she asks.

"Did you wear a watch the last time you went to Spain?"

"I did but obviously removed it before I got off the plane. I knew they had searched my room when I was in Wu's parlour that night. I used markers."

Cross smiles at this comment. Damn, she is an intelligent lady.

"You are very clever. I guess you must be to have survived this long. The compound in the mountains was abandoned."

She now looks surprised. "You evidently know I was controlled and told what to do. I have no life." Her eyes are watering. "Wu took me in and treated me better than any man ever has. Once I was trapped, everything radically changed. I was just a pawn after that and used at will." The volume of water in the tear drops break the surface tension and she starts crying.

"Does Wu know you are in London?"

Through the tears, "No, but he must suspect I am."

Jesus, he was right about all this but can't handle the emotions. Cross heads for the bathroom before he too breaks down.

Jennings has been listening to all this, numb struck. He goes and sits himself next to her.

"The man who just saved you is one of the most amazing men in the world. You can't even begin to imagine what I have seen him accomplish and recover from, Florence."

Her head turns and her eyes follow Cross just as he closes the bathroom door.

"See the laceration on his face?"

"Yes, of course."

"Our hotel was bombed in Latvia. Whatever is going on he wants it to end. This man is here to help you. We all are. We all want to end this."

Anderson shifts on the sofa cushions and calms down. Her tears dry.

"How did you know I was there?"

"We didn't. No one told us. We had our own reasons for being there."

"Davenport was predicted to win by a large margin. I was there in anticipation of that."

"Nah, we predicted him to lose."

"How can you predict that, Nick?"

He just smiles. "I could tell you, but then would have to bury you afterwards."

He gets up and locates the remote, then turns on the TV. Splashed across the news is the projected capitulation of Davenport and his support.

"See, I told you. We are not here to play games, Ms. Anderson."

Wu is walking around the war room in a hysterical state. He is beyond control. Handcock had seen his fury, but not at this level. He had heard stories so was critical of avoiding death.

"What went wrong?"

"No one has seen anything like this before," trying to calm him down. It doesn't work. "Pundits, polls, peer reviews, political experts and broadcasters all said the same thing. No one predicted the submission of Davenport's support."

The news is displayed on a large screen TV hanging on a wall in the war room. It is evident to everyone in there that something went wrong. Their man, Davenport, is now ten percent behind Carlisle.

"Something happened here."

"I'll go find out," Handcock replies, heading for the door to save his life.

63

Anderson Escapes London

Cross' phone rings, so he picks it up.

"Where are you?"

"Heading to Paris, David."

"This hour?"

"I have Florence with me."

"She was in London? Probably to meet Davenport."

"Yes, but those plans got curtailed and we had to move her."

There is silence on the other end.

Cross took Anderson to retrieve her possessions from the hotel since they didn't want to leave material evidence. Jennings had the hotel records purged so now nothing exists, and then drove them both to an airport where the Dassault was parked.

Cross continues. "There is a rally in Paris for Marchant tomorrow morning, presumably in support of Davenport. Who knows what he is going to say after tonight?"

"Davenport hasn't conceded defeat and yielded the election to Carlisle yet."

"Yes, well, he's a moronic puppet."

"Update me when you have one."

Cross stares at Anderson sitting across from him. She has her eyes shut and is trying to rest. He cannot imagine what her life has been like.

He retrieves his laptop and plugs in one of the thumb drives from Wu's desk. "I'm missing something." He has been told talking to one's self is the first sign one needs help.

He looks through the pictures to see what he is missing. As he stares into the portrait of Robertson, what is he overlooking? Cross copies the file and inserts it into software Wilson had provided in Vancouver. He looks in the background and there is a lake of some sort behind her. On the other side of that is a small structure. He expands the region and focuses on that area. The software transforms blurred images into 4K resolution. Now Cross can see the lake and a small cottage at the foot of some snow-capped mountains.

He transfers that image to a layered product within the software package and hits 'enter'. A few minutes later it spits out a location.

Cross is momentarily shocked. "Wow."

He types the address into his search engine and away it goes, chugging through algorithms and programs. Finally, the address comes up with pictures of the property.

The location is hidden, and remote. The images are older and of poorer quality, but the small cottage is exactly that. However, the land boasts a large historical castle, and an old runway resides at the side.

He reads the text and finds the runway was used by the military during the second world war.

"Interesting."

He then goes researching the history of ownership and stares at the document that opens in front of him. The last five hundred years have only seen one owner: Robertson.

Anderson is stirring in front of him, so he closes the laptop. He has seen enough, but he looks at her and wonders if she really knows who she is.

"Where are we heading?"

"The outskirts of Paris. Leslie will arrange your transportation back to Washington as soon as she can. Likely in the morning."

"You are Daniel Cross?"

This surprises him but it took her long enough to figure it out.

"I'm not at liberty to reveal my identity since it is deemed inconsequential for you to know. It could also get you killed."

She marginally laughs. "That boat has sailed, my friend. Wu signed the petition months ago and trust me, my name is on that list."

"I'm MP Michael Horseman."

She smiles. "Yeah, ok. Whatever."

The Dassault lands and taxis to a parking area. As the cabin door is opened and dropped, the familiar face at the bottom of the stairs brings comfort to Cross.

"Hello, Michael. Welcome back," as they hug.

"Madelaine, this is Laura Inglewood. Laura, this is Madelaine Couton."

"Nice to meet you, Laura. You were correct. She is stunning and ideal for France's fashion world."

This releases some tension and anxiety built up in Anderson's complexion. She smiles. "Nice to meet you too, Madelaine."

As they walk towards the vehicle, Cross turns to Anderson. "See, I told you I am Michael," and grins.

They get dropped off at a ground-floor apartment within the inner city. Cross has no idea where, yet, but can see the Eiffel Tower lit up is close.

"Get some rest. I will call you around seven."

"Thanks."

They both watch as Couton disappears into Paris' post-midnight chaos.

Cross follows Anderson into the small apartment and bolts for the TV. He goes searching for BBC International and finds it. The headline banner along the bottom of the screen is announcing the sudden death of Davenport so he turns up the volume.

"…information is sketchy and slowly coming in, but we are being cautionary as some reports are indicating a heart attack or cardiac arrest. In any event, the downfall and sudden death of a rising star, in what polling numbers had suggested would be the UK's next prime minister, is heart breaking and shocking. The nation is in mourning once again."

The screen now pans to cameras outside of Park Lane. A huge crowd is forming at the park across the road. People are crying, holding flowers, praying, hugging each other.

"They had no idea the repercussions their votes would have caused. Incidentally, how did you get the syringe through security?"

"I was exempt as Davenport's invited special guest. If that hadn't have worked, I'm diabetic so need to syringe insulin for survival."

"Are you?"

"No." She smiles and stares at him. "I have met you before." She ponders for a few seconds. "I bumped into you at another Davenport event, interestingly enough at the same hotel."

Cross smiles. "No, you didn't."

"Hey. Ok, I will give it a rest, Michael."

"We should sleep since I have work to do in a few hours."

"Marchant is another Deep State candidate, paid for by Wu."

He turns and looks at her. "We know. Were you delivering more cash for Davenport?"

"Yes."

He sighs. "I'm sick of these arseholes. They are everywhere."

"Indeed."

"We know Marchant is part of Wu's organisation. He is another trust-fund billionaire who likely killed his father to get access to it."

"He didn't, but Wu did. Marchant just helped clean it up and keep it away from the media."

"You mean he called Abrams to do that?"

"You really know how this works, don't you?"

Cross walks over and opens the sofa-bed.

"You can use the bathroom first and I will sleep on the floor. All this needs to end."

After showering, Anderson exits the bathroom in a black bra and matching lace panties.

"I wasn't prepared, and this is all I have, sorry."

Cross looks, then grabs a t-shirt from his bag. "Sure it is, honey, but here," tossing it over, smiling at her.

64

France Plucked
from Dystopia

"Good morning, Florence. I have made some coffee."

"Don't you sleep?" as she walks over in the t-shirt and sits at the kitchen counter.

"Not very often." Cross hands her a mug of coffee. "I don't know how you take it."

"Leslie can't get me out of here until later today."

That doesn't sound right. "You can stay here, and I will pick you up when I'm finished."

They are both dressed when there is a knock at the door. One of Couton's liberator friends is there so Cross picks up his bag and exits. Anderson waits a few seconds, until she hears the car depart, and then she exits and hails the cab she had arranged earlier.

Cross is now set up on a roof, and away from the gathering crowd. Marchant evidently has a huge following until he remembers what Couton had said: it is all paid for. Cross is unaware of someone else up there monitoring his position.

He removes the marksman's rifle from his bag and puts it

together. After inserting the loaded magazine, the last thing he installs is the scope.

Adjacent to the Eiffel Tower, but on the north side of the Seine River, is Avenue de New York. Next to that is a large park. Rue le Tasse runs along one side of it and a platform has been erected for Marchant's campaign event. Parts of the park are fenced off to restrict crowd size and assist safety measures. The road is also partially cordoned off to facilitate access to the stage. Police and security seem everywhere, despite assurances, observes Cross.

The assembly, now formidable in scope and size, is loud and boisterous. Some are holding placards and signs, whilst others have posters or wearing sweatshirts with a picture of Marchant printed on.

Couton had set this up. It was purposely void of security in specific areas. The scenic viewing post on Rue le Tasse was closed to the public. He is alone and waiting.

More than half an hour passes before a motorcade approaches from the direction of Rue Benjamin Franklin. The procession consists of six police motorcycles and four limousines.

"These egotistical peasants."

It grinds to a stop slowly, and he watches as Marchant climbs out, surrounded by his men who are all armed.

As he is preparing, he feels pain as a muted shot rings out.

"What the f…"

Another shot hits the chimney stack he is partially hiding behind. He gropes to find where he has been hit. He feels blood at the side of his stomach area, but the penetration appears superficial.

Marchant is walking toward the stage.

Cross hears more shots, but from a different weapon. The noise from the crowd is distracting the events up on a Parisienne rooftop.

He turns around.

"Get Marchant, quickly, and let's get out of here."

Cross is looking at Anderson but doesn't have time to say anything. He rotates, looks through the scope, aims and fires twice. His bullets penetrate the heart and Marchant keels over.

"Let's go," she yells.

Cross lifts himself up and hauls across the rooftop to the other side. One climbing rope had been suspended along the side of the building. Anderson takes it first and rappels down, with Cross close behind her. At the bottom is a small plumbing van Couton had arranged. They jump in the back as it rapidly departs for the private airport. Interesting choice, thinks Cross, since he did re-arrange Marchant's internal plumbing.

"You saved my life."

Anderson is looking at his wound and it isn't superficial. Bullets into this area of the body can lead to dangerous, sometimes fatal, complications. She has the left hand holding a cloth to stop it bleeding.

"Don't say anything. Just lay back and breath properly."

The front passenger is Couton. She is monitoring two cars way behind that appear to be following them. She quietly instructs the driver to take evasive action through old, narrow side streets and residential complexes. She knows where she is taking them, having alerted her people already, as an added contingency.

"Is your plane ready, Daniel?"

"Yes. I instructed the pilot to have the engines primed and be ready for us at the end of the runway."

"Good. We are going to take diversionary measures, so hold on."

The van veers onto a major highway northeast of downtown Paris and heads in an alternate direction. Cross looks out and they are approaching what he would perceive as a vast questionable neighbourhood.

"You do know what you are doing, Madelaine?" He chuckles a little, to remove the edge off the question.

She turns and looks at him. "I got this."

The vehicle turns off, enters a huge complex and slows down. Cross doesn't understand what is happening because he isn't in control anymore.

Couton is aware that the two cars behind have promptly caught up. They are perhaps half a block distance and edging closer when she hits her phone.

"Go."

Cross hears gunfire and explosions behind them, so he sits upright absorbing the pain and turns around. Out of the rear window he observes locals running toward two black Citroens with guns blazing, some tossing home-made missiles and Molotov cocktails. The occupants have no chance.

Couton turns to the driver. "We need to get out of here."

The driver picks up speed as they now make considerable progress out of Paris.

Cross is familiar as they reach the private airstrip. Once their van pulls in, he sees the Dassault sitting at the end of the runway. The van pulls up at the bottom of the stairs.

Anderson climbs out and helps Cross scamper to his feet. They shake hands with Couton, thank the driver before climbing onto the plane. Cross is so relieved when he hears the engines hit full throttle as the aircraft careens down the runway and vacates French real estate.

Anderson is attending to the wound as they climb away.

"You need help. Where are we heading?"

"I'm hoping Washington, DC."

"No way. Sorry, I'm not allowing that, Daniel."

"We need to escape France."

Cross asks for his phone and she hands it to him.

"Nick, job done but I require medical assistance before embarking on the next phase in the US."

He hesitates for a few seconds. "Hold on."

Cross hears him conversing with someone in the background.

"Daniel?"

"Yes, still here."

"Head to Ireland. I will text the airport location and the person who will meet you there."

"Ok."

"We saw the news here. Marchant was shot twice in the abdomen. Good job."

"Someone knew. They were on the roof waiting for me, but Florence killed him. We also had two cars follow us as we departed Paris, but Madelaine dealt with them. Someone knows."

"We knew this day would come."

"Yes, I can only hide my death for so long."

"But Florence saved your life?"

"Yes."

"Damn, another person you will have to thank." He chuckles, trying to lighten things up. "Call me from Ireland."

65

Millimeters from Death

Handcock can't hide anymore. He is seeing the demise of all they have been working for right in front of his eyes. He had been observing the cataclysmic turn of events in his living quarters, too scared to venture back into the war room.

He had arranged Wu's superior marksmen to be prepared in Paris, and now one of them is dead. Ten more hand-picked people dead in what looks like a prepared ambush. A security video he had reviewed privately a few days ago showed Cross at Davenport's event. He wasn't one hundred percent sure it was him except the features looked awfully similar. A facial scar revealed recent activity of some sort. He had taken on the responsibility of killing him and convinced Wu Cross' death was achieved. He was dead. He saw it with his own eyes.

Handcock asked their people in France to be aware of a possible attempt on Marchant's life and they had arranged surveillance. He isn't sure how to explain all these events.

But one thing is clear, when someone controls with such venomous authority and diminutive regard for those beneath them, cracks will eventually start appearing.

Handcock walks into the war room, but Wu doesn't wait for an explanation. He is beyond livid.

"Take him to the basement," pointing to two security personnel who have been waiting. "I will deal with him later."

Handcock is unceremoniously marched away and admonished to the darkest depths of Wu's citadel, conveniently eliminated for other people's wretched failings.

On the large TV screen is the news of Davenport and Marchant's deaths. That isn't irritating him the most. BBC International has been cutting into the feed of mass gatherings with a narrative broadcast in English by Gabrys at TV5, a channel they are now calling an affiliate.

"The untimely deaths of Davenport and Marchant are fueling rumours they were both representing Deep State. This is something our intelligence services have been working on for a significant amount of time. Had they been elected, Intelligence believes they would have been complicit in forming a network known as the New World Order. Control of people and relinquishment of their assets are apparently paramount in achieving this order. The flaw in their rationale is evident when one realises a majority of the planet wants nothing to do with the West's control. The entitled and privileged elites, deafened by arrogance and blinded by incompetence, don't see it though." Gabrys is fluent in the presentation given to her by MI6.

Wu's heard enough and turns around yelling at no one in particular. "Find me Lutkus," and storms out of the room, as he sees their sphere of influence diminishing.

Cross is in Cork being attended to by a physician. He calls Jennings.

"I'm lucky, yet again. I think I'm beyond nine lives at this point."

"What did they find?"

"The bullet missed a major organ by millimetres."

"Brilliant news, my friend. When will they release you?"

"They are sending me over to a psychiatric ward."

Jennings wasn't expecting that and bursts into hysterics. "It's the medication, right?"

"Possibly, but I didn't want full anesthetic so requested a local one. We depart shortly."

"You are insane."

"Utterly."

"I need to follow up with Ozolins and Rostov. I will get back to you. Safe flight."

Cross messages Moore Jr. next.

'Graeme, I need recent satellite imagery of this location,' and proceeds to forward an address.

'I know roughly where that is, but it will take some time for a satellite to be in the area. It is out in the nether regions, mate, miles from anywhere.'

Cross explains his request in brief texts.

'Jesus.'

'Something like that.'

Before he succumbs to the pain medication, Cross calls Granfield.

"David, Marchant is dead."

"We heard that at CIA and a huge cheer hit the control and conference rooms. Also, Davenport had a heart attack last night, we are being told, but await official word."

"Sounds accurate."

"You know already?" Sounding more surprised than he should be. "How are you doing?"

"I'm in Cork being stitched up."

"What?" Sounding worried now.

"I suspect Wu knows I remain in the land of the living. A sniper waited for me on a Parisienne rooftop, and we were followed escaping Paris. They were expecting me."

"Or expecting someone, not necessarily you, Daniel. Are you ok?"

Cross hadn't thought of that. "That makes this better. It was millimetres away from the bullet causing serious organ damage."

"How is Florence?"

"She saved my life."

"You saved hers too." Always the quintessential pragmatic leader, Cross thinks. "Get back to Washington, DC as soon as you can. We are ready here."

"We need to finish what we started. I will have an update on Wu, but not over the phone. I know we are secure, but so close to ending this."

"Prepare to land in Langley. I don't see a requirement to continue with this charade."

Two hours from the US coastline and Cross is coming out of his pharmaceutical-induced stew. Or trying to. Electing local anesthesia created protestations which he brushed aside. He can't afford to be out of commission. Anderson had brought him a coffee as he sat up, facing her.

"Thank you." He tries to stretch. "God, it hurts."

"You are one crazy mother."

He grins. "I have absorbed worse compliments."

"I saw other scares on your body. Some of those are recent."

"How come you didn't recognise who I am?" in a surprised tone. "Wu has Leslie and me on hit lists with bounty hunters around the galaxy given shoot-to-kill orders."

"I admit, when I first bumped into you, there was this air about you but the makeup on Horseman was Hollywood quality."

"When money is no object. It worked too."

"Of course it did. How did you stage your deaths?"

"That's the fascinating part: we used Wu's own robots."

Anderson just stares for a few minutes, drinking her own coffee. Cross looks at her. Even after her military-trained intervention, and taking care of him, she sits there radiating this warm effervescent glow.

"You don't know where Wu operates from, do you?" he theatrically asks, knowing the answer.

"No, Daniel. He is very reclusive but always had me travel to the Pyrenees retreat. However, I did first meet him in Taiwan, and he was pissed when you blew up his island."

Cross smiles at her. "I can't imagine the life you have lived, Florence. Your mother leaving you at an orphanage is despicable."

"We all have our crosses to bear, my friend. No life is perfect, even for those fed from birth with silver spoons. It isn't that we go through abhorrent experiences, but how we deal with them. Some can. Some can't."

The picture of her after the shower enters his mind, but quickly wipes that image clean.

"Briar and Hislop are disgusting. Why would Wu select people of that low quality?"

"I understand there wasn't a choice. I don't fully know the reasons," he thinks she does, "but politics can sometimes tie one's hands."

Cross relaxes for a while before calling Jennings.

"I was informed you got fixed."

"Thanks for arranging that so quickly. Yes, I'm fixed so no more children." He laughs heartily.

"Good for the planet I suspect," and snickers. "You are on your way to Langley; I was quietly informed?"

"We are done with the pretense of me being dead. I'm also

waiting for information from Graeme, but I may have found Wu's homebase."

He goes into details of what he extracted from a more methodical and thorough examination of photographs removed off Wu's thumb drive.

"That's brilliant. We will need to organise a military response if that is the case."

"Yes, absolutely."

"Keep me posted."

"How are the Baltics doing?"

"We must predict a response from Wu after the unprecedented losses in Britain and France. He will see his new world order dying right in front of him. No way he will let it go."

"I agree with you. My thought is he will push to energise Lithuania into a war with Russia. Nothing good will come from that and gets the world fighting, but a war with NATO isn't productive for anyone's gain. If Wu is going down, he will want to drag everyone along with him."

"His compound needs to be destroyed, with him inside the perimeter."

"As soon as Graeme endorses what I have asked him to do, I will get back to you."

"Ok. Good luck with the world's scumbags in Washington, DC."

"They are everywhere, mate."

66

On the Brink

Cross hasn't been to Granfield's office in months. He told himself back then he didn't want to see it again, but he was wrong. They are standing next to windows that look out onto part of the main campus. Five floors up from the concrete pads encircling a large, square manicured garden, Cross can see more multi-storey structures enclosing two other sides of the courtyard and perpendicular to each other. The CIA complex is massive.

"I have missed this place," as they shake hands and hug. Cross winces in pain but hides it.

"This is Florence Anderson, David."

"The infamous Ms. Anderson." They exchange pleasantries and shake hands.

Cross doesn't want to open about Wu's new location yet for two reasons. The first being he doesn't have confirmation and the second is the presence of Anderson. It isn't the lack of trust but the fact she is still technically masquerading as a double agent.

"Good work, both of you. The deaths of Davenport and Marchant are compelling."

"Thank you," Cross answers.

"Davenport's death was a heart attack, likely induced by the election loss, which he hadn't anticipated. He was also a big man, which never helps."

Cross turns to Anderson and smiles. He doubts the British government will push for an autopsy report being publicly filed, even if Davenport supporters demand one.

"It happens."

"Florence, sorry you had to experience such behaviour the last time you met our illustrious Briar. Thanks also for rescuing Dr. Cross."

"Involving me is new but I had a little inkling about this child trafficking ring for some time. He got creepier as the Speaker of the House seat was coming up for a vote. Once he was confirmed, things dived even lower. He behaves as if he has impunity. It's as if he doesn't expect to be caught."

Granfield looks at Cross, raises his eyebrows, and then returns his gaze back on Anderson.

"That's an interesting point because we came to the same conclusion. But then again, this is how all these cream puffs behave."

After more discussions, an interruption occurs when Taylor walks into the room. Cross stands as she bounds over to hug him. This time he can't hide the discomfort.

"Sorry, Daniel," looking apologetic. "I'm so happy to see you. You look good despite another attempt on your life."

"Thank you. Florence saved me."

"That's because she didn't know who you are." Everyone laughs.

"Good to see you, Leslie."

"You too, David. Let me take Florence away to prepare. She needs to clean up anyway after the travels. We will convene later for dinner, right?"

"Yes. Nice to meet you, Florence." Granfield is as gracious as ever. "We will meet and talk over dinner."

Taylor departs with Anderson.

"Poor girl. I can't envisage what life she has lived. But then again, we all make our own choices."

"All these peasants have used her."

As he says that, his phone starts actively pinging. He looks down and sees messages with links from Moore Jr.

"David, please bear with me. I need to look at these."

"I will get some coffee whilst you do that." He departs the room.

Cross clicks on cloud links and opens files hosting pictures. He scans through the jpeg files and finds an interesting one. The landing strip next to the castle has been converted to a taxiway and a new parallel runway had been added to accommodate the jet age. Off to the side is a large aircraft hangar that appears to be housing corporate jets, partially viewed through windows high up the structure. There is a helicopter tail showing through hangar doors half-way open. The roof has moss and grass installed as camouflage. In another file are two Boeing Max 8 aircraft parked on holding pads off the taxiway. They have simple colour schemes of red, light blue and black striping running along the side that then fan out on the tail, painted onto white airframes.

"This must be it."

His heart is pounding which is affecting his recent surgical procedure. He bends over in excruciating pain.

As he does so, Granfield walks in, places the mugs on his desk and immediately picks up the phone.

"I need medical help in here please, Angela."

"I'm ok."

"It is evident you aren't."

"I just need to slow my heart rate. Take a look at these."

He hands Granfield the phone so that he can flick through the pictures.

"What am I looking at?"

"What I firmly believe to be Wu's new digs."

"You are kidding?"

"I wish I was."

He explains how he found them and how he extracted the data.

"This is clearly going to require a military intervention."

"Agree, yes," answers Cross, just as a doctor walks in.

"Take him to the medical centre, Doctor." He turns and looks at Cross. "Take care of yourself, and then let's continue this discussion. Dinner is secondary to your medical requirements."

Cross loves this man.

Cross is laying on a medical bed somewhere within CIA headquarters. He has just been administered drugs after his wound was re-opened. His eyes want to close but he prefers to digest the pictures Moore Jr. has sent.

The property's satellite images show a fenced-off compound with active-duty military and security personnel. The security looks to escalate as the images migrate toward the castle. Barracks have been constructed to house those personnel, outside the castle's perimeter.

The construction is so old, a moat exists encircling the walls. Access is through a main gate that had been modernised beyond the drawbridge-era centuries ago. On one side of the area, there are mountains in the background.

Cross did his research, and the property is designated historical in its country and, as such, is found on some National Heritage List. He speculates bombing the shit out of it might upset some people.

He transfers the images as before so that he can expand, manipulate and process. He zooms in on one particular area of interest. There is a small bunker, but he can just make out a large door of some sort. Its location is close to the lake and wonders if this is an escape route. He traces back toward the castle and finds what could be conceived as ventilation shafts for a possible tunnel.

A few hours of recuperation have aided his immediate need for recovery. At least it is elevated to a level of tolerance, but beyond that there is no allotted time for additional convalescence.

Granfield is driving them to meet the two ladies for dinner in Georgetown, just across the Potomac River. This way they can dress down and mingle with students.

An hour into dinner and Cross is relaxed. He knows best not to mix drugs and alcohol but what the hell. A locally brewed blonde ale is on tap, so what choice was there? Also, alcohol is the universal lubricant for justice.

Sitting at the table in the quiet corner of a pub, the four are engrossed in conversation about what is next.

"Briar's a pig," announces Anderson. "He is married with children. I mean it is disgusting."

Granfield must be careful here. She was on Wu's payroll and coercing these individuals as they climbed the political fulcrum. Anderson was part of Deep State because she was helping them build the framework. Taylor got her to switch, but he's comforted somewhat in believing she wanted no part of the political structure. In the end she was just another of Wu's mules he would eventually slaughter. She brought damming material evidence to the table involving Briar and Hislop. He can't understate her involvement in testimony-gathering but the whole subject makes him want to throw up.

"What do you know about this massive trafficking consortium?" Granfield asks.

"I became aware of it as I picked up information here and there. We would meet in luxurious five-star hotels most of the time. But, for reasons I soon became aware, he chose these low-class neighbourhoods on occasion. I learnt then that they use the motels for trafficking kids, so he was comfortable in the area. He knew people and he knew who operated the properties. They were all paid off.

"I heard stories of people being killed and dumped if they spoke out of turn, but I had no supporting evidence. It was all hearsay. They were paid hush money, is my recollection. Paid to keep quiet. Unfortunately, a select few couldn't keep their mouths shut apparently, not that I blame them."

"The FBI has gathered significant data and has a massive file. These kids come from all over the world and are trafficked through international hubs," Granfield adds, in disgust. This whole vile conversation is making him nauseated. "Are there others at the Capitol involved?"

"They aren't just political figures, David. This covers Hollywood, billionaires, entrepreneurs, owners of fortune five hundred companies. It is rampant. I have seen them at their parties, and you cannot even begin to imagine what goes on." She turns away in disgust, and partly because of her involvement in such reprehensible affairs.

Granfield knows it and they are ready to crash this whole three-dimensional board game. He wants to see it demolished with the people involved still inside. Deep State, had they been in control, would have set up safehouses around the world just for the sexual exploitation of children.

It is a subject even Cross wants to change.

"How was moving to New York as a teenager? It's a very intimidating place for someone so young."

"I found my feet there. You either sink or swim, Daniel. I know you tried to change subjects but the model agency I signed up with was also an escort agency for underage kids, as it turned out. I didn't even know those existed." She sits back in her chair but looks saddened.

"I did try to change the subject." Cross sighs and needs to rest. Taylor sees his revulsion and discomfort so jumps in, and she is done talking about it also.

"We are all set to go tomorrow evening?" she asks, looking at Anderson.

"Yes. Briar wants to meet around nine. I know already what he wants because it is another seedy motel in a crappy part of town."

"We will be ready," Grandfield assures them. "Enough of this despicable shit. We have law enforcement people lined up around the world and Briar will be the first to fall."

It is late evening and Cross is in a Langley hotel ready to collapse, when Couton calls.

"Michael, are you ok? You didn't look too good when you departed France."

"Madelaine, what a pleasant surprise. Sorry, I should have messaged, but we stopped in Cork, Ireland so I could get medical attention. It was a close call."

"Someone was expecting you. We found a dead body on the roof."

He hesitates first, but then goes for it. "Ms. Couton, my real name is Daniel Cross."

There is silence on the other end. He doesn't even hear anyone breathing.

"Hello."

"I knew it. No way you are a member of Parliament. Even when I met you in Monte Carlo, you had this manner about you that isn't that of a politician."

"I'm not sure what that means."

"You saved my life that night, Daniel." She hesitates. "You blew up those yachts, didn't you?" He can feel her emotion as she is almost in tears.

"I can't be seen condoning violence and approving of murder."

He hears her shift gears and starts giggling.

"Now you sound like a politician." They are laughing and Cross needed that. "Thank you from all of France for your assistance. The people had no idea what Philippe Marchant was about. They thought he was going to be their hero, their white knight. A news anchor, Janina Gabrys if I remember, is presenting a completely different narrative. She is from Lithuania's TV5 but, suddenly, the local channels are calling TV5 an affiliate. They are buying her story."

"They should since MI6 is feeding her the script. It is Janina Gabrys, and I helped her escape Vilnius. She is broadcasting out of England."

Silence again on the other end, but not for long.

"You are an enigma, Daniel, and I am lost for words. On one of her broadcasts, she mentioned something about her, and her children being rescued from Deep State's grasp."

"That is a delicate way of describing her ordeal, but it was much worse than that. They were about to kill her." He settles down. "I never thanked you for your help. It was set up exceptionally well."

"The concession being your assassin. He was tossed in as an extra." She chuckles, aided by the consumption of alcohol Cross recognises.

"We can't plan for every unknown, but who was he?"

"They haven't identified him yet. We suspect someone associated with Marchant's security, but we simply don't know. They couldn't tell from his accent." She is laughing again, more for relief than humour. "Our French citizens had no idea how close they were to dystopia."

"Let me know when his accent can be identified," and joins in the laughter.

"When you return to France, call me."

"I assassinated a political figure on foreign soil. Not sure they will let me back into your country."

She laughs. "You are a funny man, and I will make sure they do, honey. By the way, send over Ms. Inglewood. She is absolute perfection and looks like someone from the forties. I have lined up work already and you can pose in briefs next to her." They both start laughing again. "No, seriously," through the laughter.

"Thanks. I needed that."

She feels his exasperation and pain. "I sense this isn't over for you, my friend. Please be safe out there and I will be praying for you." She sends him a kiss through the phone.

67

Deep State's Depraved Indifference

Anderson is in the motel room, and everything is set up. Granfield's people are spread out, not knowing where Briar's indiscretions will take them this time, if anywhere.

Taylor is in the room next door monitoring. Cross is somewhere, no one really knows where yet. He requested obscurity.

Daylight had disappeared hours ago and the clock ticks ever closer to nine. It is very chilly, and the streetlamps shine through the falling persistent rain.

Right on time, a limousine pulls up in the hotel parking lot. Two agents step out and one opens the door for Briar. The obese figure exits the stretched automobile holding an umbrella and walks up the motel's external metal staircase. His agents follow.

Anderson hears the door knock so she ventures over and opens it. In steps Briar.

"Hello, Florence." He hugs and kisses her.

"Lovely to see you, Jason." She's reciprocal with the insincere passion.

"My sources tell me you were at Davenport's event in London.

How was it?"

This sends chills down her spine. Who else did they see her with?

Granfield can hear the conversation and his nervousness climbs a notch. He picks up his walkie-talkie. "Get ready."

She takes a risk. "Your sources were wrong. I'm here only for you."

Anderson is playing it close to her chest and Briar could be lying, just to push buttons. Or he simply stopped caring.

"You brought my money?" or money is all he likely cares about.

"Yes." She picks up a bag and drops it on the bed.

"Good. The deaths of Davenport and Marchant are unfortunate. It means my calendar has been brought forward." He walks over to the bed and opens the bag. "Excellent. We are going to play the same routine as before."

Just as he says that the agents enter the room through the door Anderson noticed he didn't shut properly.

"You know the routine. Here is the blindfold," as he hands it to her.

She puts it on and then walks outside holding onto one of the agents. Briar picks up his bag, escapes the room and follows them downstairs.

"Here we go," says Granfield.

As the limousine leaves, Taylor darts out of the room and into a waiting vehicle. Briar is unaware he is being tracked via satellite.

"The limousine is taking a different route," Taylor says through the two-way radio.

Cross is closely monitoring the satellite feed being sent to him, although the rain is impeding its quality. He is sure where they are heading so fires up his ignition and starts driving toward a derelict district close by.

Briar's limo turns into a small industrial complex that has been neglected for years. The two-storey building used to be small commercial condominiums, but racially motivated riots followed by fires forced the tenants to move out. It was ideal for what he wanted its intended use to be, so Briar paid the owner cash for it, with deeds recorded in some dead person's name.

The windows have been blacked out and secured with old iron bars welded to the structure. Someone rolls up the front entrance and the limo drives straight into the building.

He watches as the rollup door closes and then behind Cross is an instantaneous flurry of activity.

Granfield and Taylor arrive along with other CIA agents. Cross sees SWAT vans coming down the street and, from somewhere, FBI agents arrive with their insignia on the vests.

At the side of the rollup is an entrance. The SWAT members run over and when ready, they pound the metal door with a battering ram. Once the arsenal of screws and bolts overcome their ability to withstand the forces, the door collapses on the floor. Wearing bulletproof vests, helmets and body shields, the SWAT and FBI teams disappear into the building with guns pointing.

Cross sees someone rolling up the door, so he runs over to where Taylor joins him.

"This is Speaker of the House, the bastion of moral compass. He was elected to change the corrupt establishment, only we find out he is part of the decay," says Taylor.

"Only the best, right?"

They walk inside as swaths of handcuffed adults are being led outside. Cross looks around and is shocked. What appeared to be a derelict property externally doesn't visually portray that same image on the inside. It has been rebuilt and modernised with serious input of cash. He takes a quick gander upstairs and sees what appear to be private rooms on the second floor. Confirmation of this is verified when FBI agents start bringing down live bodies, half dressed. As he walks further in, he enters what he can only describe as a movie set. Cameras are on stands for filming. Floor-mounted studio lights are set facing a bed and there is even a director's chair. Off to the side is a bathroom and a partition to accommodate dressing room and makeup areas. Children of varying ethnicities and age groups are being rounded up by FBI agents and escorted out, some with blankets around them. Most are crying.

"What the hell did we walk into?"

"The child porn industry, Daniel."

"I want to throw up. Actually, to be more precise, I need to, not want to," and steps back outside.

Taylor acknowledges Anderson who is in tears, so she walks over. She is wearing the same clothes she exited the motel room in, and Taylor is relieved.

"Is this all over?" Anderson asks.

Taylor takes her in the arms and holds her tight. She then steps back.

"Are you ok?"

"I think this was it. Briar and Wu were done with me, so I was going to be filmed and exposed, then disposed of."

Cross walks back in with Granfield in tow and they witness Briar being handcuffed, so they walk over.

"Speaker of the House wasn't good enough for you?" Cross injects with conspicuous hostility.

"Daniel Cross. You only live twice, my friend."

Even being caught in the act whilst naked children are being rescued and covered with blankets, his arrogance is astounding. Cross does not live in that world, and he wants to punch his lights out. Fortunately, his head overrides his body's rudimentary desires.

"I wouldn't underestimate me, Speaker Briar. You should know that by now. By the way, I know who your Auntie is."

Briar's eyes light up. His demeanor changes and his knees almost buckle as his face turns white.

"Death of Davenport and Marchant were just the beginning. As you stand here, police enforcements around the world are rounding up your child-trafficking co-conspirators. Deep State is history."

Granfield joins the conversation. "Senator Hislop is here too, Daniel. There are two more House representatives: elected congressmen, for fuck's sake." He looks at Briar. "If I were head of the government's judicial branch for a day, who knows what I would do with you. You are exploiting the most vulnerable in our society." He is losing it and Cross places a hand on his shoulder. "Incidentally, you and your cohort Hislop will be charged with the murders of three House representatives too."

Cross has never seen Granfield so animated as four FBI personnel approach.

"Please take him away, before I get arrested for murder."

Taylor stops them before they leave and stares at Briar.

"We caught you in the act three times. When were you ever going to stop? I told you to wait for my call." She now glares at him harder. "You should have listened, you piece of shit."

The FBI folk dragged him away.

Cross and Granfield walk over to Taylor and Anderson.

"Are you ok, Florence?" asks Granfield.

"Yes, David. Thank you. This nightmare is over for me, but not for you." Granfield hugs her.

"Leslie will take care of you. She was authorised to promise you immunity. I stand by my word. Thank you for helping put an end to this irreverent sickness."

Cross hugs Anderson. "Sorry you went through this. Now it ends. Believe every word David just told you. He's a good man."

Anderson just stares at him through red eyes.

68

Falling Chess Pieces

Cross escaped the circus surrounding the breakup of Briar's criminal enterprise. He needed to avoid media cameras so headed back to his hotel in Langley. He had been lying on the bed trying to get medical rest and well-deserved shuteye.

His phone buzzing disturbs his quiescent mental state as he is dreaming of being back in Sadeghi's arms again. The words 'dammit' escape his mouth just after he opens the call.

"Sorry, Daniel."

"My timing was all wrong, mate, and I spilt a glass of water reaching for the phone. I didn't even see who is calling."

"Well done last night."

Jennings realises Cross is on the precipice of a mental and physical breakdown. No human mind and body can endure this much psychological turmoil and not be affected. He just can't imagine what his head is regurgitating and spitting out.

"I hope I never see anything like that again. My stomach couldn't handle what I saw."

"It is all over the news this morning. Law enforcement around the world are rounding up vast numbers of people, including famous ones. It is pure unadulterated insanity."

"Good. I have an idea what to do with them."

"The gender lines aren't barriers either. This is mammoth. Well done, mate."

"I am part of a team, Nick. We are all working for the same end game." Attempting to deflect praise he thinks others are more worthy of. However, he understands why Jennings is doing the dance.

"The Kremlin targeted a few mobile launch pads last night near the Belarus border. Lutkus' focus has changed. His target is to stoke animosity with Belarus to purposely involve Russia."

"Good luck with that."

"When are you coming back here?"

"Give me a day to recover. My body needs rest."

"Of course it does. We need to plan for Wu's compound."

"I know. I have ideas about that too."

"I thought you would. Well done. Just message when you are coming."

"Probably day after tomorrow, with the time difference."

Cross falls back to sleep but two hours later his phone is active again.

"Good morning. Tremendous achievement last night."

"Yes, David. Brilliant stuff."

"How are you feeling? I saw you didn't seem to enjoy your dinner last night."

"Oh, God. I couldn't keep it down and I can't purge the images. How could they swirl around and indulge in such despicable behaviour?"

"We will never know that answer. I will pick you up for breakfast and then I have something special for you."

"Ok. Can you give me a few hours?"

After they are done eating and going over the implications of last night's events in more detail, Granfield takes Cross over the Potomac River and into downtown Washington, DC. Something has changed because now they are being driven and have Secret Service agents accompanying them in convoy.

Cross is wondering where they are heading until they approach the Washington Monument. He turns to face Granfield.

"No. Really?"

They are released at the security gate and enter the compound at 1600 Pennsylvania Avenue. Cross can't believe what he is seeing.

"The President wishes to see you before embarking on our next venture."

They are met outside the White House by more Secret Service agents and other security personnel. Granfield knows where he is going so Cross lets him lead, even though they are chaperoned. They are taken over to the Executive Office in the West Wing. They enter and head down a hallway, up some steps, along another hall, where they are eventually escorted into the Oval Office.

Behind the famous grand desk sits President Walkman. Upon entry, he immediately stands up and walks around wearing a beaming smile. He looks presidential and is impeccably dressed.

"Dr. Cross, thank you for accepting my invitation."

Cross looks over at Granfield, and then returns his focus.

"Thank you, President Walkman. It's an honour."

"No, Dr. Cross." He stops himself. "May I be permitted to call you Daniel?"

Cross is momentarily humbled. "Of course, Mr. President."

"We can relax formal protocols. You have earned it so please call me Albert."

"Thank you, Albert. The pleasure is mine."

"It's an honour for people in this room to meet you, Daniel. To finally appreciate the man who saved this country and the life of the President of the United States." He extends his hand and Cross firmly shakes it.

"Thank you, Mr. President," unable to perpetuate the trend of renouncing formality. "Mr. Granfield here told me I had no choice."

The room erupts into laughter and even Walkman joins in.

"Your humour gets you through all this, doesn't it?"

"Yes. I need something for sure." He smiles at Walkman, appreciating the warmth and genuine hospitality. "You look better than the last time I saw you." He does.

"It was a process."

Walkman introduces them to several political members who have also been invited. They include Secretary of Defense and Senator Watkins, both of whom Cross has met before. Other invited guests are Pentagon officials, most notable of those being the Chairman of the Joint Chiefs of Staff, the highest-ranking military official. Cross gulps.

"Come, let's be seated."

They move over to where exquisite hand-crafted sofas and chairs have been arranged for their visit. Most sit for the conversation but several remain standing. A number of documents rest on a varnished solid-wood table in the middle.

"David filled me in on last night's events. Quite disturbing for us all. It appears a few of those arrested are Capitol politicians." Walkman is shaking his head.

"Yes. It was sickening for those involved yesterday. The perpetrators needed to be stopped."

"I understand Briar was coerced and paid for by Deep State. I'm very troubled by these findings."

"Those are the facts as presented, Mr. President. However, this isn't over yet."

"This is precisely why I invited you here."

The next nearly three hours involve deep military discussions.

Granfield had educated Cross on what he's permitted to say and not to say.

"We don't fully understand who the enemy is over here yet," he had said on the drive over to the White House.

He had a point, Cross thought.

Cross doesn't disclose the location he believes where Wu is orchestrating his decision-making. He isn't one hundred percent sure anyway, despite the convincing evidence supporting his search. In the end, it was a strange meeting because neither he nor Granfield wanted to relinquish too much control of material facts. It would end up at the Pentagon where immense pressure would be exerted on their desire to jump in with both feet. They were not ready for that.

After gratuities and then pleasantries, it is time for them to leave. Walkman was very gracious in handling the conversation. He too comprehends the military's desire to activate their fragile egos and use hardware they keep manufacturing, but don't need.

"Well, that was interesting, David," as they leave the compound.

"I thought you would appreciate that side of it, but they left me no choice."

"I could see that." Cross agreeing.

"The military people are all gung-ho, likely the effects of too much illegal Prozac, Valium, Elavil or something else to keep them energised."

"They are all on something."

Wu is beside himself. He is watching his grip on the world falling as he grapples with crisis after crisis.

Schmidt, his man from Germany, extracted the short straw once Handcock was marched away. He is not even sure if he is still alive. Taking responsibility for events out of their control wasn't in the fine print on an agreement they all signed.

They are all aware of Briar's arrest last night on serious charges. Prior arrangements were made by someone to have news crews there fast. The timing was too impeccable to have been spontaneous. Briar most likely will not be released on bail anytime soon. It wasn't just him either. There were other members from Wu's global cartel arrested as part of the international trafficking network.

Wu was cautioned but he brushed those warnings aside.

"We are about to control half the world, with plans to take over the remaining countries. Why would they become involved in something so despicable as this?" was his tort answer.

Well, obviously they did, and he was wrong.

Schmidt must navigate very carefully from this point going forwards. He isn't even convinced anything can be gained from here. They could have eventually recovered from Davenport and Marchant, but Briar's extracurricular activities have changed the dynamics. They need the White House. If they don't control governments, then it is exceedingly difficult to access each country's military resources. The US has the largest military by far, so he needs to look at their contingency plans in order to commence recovery. He isn't optimistic.

The war room is large and boasts a formidable array of electronics including displays, computers, screens, real-time data collecting mechanisms, telecommunication devices, radar along with other bells and whistles, all built into a property made centuries ago. It is impressive and full of Wu's lieutenants working away.

"Where are we with Lutkus," Wu asks Schmidt.

"Armaments in Belarus attacked last night and hit some mobile launches across the border."

"What was our response?"

"Lutkus fired a few missiles."

Wu isn't happy at all. There isn't much left of their plans to follow anymore, so they must improvise.

"Get Lutkus to ignite a real war. Lobbing a few missiles here and there is futile. We require immediate action."

"Yes, sir," as he watches Wu depart.

69

War Cabinet, Whitehall

Cross is back in London orchestrating their final push. A conference had been arranged through Jennings and being held within the confines of Whitehall's walls. It includes war cabinet members and high-ranking military officials.

"You know how to parachute," Jennings had asked him.

"Say what?"

Laughter circulated the table which helped bring much-needed respite.

They go through the military-style operation, not once, not twice but three times. Timing is a pertinent factor in pulling this off.

Cross has questions and those are satisfactorily addressed. This may be his last mission, but he seems to recall saying that a number of times.

"This is it, Nick."

"Until the next time." He chuckles.

"I once said life can't get any worse, and then weeks later a forest fire came along."

"We just need to maintain our attention to details."

The general now talks so they listen.

"As in any operation of this nature, there will be unknowns. We must remain flexible and ready to improvise. It is almost impossible to anticipate every conceivable re-action because we don't know what we are facing. Be prepared to implement changes even without authority, but only if those changes work." Laughter fills the chamber. "Furthermore…"

There's a disturbance outside the cabinet war room, then the door opens. In walks a tall, strapping man no one is apparently expecting as the whole room stands to attention and all mutterings cease.

"Good morning, ladies and gentlemen," says Prime Minister Carlisle. "Please be seated."

Cross vaguely remembers a picture of him competing with Davenport at the polls. He leans over to Jennings and whispers.

"This is the man you fudged the polls for to beat Davenport?"

"Precisely."

"How did you do that, exactly?"

"Easy. All votes are hand-counted in each district. We just arranged for our own people to participate in the process." He turns and grins. "The people we happened to select failed in mathematics in high school."

Cross chuckles.

Carlisle walks over and takes a seat.

"I'm not here to participate in the military operational discussions nor to offer my rendition of how they should be conducted. I leave that to you esteemed cabinet and military people. I just want to wish you all good luck."

His focus now turns to Cross.

"You have been part of this charade for a while, Dr. Cross."

"Yes, Prime Minister."

"I have instructed the men and women here to ensure you are taken care of. You have brought us this far, now it's time for others to share the burden."

"Thank you."

"I admire what you have done, and I can never overstate that."

He stands up and walks over to Cross.

"Thank you for your services," and sticks out his hand. Cross accepts and they unequivocally shake hands. "Come and see me in Downing Street when this is all over, Daniel."

"I will, Prime Minister."

Carlisle turns to face the assembled figures at the table. "This man has been systematically dragged through hell. He has survived missions that were designed to kill him. Now, let's get this done since we all owe him our freedoms." The whole room erupts into a chorus of clapping.

Cross is attempting to control his emotions but fails. His eyes tear and Carlisle notices as he is about to depart.

"I can't even begin to imagine what you have been through, my friend," being less formal for a reason. "Our country's resources are at your disposal, Dr. Cross."

70

Last Non-Person Standing

Cross leaps off the dingy and wades through shallow water for the shoreline. The ten Special Air Services soldiers handpicked for the mission follow him, dragging their necessary equipment with them.

It is nighttime, so dark and cold in this part of the world. There are breaks in the clouds allowing spurious light to blanket the desolate region, emitted from a half-moon sitting nearly two-hundred and forty thousand miles away. This is fortuitous and allows Cross to survey their landing. He mentally analyses the bleak landscape and tries to compare it from satellite imagery Moore Jr. had sent.

"This looks like the right place, Commander."

"Good."

Cross points to a mound of earth fifty metres away. "Over in that direction is an entrance."

"Are we all accounted for?" asks the commander.

Each soldier calls out a number in sequence. Cross looks at their faces, all camouflaged in various dark greens, black and touches of white, and feels their strength, agilities and desires to complete this mission. Dressed in black/dark-green fatigues over waterproof rubber full-body suites, carrying armaments and ammo for war, their confidence oozes in droves. Their special training has got them this far, but the SAS is a highly secretive and classified regiment, never mentioned by the government or Ministry of Defense.

Cross has been in this position before, so he is confident also.

They approach a double doorway built into the mound Cross had pointed out. It must have a mechanism to trigger an alarm built into it somewhere, so one of the soldiers uses a device to search for electrical signals. She finds three places along the seam of the doorframe.

"We avoid these areas."

Another soldier brings a miniature blowtorch and starts cutting into one of the doors. After fifteen minutes, he is done. They carefully swing the cut-out piece outwards.

"They must have motion detectors and cameras out here, surely," Cross says.

A soldier peers through, in search of said detectors. He removes his gun and silently blows out a camera but cannot tell if it was operating.

"Now we must move," shouts the commander.

Cross and the ten soldiers climb into the concrete-lined tunnel and start heading toward the castle, carrying rifles and other ancillaries. There is sparce low-level lighting which facilitates their progress. Submerged into partially saturated land from mountain moisture runoff, areas of the concrete are seeping and have fungus growing. The smell is rancid.

At the first ventilation shaft, Cross climbs the few metal stairs so he can reach air. He takes this opportunity to send a message to Jennings.

'We are in.'

Now they pick up the tempo and start jogging, allowing them to hear alert signals of any kind. They had estimated the tunnel to be around one thousand metres. Half-way in, it banks ninety degrees to their left. They slow down and stop so one of them can peep around the corner to gather intel.

"It widens from here, and I can count three security guards. There are also rooms off to the left side because I can see doors and windows."

"How far are the guards?" the commander asks.

"Twenty metres."

"Can you take them out from here?"

"Yes."

"We have no choice."

With dexterous precision, the soldier turns and fires three silenced shots.

They navigate around the corner and enter an enlarged cavern that has doubled in width and height. There is an increase in positive gradient as it goes. Three security guards lay dead on the floor. Cross investigates the rooms as they pass them.

"Wait," he whispers. "I see uniforms hanging in open closets."

"They look like living quarters for these poor bastards," another soldier adds. "If we wear their uniforms for camouflage, our own people will shoot us."

They continue.

The tunnel is now curving to the right, the floor increasing in gradient with occasional steps added, as they approach the castle. The soldiers cling to the inner wall as they follow the curvature.

The lead soldier stops as he hears more voices. He puts his left arm out to halt the procession.

"We must be close now, Commander."

"Yes. Check our watches."

"Two minutes," Cross pipes in.

They wait until they hear the first explosion, which is their signal.

They bolt around the corner and spread out, indiscriminately firing at anyone and everyone. Surprise, as always, is the ultimate weapon. As Wu's men drop, they progress through the tunnel until it opens into a basement.

"This is it."

The dead guards present down here were armed with Chinese weapons. Their purpose evidently was to guard against captors escaping from their cells. They don't have time to survey the surroundings, nor does Cross, as they run up a large stone circular staircase to the next level.

Outside Cross hears more shells and missile strikes as the mission fully encompasses the property, the deception now in full swing.

Wu is screaming. "What's going on outside?"

"Sir, someone has blown up the hangar and now they are attacking the 737s."

"Who is?"

"They look like British military aircraft."

"How do they even know we are here? That's impossible. Our electronic protective shield is armed."

Another missile hits an unknown target outside. Wu can hear return fire from his battalions, but they were never prepared for an assault of this nature. Not for this facility. They at least have some missile capabilities, so he authorises their use.

Schmidt has never seen Wu like this. He is in the process of a full-blown panic attack.

"Enforce security. Close the screens."

Screens were never designed for a castle made of stone, Schmidt knows, but does as he is ordered.

As they climb the stairs, metal security roll-cages start to scroll down.

"Wu must be securing their operations room," Cross yells.

Shots ring out and hit the stone wall next to them, sending dust and fragments flying. A soldier turns and opens fire, killing the shooter.

Cross looks for something to jam the screen with and finds a big rock at the top of the stairs. He requests two soldiers to help, and they roll it under the cage just as it slams down on top of the stone. There is now sufficient room as they crawl underneath and head into the war zone.

The soldiers enter Wu's temple and start tossing small incendiary devices as they see fit. Explosions rip through hardware and send it flying along with bodies, as the occupants are startled. A few of his security guards return fire but they are not in the same league as SAS soldiers. Screams are heard from the lieutenants who start scurrying around, ill-equipped for such a clandestine military altercation in close quarters.

Crouching behind operational platforms for cover, Cross finds a man with an Asian accent at the centre of the room giving commands. He remembers his face from the grow farm in Taiwan. This time he has nowhere to run.

As Cross aims, one of Wu's guards from across the room shoots him in the left arm.

"Fuck."

An SAS soldier close by hears the explicit and takes out the villain.

Cross is momentarily put off by the recoil from the bullet, but soon regains his composure. His first shot hits Wu in the head, but it rebounds.

"Shit. What the f…"

Wu feels the bullet, so his natural instinct is to turn around. As he does so, Cross fires into his right eye, again, and again, and again.

The velocity of the projectiles forces Wu backwards, and he falls onto the console he was standing next to.

Cross gets up and runs over, oblivious to the bedlam propagating around him. He doesn't care. He stares into Wu's face surveying the damage his bullets have caused.

The human brain isn't there: replaced by a smaller synthetic device. He still sees lights flashing so whatever lifeform it is remains active somehow. Wu turns and looks at him. As he does so, the hole in the right side exposes a small power module.

"Your cryptic mortality galvanised me, Dr. Cross. Unfortunately, life clings to you like a malignant tumour?"

Those are his last words as Cross sticks the rifle in his head and pulls the trigger, blowing it to pieces, titanium mantle and all. He then drops the end of the gun barrel onto Wu's chest, where he believes the heart should be, and starts emptying his chamber. He doesn't give a shit about his vulnerability and exposure as bone fragments, tissue, blood, hardware and synthetic material fly everywhere.

It is chaos all around with incendiary devices exploding and the room filling with smoke. Gun shots and screams are repeatedly heard and the sounds cavitate off the cavernous stone walls. He doesn't care anymore as his job has been unilaterally terminated.

The commander sees him and screams, "No, Daniel." He bolts over and leaps to grab him in a rugby-style tackle around the waste as they both fall to the ground in a heap behind the console. The timing is impeccable as Wu self-destructs in a cacophony of noise, sparks and flashes befitting his demise.

The commander sits upright and takes a gander at Cross.

"What the fuck was that?" Cross mumbles, whilst groaning from immense pain.

Blood is running down his arm and is a deceptively distinct colour from their fatigues.

"Daniel, we need to get you out of here," the commander yells, understanding the predicament as a pool of blood is forming on the centuries-old tan stone lying under Cross' arm.

"I'm physically and mentally done, Commander. Save yourselves."

Purposely ignoring him, he leaves Cross lying on the floor and looks around the electronic equipment to find a button for energizing the rollup gates. He locates one and punches it. As he does so, he hears the motors energise.

Cross looks up and somehow, through the disharmony of din resonating throughout the castle, he filters out the sound of helicopters landing.

"Commander, the choppers are here."

The commander turns as Cross is dragging himself to his feet. His disposition is that of someone who has had enough: he is physically spent and heading into shock. He is also oblivious to the world he currently occupies, and the commander realises he needs to remove him, and fast, before it is too late.

He screams, "Someone help Cross, now."

Heading for exits down below, they move through the basement they had passed coming in. Cross must look in one of the cells as it's his nature. As he does so, the last thing he expected to see are these people.

"Someone else will get them, Cross," hollers the commander, as he yanks his right arm and pulls him out into the castle's vast court.

"I promised the prime minister I would protect you. I am not going to renege on my word, sir."

Two helicopters are sitting on the grass, rotors turning, as the soldiers run over and climb aboard.

71

Road to Freedom

Cross wakes up in a hospital bed but has no idea where. His arm is in a sling, and he knows someone has re-opened the wound in the abdomen. Sitting next to him are Jennings and Moore Jr.

He is groggy and feels like hell. "Where are we?" as he squeaks out strained vocals.

"At a military hospital in Fort William, in the northwest of Scotland. The commander had them fly you straight here. He sure as hell wasn't going to leave you, despite your request."

"What the fuck just happened?"

"The castle was overrun, and we irreparably shut down Wu's operation. The cabal is over."

"Wu was part clone. You were right, Graeme. His brain was replaced and protected within a titanium shell. He also had a mechanical heart with a self-destruct mechanism built in."

Jennings sees that he is still in shock.

"That doesn't surprise me," Moore Jr. responds. "We were aware of these procedures but didn't know Wu was part of that experiment. Looks like they left out a few zeros and ones in the software programming." He chuckles, but not in a funny way.

"Leslie and Florence are flying out. They will be here in a few hours."

"Thanks, Nick. I have something to share with Florence."

"I figured."

"What happened to the captives? I recollect something but then the commander grabbed my arm."

"We flew them down to London with the other live occupants we didn't kill. We will meet the ladies down there too, but only when you are ready."

"I think I saw Wu as one of the captives. He didn't look too good."

"You did," which is all Jennings says.

"I'm ready. Just give me a few hours more sleep. Oh, what happened to the Sanchez findings?"

Jennings realises Cross never shuts off his mind.

"It wasn't the senator, as you speculated. He was another hybrid clone. The Spanish authorities are looking for the real Sanchez, who they presume is dead. He was the senator who approved the construction project in the Pyrenees."

"That is why I asked you to exhume the body. Fascinating world." He rolls his head and closes the eyes.

They are in a conference room down the hallway from Jennings' office at MI6 in London. One of the captives found at the castle in Scotland will be ushered in shortly. Cross is seated next to Jennings and across from Taylor and Anderson. He is anxious and wonders what will happen.

At that moment, the door opens, and a lady is escorted into the room by two agents. She looks frail and tired from many months of forced captivity, but she certainly doesn't look in her mid-forties anymore.

Cross stands. "Good afternoon, Ms. Robertson," and shakes her weak hand. "I'm Daniel Cross and these are Nick Jennings, Leslie Taylor and," he hesitates not knowing the recourse, "Florence Anderson."

Robertson goes motionless. She doesn't say a word and whatever blood is flowing stops and drains from her face.

"Please, take a seat, ma'am," Cross adds, before she keels over.

The agents help her to sit down, as she maintains her silence. Finally, after what seemed like eternity, her mouth starts to open but not before tears roll down her face.

"I'm sorry I abandoned you, Florence." Now, she brings her hands to her face and lets the floodgates open.

Cross can't take it anymore. The emotions are ripping his fragile carcass to pieces, and he does not even wait for Anderson's response.

"Nick, I will be in your office. I think these two need to be alone."

"I'm following you."

Sitting in his office, Cross is a mess.

"Sorry, Nick. I couldn't sit in that room."

"When did you know?"

"Flying to France. She was sitting in front of me when I noticed the family resemblance. I did the research, but it took considerable effort and I used search engines that dove into the dark web. It's ugly down there."

"Yes, it is."

"I couldn't understand why Wu had chosen her. He must have found out and used that against her mother. Ms. Robertson doesn't need to know yet that her nephew from marriage is a paedophile, does she?"

"Certainly not, if ever, but it is obvious she regretted giving up her own daughter." Even Jennings can't conceal his emotion.

"I didn't know either," answers Taylor. "She didn't know who her mother was. She never disclosed anything about her past."

"Sometimes we don't want others to know and best kept in a sealed vault."

Cross sighs and gets up to walk off the sentiments.

"How is the arm?"

"Like every other part of my body, Leslie. Thanks for asking." He retains his seat and looks at Jennings.

"Are we in a war?"

"No. It appears Lutkus isn't that desperate now his funding source dried up, but he is responsible for deaths and must be made accountable. He doesn't foresee any future in a military confrontation; not anymore now that their Deep State aspirations have been curbed. His tenure as prime minister is over, and he will be replaced. However, before he is, there is a secret meeting in Minsk being arranged at an undisclosed location. It will involve Lutkus, Ozolins, ranking members of NATO, our friend Rostov, myself and you are invited if you wish to attend."

"When?"

"In the next few days."

"I may wish to attend that meeting. What about the sponsors?"

"We have their names, so Granfield is rounding them up too. At least the ones still alive." He looks at Cross and smiles.

Once the signatures on the multinational documents are signed and verified, the meeting grinds to a conclusion. Cross is done and the Dassault is fueled and waiting for him. He has one thing left on his mind before leaving and walks over to Rostov.

"Sergey, I have one question left."

"Only one?" and chuckles. "Please, my friend, ask."

"How did you know about Amanda Robertson?"

"Who told you I did?" His smile and posture give Cross the answer he is looking for, but he doesn't care anymore.

Cross exits the plane and climbs down the stairs, having arrived outside of Tehran. At the bottom is Sadeghi and they run into each other's arms, as if the world is ending...

Epilogue

The Daniel Cross trilogy did not start out that way. However, that is what it ended up being. Originally, I tried to entertain current events and draft them into a political thriller. I purposely brought adversaries together and had them fight a common enemy. As other incidents unfolded over the course of the last two years, I became inundated with opportunities to expand the story. Moreover, I opted to retain a number of important characters to keep the flow consistent throughout.

Despite the trilogy being works of fiction, I aimed to adapt some of my broad travel experiences into the narratives. These helped to levitate the stories, making them more alive and credible.

To enhance the feel of reality, extensive research was administered in areas where it was required. For example, countries, cities, street names and places exist. Technical aspects such as biological laboratories, cannabis, the Panama Canal, artificial intelligence, electronics, weaponry, ship building and military hardware are real. Political structures in various countries are factual. Fiction, by definition, evaporates constraints which present an opportunity for any author to incorporate their imagination. This facilitated the expanse on my own areas of expertise which further developed the stories.

Significant research was undertaken for Political Deception, and I am obliquely aware politics is a polarising and contentious topic. Therefore, I wish to add that currently I share no political affiliation whatsoever, but lean centre right. Political party names and affiliations in various stories are fictional and random but done a certain way only for consistency. I wanted to avoid being an instigator of a civil war.

Whether some disagree, it doesn't matter: Deep State exists. Recently our president used the words 'new world order', perhaps by mistake, who knows. This phenomenon also exists. A recent conference at Davos, Switzerland under the guise of the World Economic Forum, or WEF, invited an array of the world's richest people, along with high profile politicians, as guest speakers, as if money endears them to intelligent thoughts or breeds a collective concern towards the burgeoning population. It does neither. Some people want to control the planet's population, and this is not a debatable subject either. The world has the resources to easily eradicate hunger and yet leaders – using that term very loosely - elect wars instead. Make your own judgments as to why.

To add credence to this disturbing topic, I brought into the story an abhorrent reality of child trafficking. This too is real. The numerical figure used in this book for missing children in the US is reported and confirmed on several reputable websites. Huffington Post published an article in June 2015 about this very subject, pertaining to one particular country I cannot mention because it is too political, even for this book of fiction. It is a sick subject and I make no apologies because it accurately depicts society's Mariana Trench in how deep civility in some areas has fallen: human trafficking and child pornography are serious crimes coordinated globally. I am making no claims regarding who is funneling these activities. This is simply utilising my imagination to broaden the story by incorporating political figures, thereby heightening the impact.

The Deception Series is purely a work of fiction dosed with a sprinkling of ingenuity. However, I merged creativity and some experiences with existing truths and facts. Only you, the reader, can determine if I was successful.

Coming soon:

Schofield enters the Low Emission Zone in Birmingham and pulls up to a traffic light as the congestion approaches insanity in the early Wednesday afternoon rush-hours. He had tried to escape work early having arrived early but as is typical in his environment, that never works.

"Perhaps coming in late and leaving late is a better option," he says to his Indonesian secretary sitting next to him. "Or, better yet, come in late and leave earlier," as he turns and grins.

The Avron he is driving is a company car, but they had switched from the preferred BMW internal combustion models because of the forced government mandates. His research had uncovered mass corruption on the implementation of electric vehicles but he is also seeing attempts at cyberattacks on the grid system designed to charge them.

The silence of the motors shutting down is eclipsed with the romance of Barry White transmitting via his iPhone through the McIntosh high-end sound system. He turns to his companion and puts the left hand on her naked legs and shuffles it under her skirt.

"It won't be…"

Before he finishes his sentence, smoke enters the cabin from underneath and he hears the gentle thud of doors locking. He removes his hand and grabs the door handle in a vain attempt to open it. It pulls away but nothing happens.

Panic sets in as he tries to unbuckle the seat belt. His passenger is already screaming when flames shoot out from behind the large flat screen portraying complex graphics of the GPS and city traffic, the musical playlist and the vehicle's mechanical and electrical systems including speed. In the lower right corner is the batteries' temperature gauge which has overshot its limit and is flashing a warning.

The last thing he sees displayed is a message, 'Have a nice day, Dr. Schofield', as his car erupts into a ball of flames, grotesquely terminating the life of the two occupants.

www.ingramcontent.com/pod-product-compliance
Lightning Source LLC
Chambersburg PA
CBHW070326030726
47505CB00004B/1108